HIGH WATER

Douglas Reeman writes:
'Although my first full-length novel, *A Prayer for the Ship*, was not published until 1958, I have always had a great interest in ships and the sea. As a child in the 1930s I enjoyed seeing the great naval reviews and visiting the dockyards for Navy Weeks. During the war I served in the Navy and never lost my affection for the people who endured the constant dangers of sea-warfare. . . . Looking back to 1958, I can appreciate my great good fortune in doing something which keeps me in close touch with ships and the sea.'

Also in Arrow by Douglas Reeman

Douglas Reeman

HIGH WATER

ARROW BOOKS

Arrow Books Limited
62-65 Chandos Place, London WC2N 4NW

An imprint of the Hutchinson Publishing Group

London Melbourne Sydney Auckland
Johannesburg and agencies throughout
the world

First published by Hutchinson 1959
Arrow edition 1974
Reprinted 1976, 1980, 1981, 1984,
1986 and 1987

Printed and bound in Great Britain by
Anchor Brendon Limited, Tiptree, Essex

ISBN 0 09 907900 3

Author's Note

It is often said that a novelist's second book is the hardest thing he will ever have to write. This is probably because his first book was to have been *the one*, or because he never expected it to be published at all.

The writing of my first novel, *A Prayer for the Ship*, was a gentle and leisurely task. I had no previous experience, other than short stories, and had nobody to point out the pitfalls or to explain the mysteries of construction and plot. This was probably an advantage. I wrote it without notes or research, building the story around events and characters I had known during the war. It was something I felt I had to do, if only for my own satisfaction.

Eventually, I sent the manuscript to a publisher, the choice of whom was made by the simple method of studying his previous book-lists. My work was done, or so I thought.

The first excitement at being told that my story had been accepted soon gave way to something like panic when my publisher asked me what new work I had to show him. A second book? It had never crossed my mind.

And so I wrote *High Water*, basing it on the times and environment of the late fifties. It was a period when many people were just discovering the real difficulties of settling down after a war. Some lost their livelihood and savings while trying to adapt in a world they did not understand.

The skilful and ruthless affairs of day-to-day business were seen by many as an extension of combat, so they were able to delude themselves that crime was merely another way of claiming what was theirs by right.

At the time of writing *High Water* I lived aboard my own motor yacht, and well aware of the temptations for quick profit with no questions asked, and of the shortages left by war's aftermath.

If the theme of the story is different from all my subsequent work, it is because I was not then sure which way I was going. *High Water* gave me the time and the breathing space to decide whether or not I could face up to a new career. For that I am eternally grateful.

1972   D.R.

1

THE grey, stone walls of Torquay harbour reached protectively out and around the countless small craft which lay anchored and hardly moving in the warm, blue water. The sun, which poured down relentlessly from a bright, clear sky, seemed to sap the very last ounce of energy out of the after-lunch wanderers who thronged the baking stonework, as they shuffled aimlessly in search of shade, the gay, multi-coloured dresses and bathing costumes of the brown-legged girls clashing with the white shirts and braces of the perspiring business men from the Midlands, and with the blue jerseys and caps of the old fishermen who leaned silently across the breastworks, sucking at their pipes.

The high, white buildings at the back of the harbour shimmered in a fine heat-haze, and made a perfect setting for the holiday-makers in their quest for pleasure and simple excitements.

Although the summer was all but ended, everyone agreed that it had been a season to remember, and even the thought that soon the water would chill with the first touch of the cold Atlantic, and the promenades would be deserted but for the fishermen and the empty deck-chairs, could not remove the deep feeling of satisfaction, especially on the part of the boarding-house owners, and the prosperous hoteliers.

Philip Vivian was probably the only person who did not share those views, as he hurried through the slow-moving throng, unaware of the appraising glances from the groups of parading girls, or in fact of anything but the realization that he was almost certainly about to become bankrupt.

In his faded yachting cap, open-necked shirt, and khaki-drill trousers, he made an interesting figure, his tall, well-muscled body swinging with the easy grace of a professional seaman, and his tanned face proving that he at least was no temporary resident. It was his face which usually caused his few friends to think and to ponder, for although only a young man, thirty-four to be exact, he had a certain sadness, and even wistfulness, in his wide, grey eyes, which made him seem old before his time. Beneath the peak of his cap, the short, brown hair curled rebelliously, and the proud tilt of his chin, and firm mouth, gave the general appearance of recklessness.

As he approached the stone steps which ran down to the lower mooring jetties, one of the blue-clad figures detached itself from the wall and grasped him by the elbow. A smile flickered across Vivian's features, as he looked down into the wrinkled face of the old boatman. Arthur Harrap was a particular friend of his, who made a casual living by fishing and running the visitors out for short trips in his dilapidated motor-boat, the *Glory*, and his round, red face was a familiar sight indeed in most of the local bars.

'Oi bin keepin' an eye on yer boat, Cap'n,' he wheezed, 'but there ain't bin no callers. Did yew 'ave any luck?'

'Not a damn thing, Arthur. I think I've just about had it.'

He shrugged, and thrust his hands deep into his pockets, and together they stood, staring down at the rakish motor-yacht moored beneath them.

With the sun glistening on her gleaming brass fittings, she made a proud sight, forty-five feet of grace, power, and a shipbuilder's love of beauty. From her creamy, teak-laid decks, with the neatly coiled ropes, to her shiny, white hull, which reflected the dancing ripple of the gentle tideway, she looked every inch a thoroughbred.

Speaking as if to himself, Vivian controlled his voice with a great effort, so that his companion squinted up at him inquiringly. 'I've just been on the 'phone again to London, and the mortgage people won't allow me even another month to pay them, so unless you've got seven hundred pounds you don't want, I guess they'll take the *Seafox* from me,' he said bitterly.

The old man shook his head. 'It's what oi've always said, yew just can't compete with the big hire-boat men.'

He spat accurately into the water.

'But what's gone wrong this time? After all, yew've bin 'ere nigh on two years with your boat, and yew've always 'ad plenty of payin' customers before, what does it matter that yew've 'ad a bit of a bad patch lately?'

'It's like this, Arthur,' he answered wearily, as if repeating a lesson. 'As you know, when I came out of the Navy I had another job in London for a bit. I had some money put by, and that, with my gratuity, plus what I could save, I put down as a deposit for the boat with a yacht mortgage firm. I thought I could make a living during the summer months by hiring myself and the boat out for holiday cruises, and pay off the rest of the cash. I just happened to forget a few points, that's all.' He laughed harshly. 'One, I forgot that I could go a whole season like this with practically no customers, and two, I forgot that my boat's just about trebled her value since I got her, so that these bastards want to get her off me, to sell again at a nice, fat profit.'

He kicked viciously at a stone.

'God, it makes you sick! Where am I going to raise that sort of money, eh?'

They crossed the narrow gangplank, and entered the

wheelhouse, both grateful for the shade, and thankful to be out of the noise and the crowds.

As Arthur busied himself with the kettle, he watched Vivian moving slowly about the snug, panelled saloon, like a caged animal, he thought, his sensitive hands feeling and touching the well-known objects about him. Arthur shook his head sadly. He knew that if he lost his boat Vivian would lose his very will to live.

A brief shadow flitted across the open door of the sunlit wheelhouse, and a second later a large, black-and-white cat pounced heavily down the steps, and stood blinking uncertainly on the saloon deck. Having made sure that both the occupants were friendly, the cat strode stiffly to a battered cushion secreted beneath the table and began to wash.

Vivian stood looking down at the animal for some moments.

'Dammit!' he exploded suddenly. 'I'll be damned if I'm going to give up all this without a fight! I'll go up to London and see the perishers!'

He paused, and grinned ruefully. 'Don't forget to keep an eye on old Coley here while I'm away, you know, the usual.'

'Aye, Oi know, Cap'n, a pahnd of blessed fish a day. Reckon 'e'll burst one day!'

The old man brightened considerably, now that a plan of action was being evolved.

'Now don' yew worry about a thing. Oi'll run the generator, wash the deck, feed the cat, keep the local kids from runnin' abart the boat an' . . .' he paused, wrinkling his forehead. ' 'Ere, what'll Oi do if some gen'elman wants to 'ire the ol' *Fox* for 'is 'oliday, eh? 'Ow can Oi get in touch with yew?'

'Hm, you'd better ring me at the R.N.V.R. Club. That's

where I shall stay. After all, I probably won't be able to afford to renew my membership next year, so I might as well make the most of it.'

He reached for the railway time-table, feeling again that dead sensation in his stomach. He had to do something, anything. He felt the boat stir beneath him, as a pleasure launch, jammed with laughing holiday-makers, cruised past, and he knew that unless he could think of something fantastic, he would lose his home, his livelihood, and his only love, all in one swoop.

He glanced down at Coley, now slumbering heavily, and smiled, in spite of himself. A luxury yacht, an overfed cat, and himself. At least his problems were a little different from those of the noisy people outside.

Like Arthur, he felt almost relieved that he had decided on some form of action, no matter how futile it might be, and as the old man chattered and made endless cups of tea, he started to pack a small bag in readiness for an early start, first thing in the morning.

.   .   .   .   .

The R.N.V.R. Club, at the back of Piccadilly, was practically deserted as Vivian came down from his room. The afternoon sunlight pierced the lounge and the bar in great spears of harsh light, and he wrinkled his nose at the unfamiliar smell of exhaust gases which drifted in through the pillared entrance, and listened to the distant roar of London's busy streets. He consulted his watch, wondering what to do to fill in the time. He had telephoned the broker's office, and had been informed, rather icily, that he could not see the general manager until the following morning. The secretary had been very short with him, and gave no doubt as to what the verdict would be.

One of the club stewards, who was polishing some brass-work by the wide, curving staircase, looked up, surprise written on his face.

'Good heavens, Lieutenant Vivian, isn't it, sir? We've not seen you for a very long time. I do hope you're keeping well?'

Vivian murmured his thanks, and wandered into the lounge to read the magazines. The hall porter peered after him.

' 'Oo's that then, Bert?' he queried.

The steward picked up his polish once more.

'You've just had the good fortune to look at one of the best motor gunboat skippers we had in the last do, chum,' he said slowly. 'Two D.S.C.s, wounded, you know, the lot. An' look at him now. Not two pence to rub together, I shouldn't think.'

'You an' your bleedin' officers!' grumbled the porter darkly, and resumed his study of the cricket scores.

Vivian, unaware that he had caused any interest, sat lazily in a large armchair, idly scanning the bright periodicals. He felt at ease in the club, and secretly enjoyed its quiet atmosphere of memories which were very precious to him. Even the pictures around him brought back the pang of wild excitement which he had once felt when his small gun-boat had hurtled across the Channel, night after night, to do battle in a holocaust of noise and fire. Even then, he had dreamed of having a boat of his own, and, even then, he had sworn that he would never be tied to some wretched, soul-destroying office. But he had made that dream a hard reality, although now it looked like turning into a night-mare.

The long train journey from Devon, the warm afternoon, and the comfortable chair, began to have their effect, and he dozed quietly, the magazine falling to the floor.

He awoke with a jerk, to find that the club's evening life had begun, and although the sunlight was still bright, a rising murmur of masculine voices filtered from the bar. He sauntered into its friendly atmosphere, and, having ascertained that he knew none of its occupants, he asked for a beer, and then, leaning on the well-worn counter, he stared thoughtfully at the gleaming bottles, which seemed to mock him.

How long he stayed like that, he didn't remember, but suddenly he received a violent thump between the shoulder-blades with a hard fist, which made him reel awkwardly to one side, his glass rolling over in a pool of beer. He spun round to face the other man, his nerves on edge.

'What the bloody hell d'you think you're doing!'

He stopped dead, staring at the other's beaming, red face.

'God in heaven!' he gasped. 'Felix! Felix Lang! Why, you old devil! It really is good to see you!'

They pumped each other's hands, ignoring the amused stares of the others in the bar, and studied one another with apparent delight.

Felix Lang was a round-faced, heavily built man, who was inclined to run to fat. His pink, confident face, with the rather full, sensuous mouth, had the appearance of the prosperous and good-living business man, and although only four years older than Vivian, he certainly looked as if he enjoyed the more comfortable attractions of life. Of the once-feared officer who had originally commanded Vivian's flotilla of gunboats, there was little evidence but, perhaps, for a certain hardness of his dark brown eyes.

Lang waved a pudgy finger in the direction of the barman. 'Two large Pink Plymouths!' he barked, and then he turned to beam once more at Vivian.

'What a bit of luck, old boy,' he chuckled, his eyes taking in the old reefer jacket, and the neat but well-worn flannels. 'This has made up for a thoroughly dreary day. I was only wondering about you this morning. Felix, I said, whatever became of that other handsome chap?' He chuckled again. 'And here you are.'

He knocked back the gin as if it had been water.

'Now, tell me what you've been up to, old boy.'

Vivian signalled the barman, painfully aware of the two solitary pound notes in his wallet, which, with his return ticket, were about his only available assets.

Fatter, perhaps, he thought, but still the same Lang. Still laughs at his own jokes, and still one of the bravest men he had ever met. In a lightweight, grey suit, which was obviously born in Savile Row, and hand-made shoes, he looked the picture of prosperity.

As he opened his battered wallet, he felt Lang's glance over his arm, and he flushed.

'Hallo then, boy, what's that photograph you've got in there, a girl or something?'

'No, it's my boat, as a matter of fact,' he said, and handed it to Lang defiantly.

Blast him, he thought affectionately, he's landed on his feet all right, but I bet he hasn't got a boat like her. He grinned awkwardly at his own childishness, and was pleasantly surprised at Lang's sudden, obvious interest. For a moment, the casual, bantering air had fallen like a much-used mask, and in that brief instant, he saw him as a man of other, unknown talents, hitherto unsuspected.

Lang took him by the arm. 'Look here, old boy, let's go somewhere quiet, and have a good yarn. We'll have a bite to eat round at a little place I know, if that's okay by you?'

Lang piloted him out into the cool evening air, to a long, low, silver-grey Bentley saloon.

Vivian whistled softly.

'My, Felix, you are in the chips!'

Lang waved his arm embracingly. 'Well, let's face it, boy, if you don't look after yourself, nobody else will!'

As he drove skilfully through the traffic of Piccadilly, he casually questioned his passenger about the boat, the business difficulties, and even though Vivian knew he was being thoroughly interrogated, he answered readily, only too glad to be able to talk to someone about his fears.

'Hm, you have got yourself into a mess, haven't you?' murmured Lang thoughtfully at the end. 'You say you haven't actually seen the broker chappie yet?'

Vivian nodded.

'Well, that's that, then.'

Vivian turned, suddenly wild. 'What d'you mean, "that's that then"? You mean you couldn't care less, is that it?', he exploded.

He was suddenly aware that Lang was shaking, vibrating would be a truer word. His cheeks puffed out, his eyes crinkled and watered, until he suddenly burst out laughing, in his familiar braying guffaws, so that he had to swerve violently to avoid a taxi.

Vivian sat watching dumbly, wishing that the car would stop, so that he could jump out, or drive his fist into Lang's gleaming teeth.

With a great effort, Lang stopped his laughter, and pulled in to the kerb by a small French restaurant. He turned in his seat, and looked Vivian squarely in the eyes.

'I really am sincerely sorry to have behaved like that, old boy, really sorry. But you see,' and here he began to chuckle again, ' can help you!'

As Vivian still didn't speak, he repeated, 'I can help you to get that money, and you can help me too at the same time.'

He saw the incredulous look stealing across Vivian's face.

'It's all on the level. This really is our lucky day. Still, come into the joint here, and I'll tell you about it over our grub.'

They left the car and entered the small, dimly lit restaurant, where a languid young man sat softly playing a piano, and two couples slowly circled the tiny dance floor.

As they settled themselves in one of the curtained alcoves, Lang began to talk.

'It's like this, old friend,' he began. 'After the war, with a little bit of influence, and a little bit of you-know-what, I took over the managership of the London branch of the Europa Travel Agency. I expect you've heard of it, even down in Torquay?'

Vivian nodded. It was difficult not to have heard of the most go-ahead agency in the business.

'Yes, I see your posters everywhere. They really are something out of the ordinary. They seem to leap out at you, if you know what I mean.'

'Ah, there you have it, old boy. The head of the company is an old Danish chap, bit of an invalid, you know, but a brilliant artist. I brought him out of Denmark with a mob of refugees during the war, his niece too, as a matter of fact. You remember, when the Jerries were killing a lot of them off. Anyway, to continue. I ran into him here after the war, and that was that. He started the company with his money, and, believe me, he's got plenty of that, and I manage the actual travel side of the business. We started with the London office, now, as you know, we've got agents on the continent, every blessed where, in fact. The funny thing is, that the Guv'nor still likes to design the posters. It's about his only pleasure. That, and his niece, and she's really something. Wow! You wait till you see her. I could do a tumble for her in a big way, I don't mind telling you, if I wasn't already fixed up.'

'Married?' queried Vivian dazedly.

'Married? Me? Do us a favour, old boy! Marriage is all right for some, but let's face it, matrimony and I are like whisky and vinegar, we don't mix!'

'Well, I must say you seem to have done a damn sight better than I have, Felix, but I still don't see where I come in.'

Lang leaned seriously over the table, his eyes searching. 'Among other things, we arrange a lot of cruises on hired yachts, and I could keep you busy all next season, if you're interested. Wait!' He waved an admonitory finger as Vivian opened his mouth to speak. 'Right now I need you for a special trip for one customer only, over to the other side. The chap who was going to do it is no longer available.' He paused. 'And I must have a chap I can rely on absolutely. In other words, old boy, you.'

'Are you trying to make me believe that for doing that trip, and heaven knows there must be dozens of owner-skippers who'd do it for you, you'll pay me the seven hundred pounds I need for my boat?' He looked the other man hard in the eyes. 'It's crooked, isn't it?' he said quietly.

Lang sighed heavily. 'Come, come, now, don't ask me a question like that. Let us say it's a matter of essential business. Essential to me. And, of course, essential to your boat.'

He watched Vivian struggling with his emotions, and went into the attack.

'Look, Philip, I wouldn't give you a line, I know you too well of old, but believe me, you'd have nothing to worry about, you'd be an employee of the agency while you're on the job, quite legitimate in fact. There is absolutely no need for you to know anything about anybody. Just take my chap over to France, quietly, and without anyone knowing when or where. The chappie in question, Cooper, is a sort of undercover agent, who keeps an eye on all our agencies, and keeps them supplied with a little extra cash to by-pass the bloody currency restrictions. It's the only way to survive, you know. On paper it's illegal, I know, but the people who made those laws are the very people you and I fought like hell to protect. While we sweated blood, they made a tidy pile, but I don't have to tell you that, do I?' He smiled confidently. 'What have you done with your medals, eh? I don't suppose your friend the broker would accept those for credit!'

'But, seven hundred quid, I——'

'Well, it's worth it to us, you can say it's six months' pay in advance, if you like, anything, but will you do it? Because, if you don't, I'll have to get someone else. Probably someone I don't like, and don't want to help.

'You've nothing to lose, and everything to gain. No one will give you a second glance, they're used to your boat popping in and out everywhere, obviously, and on this occasion, when you come back, it'll be in your own boat! Not one that'll belong to some bloody little money-grabber!'

He drew a slim, gold case from his suit, and lit a cigarette; as he exhaled slowly, he said softly, 'Well, old boy, are you on?'

Vivian trembled violently, and forced a smile. 'I'm on. Just this once.'

Lang breathed deeply, and held out his hand.

'Shake, blast you! Now, let's have dinner.'

As he made a sign to the waiter who was hovering nearby, he grinned boyishly. 'Come round to the office tomorrow on your way to the blood-suckers, and we'll give you the wherewithal.'

He winked heavily. 'As I've always said, if you're in a

racket, and can do not a damn thing about it, then you must make the most of it!'

.   .   .   .   .   .

The grinding roar of countless cars and buses merged into one sullen symphony, and as the morning sunlight filtered through the churned-up clouds of exhaust smoke and the dust from the bone-dry pavements, the air seemed to be drawn from the glittering and noisy valleys between the opulent and colourful shop windows, and Vivian felt the overpowering desire to return at once to the comparative coolness of his room. He strode slowly down the shady side of Regent Street, glancing only perfunctorily at the busy stores, and allowing his active mind to work busily on Lang's offer of the previous evening. He did not doubt for one second that the reason for the trip was as Lang had said, but inwardly he felt that he was being offered a form of charity, for old time's sake, and that Lang was probably wrapping the whole thing up in a mesh of mystery, merely to sweeten the pill. He frowned, and glanced up angrily at the street numbers, to ensure that he was still walking in the right direction. Then he saw it, an impressive, double-windowed frontage, tastefully decorated with two of the magnificent travel posters, and a selection of carefully draped fishing-nets, imitation seaweed, and the more usual type of holiday literature.

Through the window he could see several girls busily engaged answering queries from behind a long counter, and he could count at least three glass-fronted doors opening off the main office. It was, as he had always imagined, a most prosperous concern, and it seemed almost laughable that a business of this nature should be hamstrung by foreign currency problems. Anyway, he decided, I can always pay the money back out of the boat's earnings next year. It was perhaps typical of him that he should make such a decision so lightly, which might concern his future. At that moment, the present seemed rather more important.

He thrust his way through the doors, his mind made up, and stood impatiently at the counter.

'Well, sir, what can I do for you?' A smartly dressed assistant was watching him with interest.

Vivian thought, old Felix certainly has picked a smart bunch of girls, he's learnt how to dress his window all right.

'Er, I have an appointment with Mr. Lang.'

'Oh yes, sir. Mr. Vivian isn't it? We're expecting you.'

Oh we are, are we, mused Vivian, as with a flash of nyloned legs she hurried through one of the office doors. He realized then, that up to that point he had been wondering if half Lang had told him had been bluff, but now, as the girl reappeared, and ushered him into the spacious, well-carpeted office, with all the deference of a well-trained slave, he knew that this part of the story at least was genuine.

Lang stood up jauntily, and waved him to a red leather chair, then having settled himself with a cigarette from an ornate, carved box on his wide desk, he sat back, and folded his small hands across his stomach, his head on one side, as he stared quizzically through the smoke, like a well-fed sparrow, thought Vivian.

'Well, old boy, have you come to report for work?'

'When do you want me to start?' His voice sounded flat, so he forced a smile, and added: 'I should thank you, I know. I really am more grateful than you realize.'

Lang waved expansively. 'Nuts! My job here is to make sure the whole set-up works, that's all, and frankly, I think you'll want to do business with us again. After all, I don't suppose you want a whole mob of awkward landlubbers trampling all over your beautiful boat, doing enough damage to take the edge off whatever profit you might have made, eh?' He grinned knowingly, as Vivian grimaced. 'Ah, I thought not, you always were a pusser-built bastard; well, we deal with very small parties, and more often than not we send our skippers a single customer. You know, the rich type who "just wants to get away from it all".'

He laughed heartily, as if the whole thing was a huge joke.

' 'Course, you might have to turn a blind eye if he wants you to take his secretary along too, if you follow me.'

He slid open a small drawer in the desk, and tossed a fat envelope across into Vivian's lap.

'There you are, seven hundred, in fivers. Okay?'

Vivian fumbled with the packet, feeling awkward and confused.

'Hell, man, it's like a miracle!' he exploded. He weighed it in his hand. 'Feels like one too!'

Lang grinned. 'It's all there anyway, I counted it myself. I'm sorry it has to be in cash, but it does ease the complications a bit.'

Vivian raised his eyebrows. 'How come?'

'Well, you know how it is, old boy, we make out our accounts quarterly, and as I don't want anyone to know you're working for me yet, I think it's better this way.'

'What you really mean is, that if I'm stupid enough to get nicked by the Customs going over, you don't want it known that I'm tied in with you, right?'

Lang laughed. 'You catch on fast, Philip, that is exactly it. You take the risk for me, and I pay you for it.' He leaned back, studying the other's face thoughtfully.

'How d'you know I wouldn't squeal on you to clear myself?'

'You ask yourself that, old boy,' laughed Lang. 'Would you turn me in, even if you could prove it, that is?'

'No, I wouldn't like anyone to know that the Europa

Agency has to finance its employees abroad to keep them in gin and skittles!'

Lang suddenly became serious. 'Well look, my man Cooper will be coming aboard your boat tomorrow. He's already at Torquay, as a matter of fact. I 'phoned him last night, and told him to take his gear down to your boat.'

'You *were* sure of me!' said Vivian dryly.

'I had to be. The chap I used to have doing my special trips, he was bloody useless, so now perhaps you can understand why I was so excited when I ran into you yesterday? It was a bloody miracle, I can tell you.' He opened his eyes wide. 'Would you believe it, I paid him the earth, got him a lot of jobs, and he tried to blackmail me!'

'What was his name?' queried Vivian. 'Was he one of the old naval crowd?'

'Oh, God, no! Why, Nick Patterson hadn't been anything before I gave him a job. I must have been mad in those days. Still, we got it all straightened out, and got rid of him somehow, though I believe his boat's still about the South Coast somewhere.'

Vivian stood up. 'I must be off. I take it this Cooper chap will tell me my destination when I see him?'

'Oh no, I can tell you now, it's quite straightforward, you're to go to Calais.' He hurried on. 'I happen to know that there's a big rally of British yachts there all this week, so you won't be noticed in the confusion. Cooper will be an official passenger of yours, but you can take the cash ashore. It's quite simple really, but he'll explain it all to you.'

They shook hands, and the next instant Vivian's feet were taking him rapidly through the crowded streets towards the broker's offices. He felt quite light-headed, and his humour was so buoyant, that he felt a little sorry for the firm's secretary, as she wrote him out a hurried receipt.

Mr. Grandison, the manager, seemed more than a little

shaken by the sight of so much money, and cunningly tried to question him, but Vivian, after a session with Lang's quick-witted bantering, was more than a match for him.

With the receipt in his pocket, and the humble promises that the official Bill of Sale, and other papers, would be sent on to him immediately, still ringing in his ears, he started his journey back to the sea.

. . . . . .

Vivian was giving the decks of *Seafox* a wash down the following day when, glancing up, he saw a man standing on the very edge of the wall, watching him.

'Good morning. Mr. Cooper, isn't it?'

The man nodded, and turned towards the steps.

'Here's yore passenger, then,' said Arthur hoarsely.

Vivian nodded vaguely. He had noticed that the dapper, little man in the smart blazer and white flannels was carrying two very large cases. Those, in addition to the two he had found already parked in the saloon by Arthur, made the venture seem a little more peculiar.

The man stepped lightly on to the deck, his pointed, two-toned shoes striking an incongruous note against the nautical background. He removed his panama hat, which had been shading his narrow, rather swarthy face, and offered him a well-manicured hand in a moist, lingering handshake. As near as he could tell, Cooper was about forty, with receding hair, and a pair of dark, almost black, eyes, which, set close together beneath thick brows, were the most vital part of his otherwise too-smart personality. Even his sharp-ended bow tie, and the silk shirt, gave the impression that Mr. Cooper had not always been in the money.

He handed the bags to Arthur, and said curtly, 'Please

take these below.' And as the old man shambled away, he flashed a well-trained smile, and Vivian caught the faint smell of whisky. 'I think we can get under way now, Captain, and I'll go below and unpack. You can get rid of the old man, I think.' Even his voice was carefully pitched, and was devoid of any accent.

Ten minutes later, as the twin diesels throbbed confidently, and the boat tugged impatiently at the two remaining shore-lines, old Arthur stepped ashore, with Coley tucked under his arm. The cat always had resented being left ashore when Vivian made trips over to the other side, but now his resentment seemed to have mellowed, as if he realized that the boat which was his home was safely paid for.

Vivian ruffled the black fur, and grinned at Arthur. 'I'll be back in about five days, old-timer, so long for now.'

The old man paused, as if to say something, then, with a wrinkled smile, he let go the mooring lines, and eased the yacht away from the jetty with his foot.

The grey, sun-dappled walls, with the rows of watching faces, the white boats, and the tripper launches, all slid by, and as he stood in the cool wheelhouse, his legs astride, and the wheel firmly held in his hands, he felt his heart rise with the boat, as she pushed her slim stem into the first small roller.

An hour later, firmly planted on course, Vivian was busy with the Automatic Pilot, when he felt Cooper watching him from the saloon doorway.

'All okay, unpacked and everything?'

Cooper didn't answer him, he was watching the delicate machinery moving in Vivian's grip.

'That is a very nice little thing,' he said at length.

Vivian nodded. 'Essential when you sail single-handed, as I do.'

'Your predecessor didn't have one, you know. His boat was very old-fashioned.'

'Oh, you knew that chap Patterson, did you?' Vivian looked up with interest.

'Yes, I sailed with him several times.'

'Where is he now? Are we likely to run into him?'

'Hardly,' and he laughed softly. 'He's dead.'

'Dead? Why? What happened?'

'As I said, it was a very old boat, and there was a fire, I believe, rather a bad fire in fact.'

He shook with silent laughter.

'Poor old Patterson, he did want to be such a big shot too.'

A faint, unaccountable chill crept into Vivian's spine, and he remembered Lang laughing too, and saying, 'We got rid of him somehow.' He heard himself asking, 'What sort of a chap was he?'

'All right, but, you know, he asked too many questions.'

When Vivian turned to meet his gaze, the close-set eyes were watching him fixedly, like a shark's, cold, and devoid of all compassion.

.   .   .   .   .

The navigation lights gleamed like red and green eyes on either side of the wheelhouse, and having ensured that the horizon was clear of shipping Vivian slipped down into the saloon, where Cooper had agreed to lay a meal for them both.

One of the big suitcases lay open on the deck, and Vivian looked at it in amazement. It contained a dirty, five-gallon oil drum.

Cooper nodded knowingly. 'Pretty, isn't it?'

'What's the idea of that, then?'

'You take the dear, little drum ashore, well, two of them to be exact, and if any gentleman asks you where you're going, just say you want to get some lubricating oil for the engines. You then go to the garage which I shall point out to you, and bring back two full drums of oil; the man at the garage will keep these beauties. Neat, yes?'

'Phew, it's neat all right,' Vivian pushed his cap to the back of his head, and watched while Cooper unpacked another drum.

He tested the weight in his hand.

'Hm, they're a bit heavy for drums which are supposed to be empty, he commented.

'Well then,' said the little man, with a bright show of teeth, 'you mustn't let anyone hold them for you, must you?'

Again, there was that strange undercurrent of menace in his voice.

Vivian shook his head, he was imagining things again.

'Okay, Mr. Cooper, those drums are as good as delivered.'

Cooper stroked his silk shirt lovingly, and gazed dreamily into space.

'I'm so glad you're easy to get along with,' he paused, and glanced casually round the saloon. 'After all, I hate boats to catch fire, don't you?'

As Vivian reset the Automatic Pilot at midnight, those words were still with him, but he knew that it was too late to turn back now.

2

EVERYWHERE in the Calais yacht basin groups of bunting-bedecked yachts, of every conceivable class and size, rolled gently together, their ensigns, and the excited voices of their boisterous owners, making it quite clear to Vivian that they were indeed the visiting British yacht club.

The two oil drums felt conspicuous enough as they banged clumsily against his legs, but, knowing their contents, he felt that every eye was watching him.

As Cooper had suggested, in his pseudo-American-gangster manner, before he had left the boat just previously, it had all been just too easy, the Port and Customs officials had been both too busy, and too full of good-fellowship, to worry about one more visiting yacht. He chuckled to himself, as he wondered what would happen if he absconded with the money he was carrying.

Away from the boat, and Cooper, his previous thoughts and fears now seemed a trifle fantastic. Cooper really was an odorous little man, and he would not be at all sorry to be rid of him for good.

He turned sharp right, as directed, into a dingy, little, cobbled mews, and stood for an instant looking at the small, dilapidated garage, with its battered, tin advertisement placards, their surfaces long since made unreadable by urchins throwing stones and the filth of manœuvring vehicles. The double doors leading into a large work-room leaned drunkenly, the faded paint peeled and decayed, and adding to the general air of forlornness.

He strode into the middle of the shed, blinking in the gloomy interior. From beneath the half-dismembered body of an aged trailer, a round-faced man, in the inevitable garb of all mechanics, except that his overalls had obviously never been washed, heaved himself up on to his short legs, wiping his blackened hands with an old towel. For a moment he looked Vivian guardedly up and down.

'*Oui?*' he nodded his head questioningly, then his face suddenly transformed, as his eyes became fixed upon the two drums.

'Plis, you 'ave come for the refills, m'sieur?' and as Vivian nodded, he beckoned him hurriedly into a small back office, where two identical drums stood in readiness.

While Vivian filled his pipe, and rested himself by the door, the little man chattered cheerily about the harbour, the weather, and the cost of living. Occasionally he lapsed into voluble French, and he had the greatest difficulty in following the trend of his conversation.

As he watched, the Frenchman produced a greasy instrument, like a giant can-opener, and proceeded to screw it to the bottom flange of the first drum. Feeling Vivian's interested gaze upon him, he glanced up, his small eyes thoughtful.

'I think you 'ad better go to your boat now, my friend. You will 'ave to make the two journeys this time, yes?'

Vivian lifted the new drum, smiling. 'Okay, I'll go quietly.' And with the other man's eyes following him through the gates, he sauntered back to the harbour wall.

Of Cooper there was no sign, so he returned to the garage for the second drum. The mechanic was waiting for him in the office, puffing impatiently at an evil-smelling cigar.

He nodded briefly as Vivian left, and was obviously eager to continue with his investigation, and no doubt in a hurry to parcel up the pound notes for collection.

Vivian was halfway down the mews, when he realized, with irritation, that he had left his pipe behind in the office. A good opportunity to put the wind up the garrulous mechanic, he decided, with an inward smile.

With a quick glance to ascertain that the whole area was deserted, but for a mangy dog which sniffed hungrily at an overturned garbage bucket, he slid quietly into the shed, his rubber deck shoes making no sound, and reaching the office door undetected, he paused, searching for a gap in the torn sacking across its windowless entrance. It would be interesting to see what amount of money was worth a seven-hundred-pound travel ticket.

Holding his breath, he gently eased himself against the lower part of the door, so that the excited beat of his heart seemed deafening, and then with one finger, he slowly began to raise the bottom edge of the sacking.

At first he could see nothing but the stooping back of the other man's overalls, but then, as he turned towards the table, he saw the contents of the two drums strewn on the narrow bench opposite the door. His breath choked in his throat. It had been money all right, but not the sort of cash required by a legitimate business. From one end of the bench to the other American dollar bills of every possible denomination were sorted neatly into little, fat packets. It was obvious that both the drums must have been completely filled, for the pile, even to Vivian's inexperienced eye, represented a fortune, running into many thousands of dollars, and on the Continent, where any mortal thing could be purchased for American money, it represented power untold.

Vivian drew back, confused and startled. Knowingly or

innocently, whichever way he chose to interpret his actions, he was mixed up in something a little more disquieting than dodging petty restrictions. For a moment he felt a wild fury sweep over him, and in that instant it seemed the only course of action open to him was to burst into the office, and beat the truth out of the occupant, and then do the same for Cooper. The eventual realization that he alone was the smuggler, as far as the law was concerned, acted like a douche of cold water to his reeling brain. By God, Lang must have known about this. Or did he? Vivian backed cautiously to the gates, his mind working furiously. Suppose he too was being taken in by his Danish employer, and was just being used as a tool? Whatever the outcome, it was obvious that right at that moment he had to get back to England, and get the truth out of him. Grimly he clambered down on to the *Seafox*'s deck, noting as he did so, the wet imprint of a shoe by the wheelhouse door.

Cooper had returned, sitting back on one of the cushioned benches, his legs stuck out, a general air of well-being surrounding him. His dark eyes were faintly mocking, and Vivian noticed with disgust that he was wearing silk ankle socks.

'Everything went perfectly, I see,' he commented at length. 'Not a hitch in our little drama.' He waved apologetically with his pale hands. 'Oh, I'm sorry. I forgot, you've been used to drama.'

'And what the hell is all that supposed to mean?' asked Vivian shortly.

Perhaps it would be a good idea to beat him up after all, and involuntarily he took a step forward.

A brief look of alarm flitted across the dark eyes, as Cooper hastened to assure him:

'Oh, nothing really. It's just that I've always had the highest respect and envy for you naval chaps. I——'

But Vivian, relieved of the strain of the trip, and aware that he had no choice but to go through with whatever scheme was required to get the truth about the organization, had had enough.

'You're a bloody, little liar,' he announced calmly. 'So for God's sake, let's just leave it at that.'

Cooper sat taut and watchful, like a trapped animal, his hands screwing up the corner of his immaculate blazer.

'Furthermore, we're going straight back to London, and not to Torquay,' he added, after a pause. 'I've been paid for the trip, and now I've got some other business to attend to, so what d'you think of that?'

'Gee, you must do as you think, Captain, it'll suit me better too, and goddamit, I'm sorry I riled you, honest.' His mouth hung open pleadingly.

'Forget it,' snapped Vivian. 'But just keep out of my way in future!'

As he turned angrily to the chart rack, Cooper's eyes seemed to expand, until they filled his whole face, and his loose lips quivered with the combined passion of hatred and humiliation.

Vivian would not have felt quite so confident of the future, had he turned to see the livid, sadistic face of his passenger.

.   .   .   .   .   .

With a short bow-wave creaming away from her sharp stem, the *Seafox* ploughed steadily into the busy approaches of the Thames Estuary, which, in the fine haze, shone like a dappled, pewter tray. With a practised eye Vivian noted, almost casually, the approaching coasters, and colliers, and the passing bulk of a Swedish timber-ship. *Seafox* rolled slightly in the criss-crossing wakes, but held her course, undeterred by the heavy shapes which surged past her.

All the wheelhouse windows were wide open to catch the last breath of the sea breeze, but even so, the air was heavy and thick, like the forerunner of a thunderstorm, and Vivian repeatedly wiped his damp face with the back of his wrist, as he stood poised and watchful at the wheel.

In his mind he had already decided to have it out with Lang, and find out what exactly was going on, and how exactly he was implicated.

He eased the spokes of the wheel deftly, as a waterlogged mass of timber bobbed menacingly past. He cursed softly as he resumed his course, wondering why a country such as Britain should allow her one real waterway to become such an attraction for filth and neglect.

A small, dark shape detached itself from behind a distant collier, and with a mounting wash, bore down towards him. As the fast launch drew near, he could clearly discern the uniformed figures, and the blue flag. Her Majesty's Customs.

He turned his head, but kept his keen eyes fixed on the other craft. 'Cooper!' he shouted, above the drone of the engines, 'Customs coming!'

Cooper scrambled up beside him, blinking in the hard gleam from the water. He bared his teeth, and nervously picked at his tie.

'Hope it doesn't mess things up,' he complained. 'I mean, I told everyone we were going back to Torquay.'

'Mess things up? What the hell difference does it make?'

The other man didn't answer, so Vivian turned his attention to the Customs boat, which had suddenly turned gracefully to run parallel with him, making the water between them boil and plunge in trapped torment.

Vivian eased the twin throttles, as the gap slowly narrowed. Closer and closer, while her crew lowered the rope fenders with a well-practised efficiency, and a stocky figure swung out of the wheelhouse in readiness for boarding. The name *Pursuit* glinted dully on her royal blue bows.

With hardly a bump the two hulls touched, and as the boarding officer leapt easily aboard, the Customs boat swung away, and followed purposefully astern.

Vivian waved cheerfully, his inside peculiarly uneasy. 'Come in, sorry I can't leave the wheel, I've no crew,' he explained.

The other man stepped down, nodding approvingly.

'A very nice little boat you've got here, sir,' he smiled. 'When we saw your "Q" flag, I thought to myself, here's a good chance to see what she's like inside.' His eye fell on Cooper, who stood framed in the saloon door.

'This is Mr. Cooper, the boat's under charter to him.'

'Yes, very well, sir, then I'll go and see what he's brought back from Calais, eh?'

The two men went below, their conversation drowned by the engines. The Customs officer was soon back at his side, his broad face as cheerful as before. Vivian was unable to control himself any longer.

'Here, how did you know we had come from Calais?' he demanded.

'Did I say Calais, then?' the other man's face was blank. 'I must have guessed that, mustn't I? After all, most of the yachts seem to call in there on the way home.'

He handed back the boat's papers, and waved his cap from the wheelhouse door.

'Sorry I can't stop, but we're very busy these days, y'know.' He watched as his launch crept alongside. 'Glad you had a good trip. Might see you again some time.' And with a wave he was gone.

The *Pursuit* had sighted another yacht making for the estuary, flying the yellow flag, and made off to investigate.

Vivian snorted impatiently. What had become of his old,

devil-may-care attitude? All these fanciful imaginings were beginning to be a little ridiculous, he decided. Damn the Customs, they always made him feel like that anyway. And with a further contemptuous glance at Cooper, who was busy filing his nails, he flung his full concentration into piloting his boat into the Thames fairway.

For the purpose of easy access to the West End of London, he eventually managed to berth his boat off Chelsea pier, and as he stood in the boat's tiny dinghy, making sure that the mooring lines to the buoy were quite secure, he wrinkled his nose disapprovingly at the smell of mud, petrol, and coal dust, and reached up for Cooper's suitcases.

He felt a childish surge of pleasure at the sight of two large oil smears on the white trousers.

'Here, steady on! Don't drop those cases in the water!'

'Well, I'm in a hurry,' barked Vivian. 'I must get to your office before it closes. I want to see Felix Lang.'

They rowed to the pier in silence, and after a word with the piermaster, they eventually captured the attention of a prowling taxi, and made for Regent Street.

As Vivian had feared, the lobby of the travel bureau was deserted when they arrived, and only one girl was at the back of the counter. She looked up questioningly as the ill-assorted pair hurried in.

'I'm sorry, Mr. Cooper. Mr. Lang's gone out,' she said quickly, looking at the little man with ill-disguised dislike.

Cooper shrugged. 'Well that does it, you'll have to wait till tomorrow, I guess.'

Vivian leaned across the counter, to where the girl had resumed making up her face in readiness for leaving.

'Er, look, miss,' he started. 'Where can I find him? Could you let me have his private 'phone number?'

She stopped her preparations, and studied him, liking what she saw.

'Well, if it's all that urgent,' she smiled, 'I can tell you, he's gone round to Mr. Mason's flat for a drink.'

'I don't think I know Mr. Mason,' said Vivian carefully. 'Have you got that number here?'

'Oh yes, Mr. Mason's a co-director,' said the girl airily, relieved that she was being allowed to go home at last. She scribbled on a piece of paper. 'Here, this is it. Help yourself.' She nodded to a telephone.

Vivian picked up the instrument, and turned to speak to Cooper. He had apparently vanished. Shrugging, he dialled the number, and impatiently tapped his fingers, wondering what he would say when Lang answered.

'Lang speaking. Who's that?' The voice was brisk.

'Hallo, Felix, it's Phillip,' he paused, and there was the sound of a door shutting.

'What the devil! Where are you speaking from? Is everything all right?'

'I'm in your office. I came back to London so that we could have a little chat,' he let the words sink in. 'I'm a bit worried about something.'

'Well, don't discuss it now, old boy, come straight round here and have a drink. Seven, Stafford Court, off Curzon Street.' He paused, and when he spoke again, he sounded anxious. 'But everything did go off all right, didn't it?'

'Yes. Too damn well for my liking, Felix. That's why I want that little talk.'

'Well, all right, hurry on round.'

Nodding to the girl, Vivian hurried out of the building, feeling in his pocket for a taxi fare. Lang was rattled all right. Well, we shall see, he mused.

As he waited for the chromium-plated lift in the expensive hall of Stafford Court, one of the most exclusive blocks of flats in the West End, he tried again to fit Lang into the picture. How big was this thing, and how long had it been going on?

The lift glided to the second floor, and he stepped into a semicircular hallway, tastefully decorated, and containing two doors. He glanced at the one bearing the card, A. Mason, M.C., and pressed the bell.

Immediately, the door was opened by a tall, gaunt man in a white jacket and dark trousers, whose hair was cropped to a savage shortness, and his eyebrows were raised questioningly.

Before he could say anything however, he was brushed quickly aside, and Lang stood in his place.

'All right, Morrie, go and see to the drinks,' and as the strange servant moved softly away, Lang jerked his head.

'In here, Philip,' and he opened another door into a small anteroom. He shut the door carefully, and turned, his face unsmiling, his eyes thoughtful.

'Well,' he said abruptly. 'What's all this about trouble?'

Vivian dug his hands into his jacket pockets, feeling the familiar touch of his tobacco pouch.

'That cargo,' he began, and Lang stiffened. 'It wasn't quite what we expected. In fact, Felix, it was rather a lot of American money. Did you know about it?' He waited, breathing hard.

Lang shrugged, and seemed to go limp. He spread his small hands helplessly.

'How the hell did you find that out? I told you not to ask any questions.'

Vivian felt himself trembling. 'So you did damn well know? How do you think I feel about it, eh?' His voice was harsh.

Lang walked to the window, and stood looking down at the traffic below. When he answered, his voice was tired and dull.

'I didn't want you to know a thing, because I like you too well. You know that. The fact is, I'm in this so deep, I can't help myself.'

'You seemed to be enjoying it, the last time we met,' said Vivian bitterly, 'or had you forgotten?'

'That's just it, I *am* enjoying myself, don't you see?' the voice was imploring. 'I've got all I ever wanted,' he spread his hands helplessly. 'It's just that I'm not free, oh, it's hopeless, I'll never be able to explain it all to you.'

'Well, I'm getting out of it, whatever it is, Felix. And I'm getting out right now.'

Lang laughed, it was not a nice sound.

'You're right, of course.' Then, as if he had come to a sudden decision: 'Yes, you go now. I'll fix it somehow.'

'But what *is* going on, Felix? What can't you cope with any more?'

He was being cautious now, but he was curious, and anxious too. He had never seen Lang so dispirited before.

The other man looked at him intently.

'I had an idea I might be able to get out of this business altogether, that's why I need your help, as I've never needed it before.' He grinned ruefully. 'I had the idea we might be able to glide out of this together, Philip.'

As Vivian didn't answer, he shrugged again. 'But I'll not manage it on my own, that's for sure.'

'Look, Felix, we've both been in pretty tough spots before, what in hell's name have you been up to that's so difficult now, and why didn't you level with me in the first place? You know I'm not likely to blow my top!'

Lang glanced quickly at the door, and unwittingly lowered his voice.

'As far as everyone else is concerned, you know no more than what I told you before you did that trip, right?'

Vivian nodded, frowning.

'Well, then, just come in and have a drink or two, and play the innocent, and afterwards we'll creep over to my place, and I'll give you the whole story.'

He looked anxiously at Vivian's taut face. 'What d'you say?'

'Fair enough. You got my boat for me, Felix, and I've known you long enough to realize that you don't go around imagining things. All the same, the dollars, why did it have to be dollars? And what the hell do you do with all that cash?'

There was a slight sound in the passage, and Lang shook his head gently. 'Later, old boy,' he whispered.

The door was flung open, and Vivian goggled at the girl who stood poised in the entrance. As he took in the short, auburn hair, the moist, almost mocking mouth, and the rich curves of her slim figure, barely concealed by a vivid, off-the-shoulder summer frock, she pouted petulantly, and glided to Lang's side, slipping a scarlet-tipped hand through his arm.

'Felix, darling,' her voice was a soft purr. 'I was getting worried about you. When are you coming back?'

Her eyes, however, never left Vivian's face.

Lang grinned, and looked more relaxed.

'This is my old sparring-partner, Philip Vivian, you know. I've told you all about him.'

She moved closer to Vivian, offering her hand.

'You didn't tell me he was quite so beautiful, darling.'

Vivian flushed, and over her shoulder he saw Lang wink broadly.

'Her name's Janice, by the way, a very special friend of mine.' Lang was obviously getting back into form.

Vivian, unused to feminine company for so long, merely nodded dumbly, feeling vaguely uneasy at her nearness, and almost apparent animal warmth.

'Well, come along, children,' Lang boomed. 'Let's go and meet the bottles!'

The large lounge, comfortably and carefully furnished, was full of bright colours, from the gay chairs and drapes, to the many table-lamps dotted here and there around the room. A radiogram was giving forth a noisy dance tune, and records were scattered in profusion across the thick carpet. A miniature, glass-topped cocktail bar filled one corner of the room, and behind it, a tall, middle-aged, grey-haired man, with a thin, pallid face, was filling some glasses with generous portions of whisky. As the trio entered, he glanced up, and Vivian caught a certain quick watchfulness, born of long practice. The eyes were sharp and grey, like little gimlets, and with the thin-lipped mouth, gave the impression of extreme hardness.

The only other occupant of the room sat quite still in a deep armchair, and as he rose to be introduced, Vivian saw a brief spasm of pain flit across the tanned, deeply lined face. Although rather squat in build, the heaviness of his body was immediately neutralized by the softness of his features, and the delicate texture of his skin. His keen, blue eyes had a sad, gentle gaze, only marred by their heavy, hood-like lids, and his mouth, which turned sharply down at one side in a permanent grimace, gave his whole expression an air of whimsicality.

Lang ushered Vivian forward. 'Philip Vivian, meet your new employer, Mr. Jensen.'

The long, smooth hand was surprisingly firm in his grip, and as he glanced down, he noted the fine texture of the skin, criss-crossed with tiny, blue veins. The hand of an artist. When he spoke, his voice was soft, but clear, and the Danish accent gave it a certain additional charm.

'I am very happy to know you, Mr. Vivian. I am sure we shall be doing a lot of business together in the future, but for the moment we will not talk of such sordid matters, you will please tell me about your wonderful boat.'

He frowned, and ran his fingers through his long, grey hair. 'Ah, I forgot, please excuse me.' He turned to the tall man behind him. 'This is Andrew Mason, my partner, er, give him a drink, Andrew.'

Mason nodded briefly to Vivian, and turned to his well-stocked bar. Over his shoulder, rather too casually, he said, 'All fixed up, Felix, no trouble is there?'

'No, nothing like that,' said Lang shortly. 'Philip just popped up to let me know he was back all right.'

Mason stood the glass carefully on a small mat.

'I didn't know you were coming back to London?' His eyebrows were raised in an unspoken question.

'No, I wanted to get a few small matters straightened out,' said Vivian quietly.

'Come over here, my boy,' commanded Jensen testily. 'Tell me about the boat. It's useless talking to Mason about boats, he's an old soldier, he doesn't understand the creatures!'

Vivian seated himself in a small chair by the older man's side, gripping his glass tighly, and trying desperately to keep control of his mixed emotions.

Jensen laid one hand on his arm. 'Just a moment, before you begin.' He turned to the girl, who sat curled on the floor by the radiogram, her eyes dreamy, and a slender ankle jerking in time to the music.

'Can't you turn that dreadful din down a bit, Janice?' he complained. 'It really is a most awful sort of noise.'

She pouted again, but switched off the music. Then with her knees drawn up under her chin, she sat concentrating her gaze on Vivian's face.

In a short while, he realized that Jensen was not just a polite listener, he was a thorough master of the subject, and from time to time he shot questions to him, some of which were of an extremely technical nature.

'You know a lot of the sea, sir?' queried Vivian at length.

'Ah, my boy, there was a time, before——' he stopped, and shook his head sadly. 'It was a long time ago, in my old country. We lived at the top of a big fjord, and whenever we had any time, we would go sailing in my little boat. And sometimes,' he paused, his eyes dreamy and distant, 'we would just sit. Just sit and fish.'

There was a sudden silence in the room, and Jensen seemed unaware of their presence.

Lang laughed, a trifle too heartily. 'Have another drink, old boy,' and Janice was on her feet in a flash to take his empty glass.

She refilled it, and carefully carried it back to him, lingering as she bent over the chair, allowing her loose-topped dress to confuse Vivian even more.

The door opened, and Morrie, the unusual manservant, waited politely until he caught Jensen's eye.

'Your niece has just driven up, sir,' he grated.

Jensen jerked back to life, smiling quietly. 'Ah yes, it's getting late, and I did tell Karen to call for me.'

He turned to Vivian. 'We live out of London you see, and she insists that I go home early.' He chuckled. 'I am getting old I think.'

At the sound of the outer door being opened, Vivian steeled himself. If this girl was to be another Janice, he had to prepare a suitable expression, so as not to display his confusion yet again.

Whatever control he had, whatever fears he entertained, all were scattered as Karen Jensen stepped briskly through the door. His mouth went dry, and his heart pounded heavily, for to say that she was merely lovely, was a cruel understatement. Her hair, which was long, and hung loose to her shoulders, was of such a pure yellow, that it shone in the reflected light like silver. It made a perfect frame for her small, oval face, which was dominated by the clearest blue eyes he had ever seen.

Her slim, rounded body, dressed in a simply cut, cool-looking dress, gave the impression of warmth and cool maturity at the same time, and as Vivian stumbled to his feet, he found himself looking down into those amused, candid eyes, with a new feeling forming in the pit of his stomach. Her hand was small and soft, like a tiny animal, he thought, and he marvelled at the rich, honey-colour of her skin.

'You have made another conquest, Karen,' laughed Jensen, who had been carefully watching Vivian's reactions, and to Vivian, 'Keep away, my boy, she's expensive, I can tell you!'

She smiled, showing her even, white teeth. 'Don't be silly, Uncle, you are the expensive one!'

Her voice too, with the fascinating accent, made his blood tingle, and he was horribly aware of his own shabby jacket and scuffed shoes.

'You should have been earlier, my dear,' said Jensen, as she helped him to his feet. 'He was telling us about his lovely boat.'

She turned to Vivian, her eyes wide. 'What is the boat's name?'

'*Seafox*,' answered Vivian, his throat suddenly dry.

'A beautiful name,' she said thoughtfully. 'I should like to see it one day.'

'Er, perhaps you and Mr. Jensen would care to see her while she is in London?'

His voice must have sounded almost pleading, for she laughed outright, her hair shaking and gleaming. Then, as if she was afraid she had offended him, she laid a small, brown hand on his sleeve, and studied his face gravely. 'Yes, we will try to come.'

Then she turned away, to say good-bye to Mason and Lang, and with hot, envious eyes, he followed her every movement. Only when she and her uncle had departed, in fact, did he allow his muscles and nerves to relax.

As Mason and Lang were talking quietly in a corner, he busied himself with another drink, although he knew it was not the whisky which was making him light-headed now. He turned, and saw Janice watching him seriously. She pulled a face.

'It's hell, isn't it?' she whispered, and Vivian noticed she was wearing a wedding-ring.

He warmed to her, glad of someone to talk to.

'Did it show then?' he grinned awkwardly.

'Oh no, not much!' she laughed. 'I thought you were going to propose to her.' She paused. 'You're wasting your time there though,' she went on. 'Her sole interest is looking after old Jensen, and of course, he sees that she wants for nothing.' She watched him like a cat. 'Nothing but a man, that is,' she said archly. 'And here's me, struggling with two!'

Vivian shook his head dazedly. 'You're married, I see——' he began.

'Yes, I'm Mrs. Mason!' And she turned away to the radiogram.

Vivian shook his head wearily. She was Mrs. Mason, yet she was obviously the girl Lang had been sleeping with. Most of the people he had seen today were mixed up in this smuggling venture, yet they didn't look like . . . he paused, look like what? What does a smuggler look like? A chill crept across his spine. Perhaps even Karen? But no, that would be ridiculous. I'll get the full dope from Felix, he decided.

Lang touched his arm.

'Come on, old boy, we must be off, and let these two good people rest.'

Vivian darted a glance at Janice, but she appeared intent on her records.

As they descended in the lift, Lang was humming softly, his eyes dreamy.

'You did damn well, old boy,' he said, as the doors slid noiselessly open for them. 'Now let's get away from here. It always makes me rattled talking to that creep!'

Vivian glanced at him in surprise. 'I thought you were all fixed up there?'

'As I said earlier, it's a helluva mix-up. But I'll tell you all about it in a minute.' He stiffened. 'Oh blast!' he muttered. A tall policeman was standing heavily by the parked Bentley. He looked up as the two men approached.

'Your car?' His voice was belligerent.

'Terribly sorry, Officer,' said Lang cheerfully. 'Forgot to put the lights on, I see.' He smiled disarmingly. 'I really am sorry. I'm sure you chaps have quite enough to do without running about after forgetful idiots like me.'

The policeman, taken off his guard, shifted his feet and coughed.

'Well, you know how it is, sir,' he began importantly.

'I do indeed, old boy,' Lang nodded understandingly, and suddenly held out his hand. 'Here get a drink for yourself when you're off duty.'

The policeman's hand closed on the note without hesitation, and he smiled apologetically. 'Well, thank you very much, sir. I hope you don't think I'm in the habit of——'

Lang waved carelessly, and opened the car door. 'Forget it, old boy, let's just blame it all on the Government!'

He slid his heavy body behind the wheel, and Vivian climbed in beside him. The car trembled, and slid away from the kerb. Lang glanced into his mirror.

'Bastard!' he said dispassionately.

Vivian looked at him in mock surprise. 'You really are a cool customer,' he admitted. 'D'you make a habit of that sort of thing?'

'Can't afford to rub the police up the wrong way, y'know.' His voice was emphatic. 'Otherwise they might hang about when I'm not just making a social call one day.' He chuckled. 'They're a funny lot, you know. Half the people who get pinched for motoring offences do so because they *will* argue with the coppers. S'fact, old boy, they just don't know the right approach, that's all.'

'Bit dangerous though, isn't it?'

Lang laughed shortly. 'Have you ever heard of a motorist getting pinched for attempted bribery?' He laughed again. ' 'Course you haven't, but I have a feeling I'm not the first customer that young chap's had.'

They were both silent for a while, as Lang extricated himself from the heavier traffic. He turned his head suddenly.

'Look, d'you mind if we go down to your boat?'

'All right by me. Why?'

'I'd like to see her, for one thing. And it might bring back a few memories too. Then we can have a drink and discuss the whole bloody business.'

They lapsed into silence again, as Lang made rapidly for Chelsea, the scenery changing from grey shop fronts and government offices, to coffee bars and comfortable-looking pubs, small terraced houses, and occasionally the glint of the quiet river.

They left the car at Chelsea Pier, and clumped along the board-walk to the little dinghy, which tilted alarmingly as

Lang settled himself in the stern. Vivian smiled in the darkness. Lang seemed like a child, unable to disguise his pleasure at being near a boat again.

They bumped alongside, and as Vivian secured the painter, Lang heaved himself on to the deck, and sniffed approvingly.

'Not bad, not bad at all,' he commented, and stood back, as Vivian unlocked the wheelhouse door, and flooded the boat with light.

He too began to enjoy himself, as he showed Lang over the yacht, and as the other man stood by the wheel, examining the shining compass, he caught a brief glimpse of the past. Lang in oilskin and muffler, his face impassive, but his voice excited, yelling, 'Open fire when your guns bear!' and then standing at the bridge screen, unflinching, as the enemy tracers whipped past.

Lang looked surprised at Vivian's grave expression.

'What's up, Philip? You look as if you've seen a ghost.'

He lowered his eyes, caught off guard. 'I was just thinking about the old days, Felix,' he admitted.

Lang clapped him across the shoulder. 'If it's any consolation to you, old boy, so was I.' He grimaced ruefully. 'It's all over though, I'm afraid. For chaps like us there'll never be anything else quite the same.' He peered into the saloon, and rubbed his hands. 'Well, come on, where's that drink? We've got a lot of talking to do.'

'You have, Felix. Not me!'

He produced the last bottle of gin, and two glasses, then as he hunted for the bitters, and filled a small glass jug with water: 'This is for the paying customers really. When I get 'em!' he added. 'But I think you've paid your share of my keep so I imagine you're entitled.'

They drank slowly, while Vivian waited for the other to begin. Lang cocked one leg over the other, and stared at his glass moodily, then, with a jerk of his head, he shot a sharp glance across the table, his eyes serious.

'Well, brace yourself, me boy, I'm going to give you the lot, and believe me, I shall value your opinion, whatever it may be,' he said heavily.

Vivian tensed, and unconsciously leaned forward.

'As I said before'—Lang waved his glass vaguely—'it all began when I pulled the old man, Jensen, and the girl, she was just a kid then, out of Europe. I ran into him immediately after the war, here in London; I was in a museum of all places, just filling in time between opening hours. We got talking, and instead of going out on another blind, he took me out to his house, a lovely old place at Hampton Court, right by the river. His niece, Karen, was there, although I hardly recognized her. What with the march of time, an English boarding-school, and a good home, well, she was a bit different from the little bag of skin and bones that my sailors pulled aboard, I can tell you!'

He paused, as Vivian refilled the glasses, his hand shaking. Lang had uncovered a nerve when he had reminded him of Karen.

'Anyway, the outcome of it was we went into this business. At first, it didn't go too well, what with the travel restrictions, no money, and all that, but after a while we began to pick up, and I thought everything was going to be just fine for little me.' He frowned, as if trying to erase the memory. 'Then, one day, old Jensen sent for me at his home, and when I got there, this chap Mason was waiting.' He paused, breathing heavily.

'Did you know him then?' asked Vivian involuntarily.

'Know him?' Lang laughed harshly. 'I should say I did! When I was serving in Germany, just after the war, waiting to be kicked out of the Andrew, I was making a little extra flogging stores, you know, petrol, food, all that sort of thing.

Not very pretty, I know, but I was just about broke, and I didn't have any idea what to do in civvy street. I was a proper mutt, I can tell you. Anyway, Mason was a Security bloke out there, and to cut short a sad story, he caught up with me.'

'But you left the Navy with a clean slate!' exclaimed Vivian incredulously. 'I remember reading a bit about you in some magazine.'

Lang was scornful.

'We made a deal, old boy. He sat on the evidence, and that was that! At least, I thought it was. You can imagine how I felt when I found him sitting with old Jensen.'

Vivian gripped the edge of his seat, to control his impatience and mounting curiosity. The gin, taken on an empty stomach, was making him feel slightly sick but he gritted his teeth, and listened.

'It appeared,' said Lang slowly, 'that Mason had been his friend, or partner, for some time, and hadn't realized I was working for the bureau. Jensen said he was sorry, but he wanted me to help him get some money taken abroad. He said it was most necessary, and Mason implied that if I didn't come across and lend a hand, he would send the evidence about that business in Germany to the cops! Believe me, old boy, I nearly passed out, especially when Jensen insisted that I should be cut in for a share of the profit, if I co-operated, that is! It all happened so unexpectedly, old friend, that I didn't know what to say. The choice of getting rich quick, but being drawn in on the racket, or going to jail, with no hope afterwards.' He shook his head wearily. 'I wanted time to think, but in the end, I ran a load of dollars over to France. Mason has contacts there, who get rid of the money, and buy up all sorts of stuff, property, and God knows what. I'm really a bit hazy on that score. The fact remains, that he had something on me, but even after they'd told me their schemes, I'd never have been able to prove anything against Mason. Anyway, I didn't want to implicate Jensen, after what he'd done for me.'

'But I still don't get it, Felix, why dollars?' Vivian persisted.

Lang took a deep breath. 'Brace yourself, old boy. The dollars,' he said slowly and deliberately, 'are forged! Every blasted one of them!'

Vivian whistled, amazement written in his clear eyes.

'God, Felix, this is a big thing!' he exclaimed.

He sat back limply, his mind suddenly calm, as Lang plunged on, his voice getting shorter, and more excited.

'The Jerries had Jensen in a concentration camp for years, he was a brilliant engraver, and they wanted him to produce foolproof plates for making Allied money. They were going to flood this country with it to start with, and cause terrific inflation here, then, because Jensen wasn't being very helpful, they switched to American money. No doubt they had an eye on the future. By the way, it was just about that time they butchered old Jensen's wife and child, just to help him along a bit.'

'That's what he started to talk about this afternoon,' mused Vivian. 'I thought there was something.'

'Yes, he and his brother managed to escape from the camp, and made their way to the coast, where they went into hiding. Then we happened along on a raid, and picked a few of them up trying to escape in a poor, old fishing boat. His brother was killed a few days earlier, so he took it upon himself to bring the kid with him. Not only that, old boy, he brought the whole forgery caboodle over too, plates, cutting gear, the lot!'

He sat back, nodding judiciously. 'Yes, I thought that'd shake you!'

'He's been turning the stuff out ever since, eh?' His voice sounded hollow.

'Yep. Of course, when the cash started to come in, from the travel business too, he set up shop in the cellars of his old house. I saw it, and made newer and better plates, while all the time this bastard Mason gets into bigger and better schemes for getting rid of the stuff. And so, my boy, that is it. Any questions?'

Vivian groped for the bottle, and finding it empty, he jumped to his feet, and began to pace to and fro, while Lang watched him curiously.

'You've certainly given me something to chew on, Felix. God, I can't grasp it all yet!' He ran his fingers through his hair, frowning deeply. 'You've not explained yet how I can help you,' he said abruptly. 'It seems to me the less I know about all this, the better.'

'Look,' said Lang earnestly, leaning forward. 'A few more trips and we'll really be in the chips. After that,' he spread his hands wide, 'who knows? But I, personally, think it'll get too hot, and the gaff'll blow!'

As Vivian remained silent and puzzled, he went on hurriedly: 'If someone can convince Jensen that we've gone on long enough, that it's getting too risky, then perhaps he will destroy the plates. No plates, no racket. It's that simple. Provided we do it soon.'

'What's Mason going to say about all this?'

'He is the big snag, and I'm convinced that he's got Jensen so tied up that the old boy's content to leave everything to him, just so long as the money comes pouring in.' He smiled slightly. 'As you've seen, I'm pretty well in with Mason's wife, she's a sweet kid, and if I can get out of this, I'm hoping to take her along too. At the moment, she sort of keeps an eye on the enemy camp for me.'

'Another risk, eh?' Vivian had to grin.

'Risk is right! Anyway, what about it? Will you stay and give me a hand? You'll know nothing, except the story I handed you before, so if we slip up, you won't be in too deep.' He banged the table violently. 'And we won't slip up! As I see it, we may have to pinch the plates, if that's at all possible, and chuck 'em in the drink.' He sighed. 'That'd be the ideal thing; as I said, no plates, no rackets.'

'Couldn't he make some more?'

'Never in this life, old boy. I'm convinced he really is ready to get out. For one thing, after Karen left finishing school, and helped to set up the overseas branches of the travel business, she took it upon herself to spend more and more time at home looking after him, so it's not been all that easy for him to prepare the paper and stuff for printing in his little workshop.'

Vivian's heart bounded. 'You mean she's not in the racket too?'

'Lord no! Jensen's whole life is devoted to her. I'm convinced he started doing this with her in mind. She's all he's got now. He lets her think that all he does in his workshop is design those posters you like.'

Vivian stared out of the scuttle at his side, not wishing Lang to see the hopeful gleam in his eye. It was madness, of course, but how else could he manage to hold on to her memory? He spun on his heel.

'Christ, Felix, I'm on!' he shouted, with such vehemence that even Lang jumped. 'If it's only to keep that girl out of it!'

Lang's jaw dropped, and his voice shook. 'You mean you'll really help me? My dear old Philip, I somehow knew you wouldn't let me down.' His eyes were bright. 'Just think, we could get another boat like this, and later on, perhaps another one, and start a wonderful business.' He threw out his arm melodramatically. 'We will never stop, or settle, but every waterway will have its memories, as someone once said.'

'What's the next step?' Vivian asked, as he helped Lang down to the dinghy.

'Just carry on here. Get the boat fuelled, send the bill to us, of course. I shall tell Jensen you're fixed up, on the pay-roll, as it were, but you don't know a thing, okay?'

The dinghy scraped the pier, and Lang reached up for the ladder.

Vivian spoke out of the darkness. 'That little bastard Cooper, I forgot to ask you about him. He was telling me some yarn about that Patterson bloke.'

Lang growled. 'He's a bloody idiot. Useful, I suppose, but not to be trusted, he's one of Mason's imports for con-tact work.'

He heard Vivian chuckle below him, 'I'm definitely anti-Mason now!'

Just as Lang turned to go, he called down softly, 'Thanks again, Philip, you've given me back a bit of faith.'

He waited until he heard the car roar away, and then pulled back to *Seafox*, his mind busy.

I'm a madman, absolutely useless, he thought, but obstacles like this were made for people like me. He shivered suddenly. And there was, of course, the girl.

3

THE yellow, muddied waters of the Thames churned and swirled, as the sluggish tide began to turn, and the countless pieces of flotsam, old oil drums, baulks of timber, and bottles, began their endless journey back down to the estuary. The chill in the air was now more prevalent and permanent, as if to announce, once and for all, that summer was but something to dream about, a brief and hurried memory to fortify and encourage the traveller through the bitter weather which was always too eager to follow.

The *Seafox* threaded her way daintily up the fairway, turning quickly to any touch of the wheel, to avoid the floating rubbish, like a prim, young lady gathering up her skirts to cross a muddy road, and as she skimmed past the rusty dumb barges, stubby tugs, and the occasional lighter, she looked completely out of place, a glimpse of another world.

Vivian, standing relaxed but watchful at the wheel, shivered slightly, as an unexpectedly cold gust whipped into the open wheelhouse window, and wished that he had remembered to put on his jacket before getting under way. He hated the greyness, the dirt, and the general atmosphere of gloom which seemed to pervade the London river, and his thoughts turned back to Torquay, with its salt air, and its clean, slow-moving, peaceful life. With a faint flicker of interest, he watched the Fire Boats exercising outside

Lambeth Pier, shooting great, curving jets of water into the air, and beating the surface of the river into a gigantic froth. They lowered the power of the fire nozzles as the trim, little yacht cruised past, and the firemen grinned cheerfully, as Vivian waved in acknowledgement. He ran his eye for the hundredth time over his boat, and gripped the wheel spokes affectionately.

She was perfect, there was no doubt about it, and most certainly did not belong here, any more than he did. For two days after his long talk with Lang, he had waited impatiently at Chelsea, trying to fill in time by working on the boat, re-provisioning, polishing, but mostly thinking. Twice he had telephoned Lang, and each time Lang had told him to hold on, and be prepared to do another trip across the Channel. He had rung up old Arthur at Torquay, and told him just enough to keep him from worrying, and to learn that his cat was still in good health and spirits. Arthur's voice, faint and blurred over the distance, had been full of concern and pleading.

'Yew'm better off down 'ere, Skipper,' he had said.

Better off, mused Vivian. How true. This damn waiting for something to happen was beginning to get on his nerves. As instructed, he had been down to the fuel barges to fill up his tanks, and now, as he made his way back to Chelsea, he felt more convinced than ever that it was useless hanging around, just waiting for something, or somebody, to make a move.

The bright shape of a racing dinghy careered from behind some moored barges, and with her sails swollen by the freshening wind, tore at right angles across the river, her lee gunwale digging into the water, sending up a shower of spray. The two figures in it leaned far out over the weather side, their oilskin jackets wet and glistening. Vivian measured up the shortening distance, and began judging the angle of the little boat's next tack. Even at that distance he could see one of the figures was a girl, her head wrapped in a bright scarf, her teeth white, as she laughed with excitement. Reluctant to spoil their pleasure, Vivian pressed the horn once, and started to turn the wheel to starboard, then, with sudden alarm, he realized that the dinghy had changed course again, and was bearing straight down on him. Cursing all sailing boats, he heaved one gear lever astern, and put the wheel hard over. The diesels' roar rose to a shuddering rumble, as *Seafox* began to turn, and fall back on the tide, broaching round as she did so. It was some moments before he had her on course again, and by then the dinghy had wheeled round to run on a parallel course, barely twenty feet away. Vivian wrenched open the wheel-house door, jerking the megaphone off its hook.

'Hey there!' he yelled. 'What the hell d'you think you're doing? Are you asking for a ruddy smash or something?'

As the girl turned on her precarious seat, the headscarf slipped about her neck, and a mass of gleaming, yellow hair swirled joyously around her laughing face.

'Why, Mr. Vivian,' she called. 'What a welcome to give a fellow-sailor!'

His throat contracted, and felt suddenly bone dry, and for a few seconds he stood staring at her, the megaphone hanging foolishly from his hand.

He was dimly aware of the amused stare of the man who sat close by her, one elbow negligently resting across the tiller, a young, fresh-faced fellow of about the girl's own age, with dark, curly hair shining with spray.

He sought round in confusion for something to say.

'Er, come aboard, won't you?' he called at length. 'I didn't realize who it was,' he ended lamely.

55

She nodded in that grave manner which he remembered so well.

'Obviously, Mr. Vivian. It would appear that this is not your normal greeting.'

Before he could answer, she jumped lightly to the sheets, and with very little fuss, the sails vanished, and as the motor yacht slowed, the little boat eased alongside, and moved carefully down to the stern, where they secured it, and while Vivian tried to watch the river, the boat, and listen, all at the same time, the two visitors appeared, laughing and breathless, at his side.

The girl was looking even more beautiful than before, he decided, her face, apparently washed and blown free of make-up, looked more golden than ever, and even her hair, tangled by the wind, and which she now combed with her fingers, made his heart throb painfully.

He was again aware of the other man, who was apparently taller than he had realized, about his own height, and whose handsome face was only marred by his rather arrogant mouth.

'My name's Muir, David Muir,' he said suddenly, his voice a soft, well-modulated drawl. 'Sorry to barge in like this, but little Karen wanted to see your boat apparently. I gather you know each other?' His eyebrows rose questioningly.

Vivian nodded, watching the other man, and feeling vaguely resentful at his casual and familiar use of the girl's name.

Karen stood back, looking from one to the other, an amused smile on her lips.

'Well, you did say I could look at the boat, didn't you, Mr. Vivian?' She swung round, and opened her arms wide. 'She is very beautiful, don't you think so, David? I would love to have her all to myself.'

Muir smiled indulgently. 'You'd soon want something with sail on it, though. You might just as well be driving a big, comfortable car, eh, Vivian?'

'You don't have to get your feet wet, just to prove you're a sailor,' said Vivian coldly. 'And in any case, I haven't the time, or the inclination, to potter about the Thames all day!'

He regretted the outburst instantly, and tried to cover his anger by taking a quick glance at the river ahead. In the window glass, he saw Muir's reflection, as he made a grimace, and turned quickly to the girl.

'Look, have a look round, if you like, I'll have to stay here till we get to Chelsea.'

'I'll wait then, until you can show me.' And she sat quickly on the side seat, smiling happily.

Muir shrugged, and slumped beside her, yawning.

'I gather you've only met recently?' he asked at length.

Vivian waited until a tug and her brood of barges had swished past before he answered, and he felt Karen watching him.

'Yes, I charter the boat to Miss Jensen's uncle, for the travel bureau,' he said shortly.

'H'm, nice work too, I should think, he's a charming man,' he added, with a quick glance at Karen.

She patted his hand, and Vivian's inside took another plunge.

'Never mind, we can't all be hard-worked men like you,' she smiled. Then, turning to Vivian, she added: 'David and I belong to the same sailing club. It's quite good fun, really.'

I'll bet it is, thought Vivian savagely. But he smiled back, his face muscles tight.

'I used to do quite a bit of sailing, when I was in the Service,' he began, but his words were unheard, as the others were standing, and pointing at some passing sailing dinghies.

He sighed, and cursed himself for being a fool. She was just a dream, and just as unattainable.

That's decided for me, he thought. I'll 'phone Felix tonight, and tell him I'm going back to Torquay, unless he can come up with any definite plan.

With Karen and her friend on deck, handling the ropes, *Seafox* glided gracefully to her buoy by Chelsea Pier, and Vivian's spine tingled as he heard her laugh gaily, while Muir made three attempts before he could fix the snap-hook on to the buoy-ring. He put the gear levers into neutral, and pulled the throttles. The engines roared and died away, leaving only the sound of the water lapping against the white hull.

Vivian felt suddenly tired and dispirited, and as he glanced around the wheelhouse, he experienced a strange, brittle nervousness, which was quite new to him. It was only a matter of days ago that to own the boat had been the most important desire in his life, the culmination of all his plans and requirements, but as he watched the two figures playfully coiling the ropes on the foredeck, he knew deeply, and at the same time bitterly, what he most wanted, and what he most lacked.

Karen's scarf lay where she had thrown it, rumpled and damp, and with a strange tenderness he stooped and picked it up from the deck, and ran it through his hands. A shadow had fallen across the door, and he looked up quickly, to find the girl standing silhouetted against the grey light of the river. A surprised, or perhaps puzzled, expression stayed briefly in her eyes, and her lips were parted, as if she was going to speak, yet could not find the words.

Vivian held out the scarf to her, and smiled to cover his

embarrassment, and she took it from him, her eyes still troubled, and not leaving his.

'David's going to scull the dinghy over to the pier,' she said, her voice was low. 'Felix Lang is waiting there. He has his car.' She sounded as if she was sorry.

As Vivian didn't answer, she laughed quickly. 'It doesn't look as if you'll have time to show me round, does it?'

'No, I suppose you'll have to be going back to the sailing club with him?' He nodded in the direction of the dinghy, which was already moving away.

'I hope you didn't mind what David said about the boat, he doesn't understand, and in any case, I think it's lovely.'

'Oh, the boat. Yes,' stammered Vivian. 'Yes, she's a beauty.' And again he stopped helplessly. From the corner of his eye he saw the dinghy rowing back.

She laughed suddenly, and shook back her hair. 'You really are a strange man, Mr. Vivian,' she said, standing back to look at him. 'One minute you are a great talker, and the next,' she looked very stern, 'you look like this! Can it be that I have such a bad effect on you?'

'Good Lord, no!' answered Vivian gruffly. 'I'm just a bit stupid today. Please forgive me.'

'I shall do nothing of the kind. Look, why not come down to the house tonight. Uncle Nils is giving a little party, you know, and I'm sure he'd love to hear you talk about the sea again.'

Vivian rubbed his palm across the edge of the chart table, his eyes lowered. 'I'd like that very much, Miss Jensen, if you're sure it'll be all right.'

'I'm quite sure it will be all right,' she mimicked, and he smiled, in spite of his emotions.

'David likes to talk about business matters, you know!' she laughed again. 'I suppose, as he's an up-and-coming young stockbroker, he feels it's not right to be too flippant all the time!'

Lang's body clambered up over the rail, his face split into a grin. 'Hi there, Philip, all getting acquainted, I see?'

'Philip is coming to the house tonight, Felix, can you bring him in your car?'

'Sure, that'll be fine.'

Vivian didn't even listen to the conversation, his attention had been riveted by her use of his name, and again he felt the pain inside him.

'We'll leave the dinghy at the pier, David,' Karen called, as she began to button her jacket. 'We'll call back for it in the week. Are you coming now, Felix?'

'Righto. I only wanted to tell Philip he's wanted for a trip across to France in a couple of days' time.' He darted a quick glance at Vivian. 'Okay?'

Vivian nodded, aware only of the girl.

'Well, that's settled then.' The boat moved away. 'Call for you at eight, old boy!'

Vivian waved, and watched them out of sight.

He walked slowly aft, to lower his own dinghy in readiness, trying to concentrate on Lang's news. Ah well, perhaps it didn't matter after all. Felix didn't appear to be worried anyway. He halted, his eyes fixed on a small wallet lying by the stern rail. He picked it up, and opened it. It was a driving licence case belonging to David Muir. He must have dropped it when he jumped up from the boat. I'll give it to him tonight, he thought.

He was just going to stuff it into his picket, when he noticed another, thicker card, pushed behind the licence. By nature a curious man, he slid it casually into view, then froze, his heart pounding.

As he opened the card, he saw the coat of arms, Muir's

name and personal details, and across the top, the stamp of Her Majesty's Customs and Excise.

.   .   .   .   .

The evening was quiet and warm, and only the merest breeze ruffled the thick leaves of the old oak trees that lined the road, which, apart from the late, home-going business man, and the occasional, pleasure-seeking car, was deserted and peaceful.

From beyond the banks of trees came the ageless peal of the great clock in Hampton Court Palace chiming the quarter hour, but the two men, seated motionless in the darkened, parked car by the roadside, showed no sign of having heard.

Lang leaned forward on the steering wheel, the reflection of his cigarette glowing in the windscreen, a frown of concentration creasing his forehead.

Vivian, half-turned in his seat, sucked on an empty pipe, and watched the other man with something like apprehension in his eyes.

'Well, that's the set-up as I see it, Felix,' he concluded. 'Your little racket has got a bit hotter than you anticipated. The question is, what do we do now?'

Lang turned slowly, the ash dropping on to his lap.

'Not a stockbroker at all, eh?' he mused, as if he had not heard the question. 'Well, that is a turn-up for the book, that is.'

He flicked absently at the ash, then, with a quick change of mood, as if to announce that he had come to a decision, he turned the ignition key, and pressed the starter.

He laughed shortly. 'We'll have to get organized, but quick! I'll have to get old Jensen on one side. After all, there's not much we can do until he's had his say.'

'He must be a pretty cool customer, this Muir,' said

Vivian, as the car swung back on to the main road. 'Fancy using Karen as the method of introduction.' He paused. 'You don't suppose he's on the level, do you? After all, he might not have wanted her to know his exact job.'

Lang snorted. 'Nuts, old boy, if he was on the up-and-up, he'd no doubt have matrimony in mind, so deception is a bit useless, isn't it? Oh no, my friend, I've had a feeling something would happen one day, as I told you, but Christ, I didn't think it'd be in the family, so to speak!'

'He must be a bit of a rat to use a girl like Karen for his dirty work.'

'He'll probably tell you, if you ask him,' jerked Lang, 'that he's just doing his duty! They all do, you know.'

There was a crunch of gravel, as the tyres turned on a wide, curving drive, which passed through twin, wrought-iron gates, and between dark clumps of bushes and birch trees, and as the car slackened its pace, Vivian saw the lighted windows of the large, red-walled country house close at hand.

Lang nodded. 'This is it, grand old place, built about the same time as the Palace. Wouldn't mind it myself.'

As they were ushered into the long entrance hall by a pleasant, middle-aged servant-woman, Vivian glanced round in admiration at the huge raftered ceiling, the gleaming brasses, and polished wood floors. He noticed, too, that everywhere there were vast bowls of beautifully arranged flowers.

The lounge into which they were shown was also well supplied with cut flowers, and again Vivian was struck by the serene air of grace and comfort which seemed to pervade the whole house.

Nils Jensen began to lever himself from his chair, but Vivian stepped smartly across the room, and forestalled him.

'I'm glad you could come, my boy,' he nodded, with a gentle smile. 'We will have another talk soon, yes?'

He sat looking dreamily at Vivian, his delicate hands beating a silent tattoo on the chair, and in his dark blue velvet jacket and old world cravat, he looked as if he and the house were part of each other.

Mason and his wife sat moodily on a sofa, sipping their drinks, and listening to a fat, red-faced little man, who Vivian later discovered was a local J.P. Janice Mason's face brightened as he and Lang entered the room, and she raised her glass in welcome. She was apparently more than a little drunk.

There were several other people, local friends of Jensen, standing or sitting in small groups, sipping their drinks, and laughing gaily. Although informally dressed, the quiet elegance of their clothes made Vivian wish once more that he had been able to afford what, up to now, he had regarded as unnecessary luxury.

Karen was standing with one group by the long french windows, which overlooked a sloping lawn, that ran straight down to the river's edge. She was dressed in a soft, pale blue cocktail dress, her slim shoulders bare, and he noted, with disgust, that Muir hovered attentively at her side.

There was a fresh burst of laughter, and she twisted slightly, the lights gleaming on her smooth skin. He smiled nervously, wondering what she would do, and to his intense delight she turned, spoke quickly to the others, and then crossed the room to confront him.

'How nice, Philip,' she said softly. 'I'm glad you were able to come. Do you have a drink?'

He shook his head.

'Come with me,' she commanded, and he willingly followed her slight figure to a long table, well stocked with bottles, and little glass dishes of canapes of every size and description.

'Quite a spread,' murmured Vivian approvingly.

'Come, we will drink a proper Danish toast together,' she said, and, picking up a bottle, she filled two small glasses with a colourless liquid.

'Schnapps?' queried Vivian, and she nodded.

'Do you enjoy our Danish speciality then?'

'I had a little once, when I slipped across to Copenhagen from Germany,' he answered, as he took the glass from her.

She wrinkled her nose. 'Everybody goes to Copenhagen, and then thinks he has seen Denmark. But it is just another rather nice town really, you know.'

'I take it that where you come from is the real thing?' Vivian grinned broadly.

'Oh yes,' she studied him seriously. 'My home is in Vejle. A lovely part of the country on the Baltic, right at the end of a deep fjord.' She smiled excitedly. 'You would love it, there are plenty of little boats there, and clear, deep water, it is very beautiful.' She stopped, and looked up at him, her eyes laughing. 'But now we drink, to your *Seafox*. But don't forget, you must drink it straight down, no cheating?'

They clinked their glasses. '*Skal!*' she said, smiling.

The drink seemed to run straight through him, like liquid fire, and he spluttered, gasping for breath.

'Phew, I'd forgotten how potent it was!' he gasped.

'But very nice, yes?'

'Oh hallo, Vivian,' drawled a voice at his elbow, and he turned, trying to erase the resentment from his face. Muir, immaculate in a light gabardine suit, was regarding him with interest.

'All ready for that trip you're making?' His voice was casual.

'Practically,' answered Vivian shortly.

'Where are you off to, this time?'

'Don't know yet.' He hoped he, too, sounded casual.

Muir appeared to have lost interest, and he turned to the girl.

'Coming, Karen?' he inquired. 'Betty and Paul are just leaving, and I think they want to talk about that dance for next week.'

She put down her glass, and Vivian felt he wanted to seize her, and take her away from everyone, then and there.

'I hope I shall see you for another talk this evening, Philip.' Her voice was soft. 'Don't slip away like you usually do, will you?'

She left him, and he watched the group move into the next room, his heart filled with uncontrollable emotions.

A slim hand slid through his arm, and he looked down into the face of Janice Mason, who gave him a mock salute with her free hand.

'Care to fix me a drink, Captain?' Her words were slightly slurred.

He frowned, and shook his head. 'You've had enough, my girl, but I'll get you just a little one.'

She downed the gin he handed her without effort, and smiled at him sadly. 'I see that you were thwarted again?' As he made no comment, she nodded towards the other room. 'That man Muir, I mean.'

Vivian shrugged. 'I'm not giving up hope.'

She beamed. 'Good boy! After all, remember that envy always walks hand-in-hand with extreme joy.'

He looked at her in amazement. 'You must be more sober than I thought, to come out with a mouthful like that!'

'H'm, just a bit depressed, that's all.' And she deftly refilled her glass.

It was then he noticed that her husband and Lang had disappeared, and turning to find Jensen, he saw that his chair was also empty. So the conference had started apparently.

He turned back to the girl. 'Well, I'll look after you till the others come back.'

'To hell with the lot of them,' she muttered. 'I'd give my arms and legs to be like all these people here.' She waved vaguely about the room. 'Nice, ordinary, simple, honest little people,' she said vehemently, her eyes flashing. 'No bloody rackets, no big deals, no nothing!'

Vivian glanced round nervously, but the other guests appeared to be happily occupied.

'Here, keep control of yourself,' he hissed. 'No point in busting up the party.'

She looked at him in contempt, or was it plain misery. He couldn't be sure.

'Philip,' her voice was so husky, he could hardly hear her. 'I hate the sight of my husband. Does that surprise you?'

'I rather gathered that——' he began.

'But Felix will be able to help me, won't he?' Her voice was imploring.

'I guess Felix'd fix anything, if he wanted it badly enough,' he said firmly. 'Come on, we'll go for a stroll round the lawn, till you feel a bit better.' And steering her by the elbow, he guided her out through the french windows, and into the moonlight.

He was quick to realize his mistake, for as the cool air struck Janice, she reeled heavily against him, giggling foolishly, and as he grabbed her roughly, to stop her from falling, she clung about his neck, her eyes swimming.

They were both suddenly bathed in light, as one of the french windows opened behind them, and before Vivian realized what was happening, Mason stepped quickly down on to the lawn, and seized her arm, dragging her heavily back into the shadows.

His face was livid, as he stared from her to Vivian, his thin lips working with pent-up rage.

'You little fool,' he hissed. 'Can't you keep away from any man for a few minutes?' And with a sudden jerk, he struck her across the face with the flat of his hand. She staggered back, her hands to her cheek, sobbing quietly, while Mason stood glowering at her, his breath heaving.

'Now, just a minute, Mason,' began Vivian, his face set in a grim frown. 'She's just a bit done up, there's no need for you——'

'Shut your mouth!' Mason's eyes glinted wildly. 'And if I catch you messing about with her again, I'll fix you too!'

A tight feeling clamped Vivian's skull as, without effort, he reached out and gripped the front of the other man's jacket, and pulled him easily towards him. When he spoke, his voice was strange, and flat.

'Don't threaten me, Mason! Or you'll get the treatment you deserve!'

He gave a twist to the jacket, and a sharp thrust, and Mason reeled against the wall, his face white, and his small eyes popping with fright and hatred.

'All right, you two, I think that'll be enough for now!' Jensen's soft voice had a sharp ring of authority, as he limped out of the lighted room, followed by Lang, his round face anxious.

'Sorry about that, but I don't like people around me hitting women!' Vivian's arms fell to his sides.

'All right, all right,' snapped Jensen. 'Now you've had your say, get into the study, and Lang, give him a drink.'

He turned to Mason, his hooded eyes cold. 'And you, Andrew, I think you'd better take Janice home.' He raised his hand, as Mason began to speak. 'No, Andrew, I think

67

it's better this way. We've a lot to do, and we've no time for personal bitterness.'

Mason shook himself, his chest still heaving. 'Very well,' he croaked. 'But keep that—that gentleman away from me!'

'I think I'd better keep you away from *him*,' answered Jensen dryly, then with a quick glance round, he stepped into the brightly lit study, and closed the windows.

He sank wearily into his chair, and watched Vivian's taut face, as he took the drink from Lang, and tossed it back without apparently noticing it.

'The lout!' muttered Vivian eventually, surprised to find that he was still shaking with rage.

'Finished?' Jensen's voice was brittle, like a small bell.

Vivian snorted, and banged down the glass. 'Yes,' he snapped, 'except that I don't like your friend very much!'

'So we have gathered, my boy! And from what I've seen and heard this evening, I have had to revise my opinion a little also.'

He tapped slowly on his chair, the hands working, while his body lay back, still and restful.

'Go and pay my respects to the guests, Felix, they'll be wondering where everybody has got to, and no doubt they'll be ready to go anyway.'

Lang hurried away, shooting a curious glance at Vivian as he did so. Jensen sat silently listening to the sounds coming from the other room, then with a little sigh, he turned his attention to the other man.

'I gather from Felix, that apart from being a very hot-tempered young man,' he chuckled slightly, 'you are also completely trustworthy. I also know that you are fully aware of what is going on around you at the present moment. Well?' He leaned forward, his eyes compelling in their sudden brightness.

'I know enough,' said Vivian carefully.

'Enough! What is enough?' snapped Jensen, his hands tapping their impatient rhythm.

As Vivian lowered his eyes, he hurried on, his tone impulsive.

'Very well, Mr. Vivian, I will tell you! You know about the money, and where it comes from, eh? And you proved your loyalty to me by finding out that handsome, but foolish, young man David Muir. That, in my opinion, is enough!' He paused for breath, the deformed corner of his mouth twitching uncontrollably.

'Now, just a minute,' said Vivian awkwardly, 'I was mainly concerned in my own safety, for one thing, and for another, I didn't much like the idea of your niece being led up the garden by Muir.'

'Any more than you like the idea of her being deceived by me, and by this whole unlawful affair, is that not so?'

Vivian winced, it was like talking to a mind-reader.

'You do not have to explain, my boy, it is quite clear to me,' he smiled briefly, 'as is the most obvious fact, that you are in love with my little Karen.'

He leaned back, satisfied with the effect of this bombshell on Vivian's defences.

'My feeling for Karen,' he spoke her name carefully, as if he was handling a precious jewel, 'is *my* business!' he said coldly.

Jensen's squat figure shook with silent laughter, but he stopped, as Vivian frowned angrily.

'Please, do not misunderstand my rudeness,' he explained, 'it was just that your feeling for Karen is the one reason for my having you here tonight.' He paused, allowing his words to sink in. 'To me, also, she is everything,' he said softly. 'As you know, I believe, I was a prisoner of the Germans for some time, when they discovered that I might

69

be of some use to them. During the time I was in Sachsen-hausen concentration camp,' he smiled wryly, 'ah, I see by your face that you have heard of it! Well, while I was there, I lost everything, my family, which nearly killed me, and but for my desire to escape, and to take my revenge against those swine, I would have died too! As you can see, they left very little of my own body intact too! But when I got away to England with Karen, I rebuilt my life around her. I was determined that she, at least, would never know the meaning of fear and want, and that she would one day be able to enjoy the type of life I once knew!'

'I think I can understand all that,' Vivian said quietly.

'Yes, I thought I had you figured correctly. Anyway, to cut short this miserable story, when I found the means to make money, literally, I did not hesitate. Why should I? After the war, I could get nothing back. My home had gone, everything was different. I was a stranger in my own country. While all around us we see today our former enemies strong and powerful, snakes in a different guise!' He spat out the words. 'Oh no, Mr. Vivian, I do not hesitate! Because if I must transact business with these sort of people, I will do it the way they taught me!'

'What do you want me to do?' Vivian asked quickly.

'I want you to sail for France, at once. To make one last trip for me. Then I will finish with the whole business. I will be satisfied.'

'Where to, this time?'

'It's only a little beach, I could show you on a chart, but it will not be difficult for you to find. But it may be dangerous, I will be quite frank about that.'

'How so?' Vivian was amazed to find himself so calm.

'I feel the authorities will be suspicious, so you must be very careful.' He nodded abstractedly. 'Very careful. Mason knows about this, but he doesn't know it's the last time I shall produce any money. I think it better to tell him later. He is, I'm afraid, a very greedy man, and that may well be his undoing, but it is not to be ours.' Then, with no apparent connexion, 'Can you drive a car?'

Vivian nodded.

'Good, then you must take me now to your boat, and we will look at the charts together. I will drive back slowly myself.'

'Will I have any passengers on the trip over?'

'I'm afraid it will be necessary to have Cooper, and another man.' His voice was apologetic. 'I want you to pick them up off Ramsgate, just in case you are seen sailing from London. You are not likely to be suspected of going on a difficult trip, if you start out alone,' he explained.

'I always seem to be sticking my neck out,' grinned Vivian. 'At least I know what I'm supposed to be doing this time.'

The old man grasped his wrist in a strong grip. 'Make no mistake, it may be dangerous, so be careful.' He smiled in his quaint manner. 'For her sake, if not for your own!'

Vivian flushed. 'I'll not stand a chance,' he muttered.

'We have a saying in Denmark,' he smiled sadly, as if at a memory. 'Love is like a beautiful flower. It is not enough to admire it, you must also cherish and protect it, and be prepared to devote your life to it.' He chuckled. 'At least, I think that's how it goes.'

Lang hurried back to the room. 'I've got the car in the drive,' he said quickly, 'and nearly all the guests have gone.'

'What about Karen?' asked Jensen, his eyes at the window.

'She's slipped off too. She said she was going for a quick drive with our friend Muir.'

'Good, let us be on our way then.' He swung his body

awkwardly, as he turned towards the door. 'I will join you outside.'

Lang and Vivian crunched down the driveway, to where the car was parked.

'Good luck, old boy,' murmured Lang. 'It looks as if things will be working out all right after all.' He thrust out his hand in the dark, and Vivian saw the dull gleam of metal. 'Here, stow this away somewhere.'

Vivian's hand closed on to the butt of a heavy, automatic pistol, and he tried to push it away.

'I don't want that, Felix. I'm not going to use a gun, whatever happens.'

'Is your yacht insured?' asked Lang suddenly.

'Of course, but what the hell has that got to do with it?'

'How many times have you had to claim on the insurance?' persisted Lang.

'Never. But I still don't see——'

Lang cut him short. 'No, but you keep it, just in case of accidents, don't you?'

He thrust the gun suddenly into Vivian's coat pocket. 'Well take this, old boy. Just in case of accidents,' he added meaningly.

They both straightened up as Jensen limped out of the gloom.

'Come, we must be off!'

And as the car began to move, he called softly to Lang, 'Stop worrying about Janice Mason, Felix, something will work out in the end.'

Lang grunted with surprise. 'No harm in hoping.' His other words were drowned by the car's powerful engine, as Vivian drove skilfully through the open gates.

He remembered the drive long afterwards, for during the whole journey, Jensen talked tirelessly, and yet at no time did Vivian feel anything but captivated by his companion's quiet, gentle voice. Mostly the talk was of boats, and of Denmark before the occupation, and in his mind's eye Vivian could clearly visualize the sort of carefree and happy life which Jensen had once led, and how the terrible bitterness and hatred, born of his suffering, had warped his mind away from his natural honesty.

Even when he was aboard *Seafox*, Jensen seemed unwilling to listen to Vivian's point of view, or to ask if his reactions might have been the same. It was almost as if he was being driven by some strange, ungovernable force.

He stood watching with interest, as Vivian spread a chart of the Channel across the table, and switched on the small chart-light, then, his eyes squinting, he made a small mark on the French coastline with a pencil.

'Here it is, now let me hear what you think.'

Vivian got busy with pencil and parallel rulers, working quickly and skilfully, stopping only to jot down notes in a small rough notebook.

He nodded thoughtfully. 'It's a beach, isn't it? And according to the chart, it's completely deserted around that part of the coast.'

'Yes, the beach is too small for much use, only about a hundred yards long, and all the rest is rocky, and too deep for holiday-makers, and that sort of thing.'

Vivian nodded again, his mind visualizing the scene that the chart, with its tiny figures and wavy lines, automatically formed in his brain.

'H'm, I could anchor right in close, even at low water.'

'Yes, now, can you be sure of being there tomorrow night?'

'Well, let's see.' Vivian carefully consulted his tide tables, and ran off a quick course on the chart, the pencil making the only sound in the wheelhouse, as Jensen watched anxiously.

'Yes, that'll be all right. I shall sail tomorrow morning, about seven. That means, all being well, I shall be off Ramsgate at approximately twelve-thirty in the afternoon, or thereabouts.' He paused. 'What about Cooper and the other man, how will I pick them up?'

'That'll all be taken care of. They'll be out in a motor-boat, on a fishing trip, if anyone wants to know! Go on,' he added impatiently.

'In that case, I'll carry on round the coast, as if I was making for the Isle of Wight. Then, when I reach the Royal Sovereign Lightship,' he tapped the chart again, 'that'll be about seven o'clock, and there'll be no moon, I'll swing south, and straight across the Channel to this beach of yours.'

'Very good. I see you know your stuff!'

'I had plenty of practice during the war,' answered Vivian dryly.

Jensen straightened. 'That's that, then. You be there at midnight, and flash a red lamp at the shore. Make the letter V. If you get the letter G back, take the stuff ashore in the dinghy.' He gave Vivian a piercing glance. 'If you get at all suspicious, then don't go ashore. Get out of it as quickly as you can.'

Vivian grinned, inwardly excited. Just like old times, he thought. It'd have to be good navigation too. One small beach, midway between the bustling town of Dieppe and St. Valery. Even without other complications, it would be quite an effort to get to the place dead on time.

As if reading his mind again, Jensen laid a hand on his arm. 'Don't forget, no risks, if you can help it.'

Together they looked at the bulky suitcase which Jensen had brought in the car.

'Where shall I stow the money, I wonder?' said Vivian, a puzzled frown on his features.

Jensen opened the case, revealing the contents, which to Vivian looked like an oilskin bag, about the size of a pillow. When he lifted it from the case, he marvelled at its weight. A great deal of money had been forced into this packet, he thought.

The other man was watching him, the hooded eyes bright, like a cat's.

'Can we get down into the engine room?'

As they scrambled down into the neat but cramped space below the wheelhouse, Jensen nodded approvingly at the twin engines, which lay inert, as if sleeping, and filling most of the space. Kneeling carefully and painfully on the deck, he peered down at the port engine, and eventually he pointed at the giant flywheel at the forward end, its sharp teeth shining with grease.

'Under there, that is the place!'

Vivian understood in a flash. Between the flywheel and the bottom of the hull was about eight inches of hidden space, well sheltered by a maze of pipes and wires. While the boat was under way, no searcher, should there be one, would dare to thrust his arm anywhere near that spinning wheel, when, at an unexpected lurch of the boat, or an error of judgement, his arm would be torn from its socket by the cruel teeth.

He whistled. 'Quite an idea!'

'Have you a couple of small pieces of ballast? I can put the packet down here, and the weights will keep it in place.'

Vivian hurried aft, and returned shortly with two small but extremely weighty pieces of iron from the after bilges.

The preparations complete, Vivian rowed Jensen ashore to his car.

He watched the car's lights fading into the darkness. He and I are very much alike, he mused. It was a frightening thought.

4

AN EARLY morning tug chugged downstream, two of her crew standing with huge mugs of tea, throwing pieces of bread to a wheeling flock of screaming gulls.

A feeling of urgency transmitted itself to Vivian, and he glanced at his watch. Six-thirty, and the uncertain ripple of the river was beginning to change, the waves slapping against the piles around the pier, as the tide started to turn.

He stepped into the wheelhouse, and slipped into his waterproof jacket, and zipped it up to his neck. He jammed on his cap, and at that moment his eye fell on his reefer hanging on the saloon door, and with a frown he pulled out the pistol, and stood looking at it in the growing light.

He jerked out the magazine from the butt. Fully loaded. He snapped it back, and put on the safety catch. For a brief second he was tempted to throw it overboard. But, as Lang had said, it might be useful. He grinned ruefully, it might even be the thing for dealing with Cooper, as he seemed to love drama so much. He looked about him thoughtfully. The First Aid box, that was it. He lifted up the tray of bandages and bottles, and slid the gun underneath. He smiled, as he noticed the directions on the top of the box: 'Be prepared for anything!'

He squared his shoulders, and prepared to cast off. With a cough and a roar, the two engines came to life as he pressed the starters, then, as they settled down to a steady rumble, he went on deck and cast off from the buoy. *Seafox* started to drift away on the tide, but as he stepped behind the wheel, and pushed the gear levers forward, the screws dug into the murky water, causing the boat to nose steadily forward.

Throttles half open, and wheel to port, he felt a thrill of excitement run through him, as the yacht swung in a tight semi-circle, and headed downstream.

He fell into procession with an old timber ship, flying the German flag, and a smart, Swedish cargo ship, and as the grey banks slid past, with their gaunt warehouses and loading jetties, he knew that the moment for turning back, or changing his mind, had gone.

Tower Bridge loomed ahead, her twin arms raised in salute, and he caught a brief glimpse of the scarlet buses, and packed ranks of cars and lorries, waiting to continue their ordered and relentless journeys.

He knew that many eyes were watching his boat with envy, and he wondered what they would think if they knew his purpose that morning.

On, on down the river, twisting and turning through the shining strip of busy waterway, through the dock area, until at last the banks grew wider apart, and the jetties and wharves gave way to mud flats, and ocean-going ships.

A police boat turned lazily away from a cluster of barges, and his heart quickened as it steered towards him. But it cruised past, the blue-clad occupants hardly giving him a glance.

All at once it was different again. A sharp tang of salt replaced that of smoke and dirt, and the yacht seemed to feel, and welcome it, as she dipped happily into the choppy waters of the Estuary. He breathed deeply, and stretched his arms, and as the long, spider-like line of Southend Pier appeared faintly through the fine, morning mist, he began to hum to himself.

It was lucky that the weather was so good, he mused, for had it turned against him, it would have been asking for trouble. No doubt the police boat would have shown some interest at a lone yacht proceeding to sea in the middle of a raging storm.

The hours slid rapidly by, and the motion of the short, steep wavelets became more pronounced, as Vivian altered course to turn round the North Foreland, making *Seafox* roll more heavily in the beam sea. He cursed silently, wishing that he could push on without his unwelcome passengers, and for a moment he toyed with the idea of leaving them behind in Ramsgate. No doubt Cooper would take a poor view of that, he chuckled.

Lifting his glasses, he examined the sun-swept coastline, letting his glance linger on the tiny catwalk around the top of the lofty North Foreland lighthouse, and he wondered if he too was under their scrutiny.

He checked the compass, and altered course again, to pass closer inshore, it was getting near time for the rendez-vous, and a feeling of tension held him in its grip.

The grey breakwater of Ramsgate harbour loomed ahead, and he began to think that the arrangements had gone astray, when all of a sudden he saw two small fishing dories wallowing and pitching about half a mile away on the port bow. There were no other vessels in sight, so with the engines at dead slow, he headed towards them.

When he drew near, he quickly recognized, with a feeling of repugnance, the rakish panama hat that perched on one of the occupants of the nearest boat.

As he let the yacht idle alongside, Cooper grinned up at him, and raised a hand in mocking salute, showing his teeth in an insincere smile.

'Hiya there, Captain, right on the button, I see!' And he reached up awkwardly for the rail.

The man in the bows of the dory turned his face towards Vivian, and he saw again the dull, impassive manservant from Mason's flat, Morrie. He merely nodded, and began to wind up a fishing line.

With a scornful laugh, Cooper turned, and kicked the winder from the big man's grasp, sending it spinning into the sea. Morrie stared at the water impassively, as if he couldn't understand what had happened, and then with a heavy shrug, clambered up on to the yacht's deck.

Cooper joined him, and waved to the small, dark man in the other dory. 'Okay, pal, go on back now, we're going on to Cornwall, to do a bit of real fishing. I'm fed up with this rod-and-line racket, it's kid's stuff!'

'What's the idea of the two boats?' queried Vivian, as he joined the other two.

'If we'd just sat around in one boat after planning a day fishing, it would have looked as if we had been waiting to hitch a ride. You've gotta do these things right,' added Cooper importantly.

Vivian smiled to himself, it was as Lang had predicted, Cooper had to dramatize everything.

They waited until the boatman had taken the other boat in tow, and then Vivian got under way once more, steering parallel with the shore. Destination Cornwall, if anyone's watching, he thought wryly.

Through narrowed eyes, he watched Morrie, as he moved heavily about the deck, his broad shoulders bent, as if with the weight of his huge frame. A nasty customer in a fight, he decided.

After a while, the big man entered the wheelhouse, and stood silently watching Vivian's actions.

'Here, take a trick at the wheel,' said Vivian suddenly. 'Ever done any before?'

Cooper's laugh drifted up from the saloon. 'Sure, let him steer, the big dope'll go to sleep otherwise!'

Vivian darted a glance at Morrie, but the dull, brooding expression was unaltered, until, as he took the spokes in his square hands, a brief glimmer of pleasure crossed his face. He gripped the wheel with confidence, making it look like a toy, and said softly: 'Yes, I've done this before. Many times,' and he nodded his bullet head slowly.

He didn't elaborate, so Vivian left him to it, and joined Cooper, who lay back on the settee in the saloon, humming a dance tune, and beating time with one of his pointed shoes.

'All set?' he cocked a sharp eye in Vivian's direction. 'Got the stuff all right?'

Vivian nodded. 'It's stowed away below,' he answered briefly, a new pang of irritation making him want to turn back and drop this odious little man ashore.

Cooper sat up, and yawned, scratching his stomach absently.

'Don't take any notice of old Morrie. Used to be a sailor during the war. Bit bomb-happy, but a useful sort of guy to have in a scrap.

'Ah well,' he pouted like a child. 'Guess I'll take a little nap. Give us a call when we get near something.' And with that, he leaned back in a corner, the panama tugged down over his eyes.

Not another word was spoken, although several times he tried to draw out the strange Morrie, only to be met with an almost dumb barrier. So he gave it up, and concentrated on the business of navigation.

When the first streaks of evening crossed the clear sky, he saw the steady eye of the Royal Sovereign Lightship, with the dark mass of Eastbourne spread across the coast behind it, and in the far distance he could just see the pale blob of Beachy Head reflecting the last of the fading light.

Humming softly, he altered course, and gently the *Seafox* turned her trim stern towards England and, like a pale ghost, headed for the open sea, and for France.

. . . . .

Vivian switched on the small light over the chart table, and glanced briefly at the thin pencilled line, then, he snapped the switch, and once more the wheelhouse was in pitch darkness, but for the soft glow from the binnacle. He eased the spokes carefully, his eyes watching the swinging compass card. It was getting close, he thought, he'd soon know if he had lost his touch.

A match flared suddenly behind him, and he felt Cooper peering over his shoulder.

'How close?' his voice was hard.

'If I've done this correctly, we should be about five miles off the headland.'

He nodded towards a pale glare, which encircled the land like a halo. 'That's Dieppe over there. It won't be long now.'

'Good. Now what about the dinghy?'

'I've sent Morrie to loosen that. But we won't bring up the money until we're sure everything's all right.' A tingle of excitement ran through him.

'You're obviously born for this caper!' Cooper laughed in the darkness.

Vivian felt in control of the situation, and now that the operation had started, he was eager to get things moving.

'Look,' he said suddenly, 'if we're challenged, I'll switch on the navigation lights again, and we'll have to say we were making for Dieppe. We might be able to bluff it out.'

'And if not?'

'We'll make a run for it,' said Vivian grimly.

The little yacht crept forward, towards the darkening mass of the land.

Here and there, a buoy flashed its warning to the unwary, and overhead, a brightly lit airliner droned noisily towards Paris. Vivian tensed, as an unwinking, green light appeared in the far distance. But after a few breathless moments, it vanished round the headland. No doubt another yacht heading for home.

The boat's speed slackened, and as if she was feeling her way, she ploughed forward towards the hardening line of the shore.

'Right!' snapped Vivian, and deftly he eased the levers into neutral.

The pulsating roar of the engines died to an even growl, and the boat rolled uneasily in the swell.

With his flashlight in his hand, he groped his way on deck. Silhouetted against the white hull of the dinghy, Morrie's dark shape loomed like a rock. He too was waiting for something to happen. With a quick intake of breath, he pointed the torch, and pressed the button. Three shorts and a long. In the darkness, the beam seemed like a searchlight, and he found his heart pounding, as he strained his eyes towards the shore.

Then, as he raised the torch again, he saw it, a brief pinpoint of light, stabbing out towards him. Two long flashes, and then a short one.

He stepped back to the wheelhouse, and in a second the engines rumbled into life, as they pushed the boat ahead, but so slowly, that the bow wave hardly made a ripple. It was rather like driving a car without lights into a forest, he thought. The black arms of the shore seemed suddenly to leap out, as if to encircle him, while from the corner of his eye he saw a thin, white line, where the surf beat steadily against a line of savage rocks. It had been a good landfall, he decided. Then, having taken a quick bearing from the buoy on the headland, he stopped the engines, and in the silence which followed, the gentle slap of the waves against the hull sounded loud enough to be heard a mile away.

He knew the depth of the water, the figures from the chart had imprinted themselves on his brain, and he had greased and marked the anchor cable in readiness for this moment, so without waiting further, he went forward and began to veer out the cable. After what seemed like an age, the white painted mark on the chain appeared from the chain-locker, and *Seafox* swung more easily, secure to her anchor.

With a splash, the dinghy hit the water, and leaving Morrie to watch it, he scrambled down to the engine room, cursing the hard, unyielding shapes that seemed to try to block his passage. He heaved the package from under the flywheel, and went on deck, where Cooper, his coat collar turned up, and now wearing a dark woollen cap, waited impatiently.

He jumped down into the dinghy, wedging the parcel under the seat.

'Which one of you is coming?' His voice sounded strained.

Without answering, Cooper jumped down into the stern, breathing heavily.

As he shoved off from the yacht, Vivian called out to Morrie: 'Are you sure you'll be all right? If I flash my torch quickly, get the engines started and get the anchor up.'

The dark figure raised a hand, and then, as if dismissing them from his mind, he sat down on the deck.

The oars creaked, and the little dinghy bounced unevenly in the choppy water, as Vivian pulled to the pale blur of the small beach. Cooper, clutching at the boat's sides, seemed to rise and fall in front of him, like a puppet.

'Ah, there he is,' hissed Cooper, and leaned forward, his eyes gleaming.

Vivian stopped rowing, and craned round, in time to see a black shape wading through water, to take the boat safely to the beach. In silence they pulled the boat up the sand, out of reach of the clutching surf, and then, in single file, followed the other man towards the short cliff beyond, their boots crunching noisily. Once, Vivian stopped to look back, but of *Seafox* there was no sign. This place had been carefully chosen, he thought. He nudged Cooper from behind with the parcel.

'Why can't we give him the stuff here and now?' he whispered.

Cooper chuckled mirthlessly. ' 'Cause he wants to be sure, I guess, and anyway, he's got a parcel for me too.'

They lapsed into silence again, until they saw in the distance, behind some tall trees, the humped walls of a house.

'This is the joint,' muttered Cooper.

And joint it was. As they shut the front door behind them, their guide switched on a light, flooding the entrance hall with sudden brightness from a naked bulb. Vivian blinked. The walls were dirty, bare, and cracked, and the floor merely uncovered boards, and when they entered a large room at one side, that too was empty, but for an old table, and a few empty packing cases. He was relieved to see that the windows at least were carefully covered, with old blackout curtains, he guessed. His gaze eventually fell, and was riveted upon a garish, chromium-plated portable radio, which stood on one of the packing cases. Its obvious newness, and brassy appearance, clashed so much with the general atmosphere of complete desolation, that he gasped aloud.

Cooper crossed quickly to it, and ran his hands over its shining dials.

'Gee, this is the McCoy, all right!' he grinned.

'You mean it's for you?'

'Sure, I told you we had to collect something,' answered Cooper innocently.

'And you mean we came up here just for that, that monstrosity?' exploded Vivian angrily.

Cooper's eyes clouded. 'Aw, shucks, we couldn't do business down on that bloody beach,' he complained. 'Besides which, I wanted to collect this. You can't get 'em in England like this, you know.'

'I should hope not!' And he turned to the other man, who had stood patiently in silence, his eyes fixed on the parcel under Vivian's arm.

Although he, too, was dirty, and roughly dressed, his smooth, clean hands dispelled the lie. He too, was obviously part of a well-laid plan.

He was a thickset, little man, with quick, sharp eyes, and a small, black moustache.

When he eventually spoke, his voice was sharp and brittle, and his English slow and careful, as if he was unaccustomed to it.

'Now that we all know each other, perhaps we can get on with the business?' He darted a nervous glance at the walls. 'It 'as been getting very hot lately 'ere.'

'Sure, sure, give him the stuff,' snapped Cooper disinterestedly. 'We don't think much of this joint either, do we, Skip?'

The little Frenchman ripped off the waterproof cover, and placed the parcel tenderly on the rickety table. And as he sorted over the masses of little bundles of dollar bills, Copper watched him with a pitying grin.

'Makes you sick, doesn't it?' he smirked.

In his tight, woollen skull cap, he looked rather like a chimpanzee, Vivian thought.

The other man had apparently satisfied himself that all was well with his parcel, and began stuffing the packets into a special lining of his old overcoat. Eventually, when he had finished, he looked plumper, but not enough to suggest that he was carrying a fortune in forged notes.

Cooper whistled admiringly. 'I guess you learnt that one in the Resistance, eh?'

The man looked at him thoughtfully, his eyes dark.

'Yes, my friend,' he said at length. 'During the war I was always hiding from someone. Now,' he shrugged, 'I am still running, but there is a little more profit in it.' He permitted himself a wintry smile.

'What's all this trouble you've been having lately?' Vivian forced himself to sound casual.

'The Sûreté have been very active. I have very good, er, informants dotted about, and they have told me that it is getting near time to change the tactics.' He smiled, as if relieved to have got through the sentence.

Vivian glanced at his watch. 'All right then, I think we'd better start making tracks for the beach. It's a fair way in the dark.'

Cooper glanced round. 'Yep, let's go, back to dear old England.' And he tested the weight of the radio.

Vivian began to zip up his jacket, when he realized that the little Frenchman had frozen, as if turned to solid rock. His mouth hung open, and his eyes were wide and anxious.

Suddenly he gestured frantically to Cooper. 'Quiet, you fool!' he hissed, and as Cooper looked up tensely, 'Zere is someone coming!'

'Where? How d'you know?' snapped Vivian.

'A car, I 'eard it turn off the road at the back of the house. I put a sheet of metal on the road for that purpose. I 'eard it bang!' His face was white, and he had the look of a trapped animal.

In two strides, Vivian was at the door, and with a flick, plunged the room into darkness. In the silence which followed, and above their heavy breathing, he heard the sound of a car engine.

He wrenched open the door, and peered into the darkened hallway. As he watched, his heart pounding, the cracked front door was bathed in light, as a car pulled up in the driveway. Suddenly the lights were extinguished, and a car door slammed. His hopes sank, this was no accident. Someone had arrived for a purpose.

The Frenchman put his lips close to Vivian's ear.

'Zere is only one, I think!'

Vivian nodded, and eased the door until it was open only a couple of inches.

'Maybe there are others at the other side of the house.'

He stiffened, as there was a metallic click behind him. He remembered it as the sound of a safety catch being released.

'For Christ's sake, no shooting!' he whispered sharply. 'Get over by the window, and get ready to bust out!' And to the Frenchman: 'Quick, get behind the door. I'll keep here, and grab anyone who comes in!'

In the stillness of that dead house, he stared at the place where he imagined the front door lay, until his eyes ached, and spots danced before him. There was a scrape of feet on the step, and as he held his breath, the door creaked open. Then complete silence for a few moments. He must be feeling for a light switch, he thought. He remembered at that instant that the switch was not near the door. This, then, was a stranger to the house.

His racing thoughts were scattered, as the boards rang hollowly to careful, groping footsteps. With his nerves screaming, he listened, and counted them. A few steps away from him, and the creak of another door. A pause, then across the floor towards him, stopping once to get new bearings. He imagined he could hear breathing, or was it his own heart beating?

He heard the rustle of cloth on wood, as a black shape brushed the door post, and almost simultaneously, he felt the door swing inwards. The pale shape of a hand hung, disembodied, inches from his face, as it felt for the light switch. It was now, or never.

With a frantic lunge, he leapt forward, his arms sweeping together, like a rugby player. As they encircled the body, he heard a quick intake of breath, and at the same instant he yelled, 'Lights, for God's sake!'

There was a wild scramble in the darkness, and he heard Cooper's curse, as he collided with the table, then they were blinded with light, and he found himself staring down into the face of Karen Jensen, her eyes wide with terror, and her mouth opened as if to scream.

Like a tableau in a theatre, they all stood transfixed, Vivian with amazement and horror, Cooper with stupefied tautness, and the Frenchman with an expression of blank watchfulness.

Vivian trembled, as he released her gently, but even when he stood back, she still remained in the position of one terrified, one hand clutching the front of her red ski-jacket, her lip trembling.

'Karen!' he gasped at length. 'What are you doing here? How *can* you be here?'

She swallowed hard, her throat quivering.

'It's too difficult to explain,' she began, her voice small and weak. 'You have to leave here, now!'

'Now, just a minute,' began Cooper, and her eyes turned to him, taking in the pistol in his hand.

Vivian silenced him with a glare, and turned back to the girl. He was still quite sure he was dreaming, and that in a moment the real nightmare would begin.

'Look,' he said softly. 'We don't know how you got here, and I'm terribly sorry if I frightened you.' He looked at her helplessly. Not that it matters now, he thought bitterly, she knows what I am now.

For a long moment, she just looked at him, as if trying to memorize every detail of his features, then with a burst of sobbing, she flung herself into his arms, her yellow hair enveloping his chin.

'Well, I'll be!' choked Cooper in amazement, while the Frenchman began unhurriedly to button up his coat.

'All right, Karen, all right,' he murmured softly, while her body shook uncontrollably. 'I'm afraid this is the end of me. You see what I'm really like!'

She turned up her tear-stained face, struggling with the words. 'That's just it, Philip, I *do* know! I know everything!'

He tensed. 'How did it happen?'

She shook her head violently. 'There is no time, you must get away, now!'

He nodded quickly to Cooper. 'Right! Down to the beach, hurry!'

'Please take me with you, I cannot go any further alone.' Her voice was near to breaking point.

There was a sudden roar of a car engine, and then silence, and he realized the other man had gone.

'He's taken your car, I'm afraid.'

'It doesn't matter. It belongs to the travel bureau in Calais.'

'Good heavens! D'you mean you've just driven all the way from Calais, to warn us?' He was shouting.

'To warn *you*, Philip,' she answered, suddenly quiet.

He pulled her roughly to him, feeling her slim body close to his. Then he looked quickly at the tiny sandals on her feet.

'Here, I'll carry you, you can't get down to the beach like that!' And he swept her up into his arms, his heart suddenly singing with reckless excitement.

He brushed out the light with his elbow, and then, with careful steps, he strode down the stairs, and away from the deserted house. She was so light, that he cradled her in his arms with ease, and as she clung quietly to him, her arms about his neck, he still could not believe this was happening to him.

As he hurried through the rough, stubble strewn ground, towards the cliff, she began to talk again, in a quick, urgent voice.

'David Muir, you remember him? Yesterday I found out that he is a Customs officer, looking for smugglers.' She dropped her voice, until he could hardly hear her. 'I heard him talking on the telephone to his chief.' She gripped him tighter, as he stumbled over a rock. 'He said that you were using your boat for smuggling drugs, and that they will catch you this time on the way back!' She sobbed again. 'And he said many other things. Many things!'

He forced himself to think clearly, but there seemed to be too much to understand.

'How did you get here so quickly?' He swerved to avoid a rotting tree stump. 'And how d'you know there's going to be trouble? I mean now, at this place?'

He felt her head shake, as if words would be insufficient.

'In Calais, when I was trying to get the car, my uncle telephoned to say that there had been a . . .' she faltered '. . . a leak, I think he called it. The police are watching the ports, and all the main roads.'

'Bit of luck he chose this little place for me to land!' Vivian spoke with forced cheerfulness.

'Oh, he has been very careful,' she said, unable to keep the bitterness from her voice. 'To think that all these years I thought he was making money honestly. I do not mind so much what he does, or what he has done in the past. It is what he has done to you that I care about!'

She spoke with such vehemence, that he felt a surge of shame running through him.

'It's as much my fault as anybody's,' he muttered.

'That is untrue, Philip. When I heard David Muir on the telephone, I went straight back to the house, but you had gone. I confronted him with the things I had heard, and he admitted everything.' Her voice trembled again, and for a moment he feared she would break down, but when she continued, her voice was firm and clear, and he could feel her breath warm on his cheek. 'I told him it must stop, that we must warn you, and finally he agreed. We knew that it might be dangerous if I came to Chelsea, or even tried to contact you at Ramsgate. They might have been watching for something like that, so I flew straight to Calais. You know the rest,' she ended simply.

He hugged her to him. 'You're wonderful, and that's all I can say!' he said, and there was a lump in his throat.

She felt him go suddenly tense and stiff.

'What's the matter, Philip? Why have you stopped?

He glared round in the darkness, trying to recognize the black clumps of bushes, and the sudden, uneven furrows of torn earth. His heart began to pound again, and his shirt felt damp with sweat. This was not the right path as he had remembered it. In a rising panic, he strained his eyes in every direction, but there was nothing to guide him to the cliff path, and even the house had been swallowed up by the night.

'Just a minute,' he panted, and lowered her gently to the ground, where she swayed uncertainly on the rough earth and stones. As she watched him, he sniffed the air, trying to get the scent of the sea, and then standing quite motionless, he endeavoured to pick up the sounds of surf. She saw his teeth bared in a grin, white against the shadow of his face.

He took her hands in his, feeling their soft warmth. 'I'm afraid I've lost my bearings. I think I'd better circle round a bit, and try to pick up the road. Then we'll work from there.'

'What shall I do?' she shivered slightly.

'You stand just there, Karen, and I'll be able to see what I'm doing then. Don't worry, I'll not let you go. Now, or ever,' he added, and he gave her hands a quick squeeze.

She seemed to shrink, as he backed away from her, and began to move in what he believed was the direction they had already been travelling. He swore silently as he stumbled against an old post, and as he recovered his balance, he heard the distant sound of a car. Again he cursed, but it might show me the blasted road!

There was a squeal of tyres, and two powerful headlamps swung, like twin sword-blades, across the barren landscape, splitting the night in two, and even as he watched, another car rocketed round the side of a little hillock, close on the tail of the other. Sharply displayed in the glare, before the cars swung round to a careering halt, he saw the old house, its empty windows like blind eyes. Even then, he didn't comprehend, until he heard the slam of doors, and the sharp shouts of command. Then he turned desperately away, and ran back through the field, heedless of the obstacles which threatened to send him flying. He reached her breathless, and seized her by the arm.

'We'll have to get a move on!' His voice sounded like a strangled gasp. 'The police have arrived!'

With the road and the house behind them, they started off again, and once, when he darted a glance over his shoulder, he saw the winking of torches around the old building, and any second he expected to hear a shouted challenge.

He forced through some bushes, holding the clawing branches back for her, and as he saw the thorns tearing at her skirt, he felt a wave of helpless rage, and a cold fury at himself, sweep through him. It was all his fault, something kept saying, and she was suffering for his stupidity.

'My shoe!' her voice called him back to his senses, and he felt her pull heavily on his arm, as she hopped awkwardly on one foot.

'Where did it go?' He peered about them, but the darkness mocked back at him.

Then, as he heard the sound of a dog barking, he gathered her up in his arms, his chest heaving. 'Come on, we'll keep going, or we're done for!'

Suddenly, like a slap in the face, a breeze, filled with salt, seemed to rise up from his feet, and he found himself groping along the edge of the shallow cliff, while in the distance he could hear the harsh roar of the sea breaking over the rocks.

Without even a pause to look back, he blundered down the path, gritting his teeth, and aware only of his precious burden, and the necessity to reach the boat.

'Fer God's sake! Where have you bin? I can't move the dinghy on my own!' Cooper's voice was high pitched.

Vivian thought it just as well, otherwise he and Karen would have been left to fend for themselves.

'All right,' he snapped, trying to control his strangled breath. 'We'll do it now.' And he lowered the girl on to the sand.

'Did you flash the boat?' he said, as an afterthought.

'Sure, sure, I flashed, and I heard the anchor come up. So for gosh sakes, getta move on, willya?'

Together, he and Vivian dragged the dinghy down to the water, and the surf boiled noisily, and cold around their feet. Vivian noted, with amazement, that Cooper had somehow found the time to stuff the radio into the sternsheets.

He swung the girl off her feet, and placed her carefully into the boat, then, as Cooper vaulted ungraciously in after her, he put his weight against the bows, and as it slid into deeper water, he, too, clambered to his seat, and got out the oars.

He pulled with his last strength away from the beach, his eyes flickering from the blackness of the land to the pale oval of the girl's face, while Cooper beat his hands on the gunwale with frustration at their slow passage.

Out of the stillness, they heard the growing rumble of the yacht's diesels, and a few moments later, they bumped alongside, and Vivian steadied Karen, as she climbed on deck.

The next minutes were a nightmare. They hoisted the dinghy, and Vivian took the wheel from Morrie, whose face, briefly illuminated by the binnacle light, was as impassive as ever, and even unsurprised by the extra passenger, and gently eased the engines ahead. Slowly *Seafox* swung about, her screws beating up little plumes of phosphorescence, and still nothing happened. Ten minutes passed, and he opened the throttles a little more, still waiting for a spotlight to settle on them, or a shot to ring out.

Cooper clung to the side of the bridge, peering back, and every so often muttering, 'Boy, that was sure close!' while Morrie merely stood silent, his very size helping to heighten the tension.

As he swung the wheel a couple of turns, the deck canted

and he felt the girl's hands holding his belt from behind, for support, and her very presence gave him strength. He reached behind him, and pulled her to his side, one arm encircling her shoulders, and for a while there was silence, but for the steady rumble beneath them, and the slap of water around the raked bows. When he had steadied the boat on her course, he sighed heavily, and glanced at the luminous dial of the wheelhouse clock: 3 a.m. Less than two hours had passed since he had stood in that bare room, watching the Frenchman counting the forged notes.

'Here, Morrie, take over,' he said suddenly. 'Keep her North, twenty East.' And as he handed over, he turned to Cooper. 'And you keep your eyes skinned. We're not out of the woods yet!'

'Gee, they won't catch us now, will they?' His tone was uneasy.

'They might have a few coastguard cutters about, you never know.'

Then, softening his voice, he looked down at the girl, her hair gleaming like silver against the dark windows. 'Come on below, where I can see you,' and unprotesting, she allowed herself to be guided down the steps to his cabin.

She stood quietly, swaying to the motion of the boat, while he made sure the scuttles were covered, and the door to the wheelhouse was shut, and as he snapped on the lights, she lowered her head, as if her strength had at last ebbed away.

He was aghast at what he saw. Her scarlet jacket was stained and creased, while her skirt had been torn in several places. Of her stockings, but a few wisps remained, and spots of blood showed on her slim legs, where the thorns had done their work. Gently, he prised the remaining shoe from her grasp, and she looked up at it in apparent surprise, as if she couldn't remember carrying it, and as their eyes met, he was shocked to see the deep hurt which was stamped clearly in their expression, and once more he cursed himself for causing her this pain.

'You must lie down, and try to get some sleep.' His words sounded inadequate. 'You'll feel better tomorrow, and we'll decided what's to be done then.'

'All right, Philip,' she answered in a small voice, and she sank down on to the bed. 'What will you do?'

He tried to smile. 'Oh I don't know, I'll think of something.'

With a great feeling of tenderness, he saw her fall back on to the pillow, her eyes closed.

'Call me if you want anything.'

She nodded heavily, and he stepped back, closing the door quietly.

All was quiet in the ebony desert which surrounded the yacht, and only an occasional white crest marred the heaving, oily swell. They were alone, and already the lights of the French coast had become tiny pinpricks in the far distance.

'All right, Morrie?'

The figure twisted slightly. 'Yes, I will stay on the wheel, I like it.'

'Very good, it'll be a big help, if we can split the duties.'

He turned to Cooper, who was wringing water from his trousers. 'And what about you?'

'I'll live,' he muttered. 'But I won't be sorry when we get out of this.'

Later, he went below again, and stepped softly into the lighted cabin. Karen lay on the bunk, one leg hanging over the edge, swaying with the boat. She had undone the front of her jacket, and he could see the gentle rise and fall of her breast. He smiled fondly, as he lifted her leg on to the bunk and covered her body with a blanket. For a while he stood looking down at her, watching her quiet breathing, and wishing he could smooth the slight frown from her face. Then, quickly, and almost shyly, he stooped, and kissed her lightly on the forehead. She moaned softly, and he stepped back, shutting off the lights.

As he returned to his worries, and his new problems, the picture of her face on his pillow remained fixed in his brain.

5

As THE light strengthened, and filtered into the boat, Vivian yawned, and wriggled his aching shoulders. His eyes were sore and red-rimmed with concentration, and his limbs felt strained from the constant pitching of the hull beneath him. Involuntarily he ducked, as a rearing wave broke desperately over the sharp stem, and sent a stream of salt spray slashing at the windows in front of him, making his vision a strange, shimmering distortion. The weather was deteriorating fast.

He wondered what would happen when he eventually made a landfall, whether or not a reception committee of Customs officers and policemen would be awaiting him, or whether he was being too careful by driving the boat up the Channel, in the teeth of a howling gale.

Another wave punched the stout hull, and he heard something fall and break in the galley.

The sound of a heavy tread on the saloon steps made him turn, to find Morrie blinking vaguely through the side windows at the pitching waters.

'Morning,' nodded Vivian shortly. He was too tired, and too strained, to try to manufacture conversation. 'Come to take over?'

Morrie swayed heavily, and put out a hand to steady himself. 'Yes, you will be tired, I think,' he announced gruffly.

Vivian watched him take the helm, and stood back, his eye on the compass. There was no need to worry, for within seconds the big man had the boat under control, and hunched his ugly body, as if to take on the sea as an adversary.

Vivian yawned again, and staggered down into the saloon. It looked desolate and unwelcome in the grey light, and the deck was littered with books, which had jerked free from their shelves. He noticed, as he began laboriously to gather them up, that one of them was the railway time-table. He smiled ruefully, as he stuffed it in the rack, remembering as he did so, the last time he had used it. If it hadn't been necessary to go to London about the boat, all this would not have happened.

He heaved his aching body up on to the settee, and lay back in one corner, his foot braced to take the sudden plunges of the boat.

He found that he was staring at the portable radio which Cooper had managed to save from the operation the night before. It lay on its back, in a corner of the saloon, carefully sandwiched between some of the chair cushions, and shining dully, its chromium fittings looking cheap and vulgar.

He sat looking at it with dislike for some time, wondering what had given Cooper the courage to hang on to the thing when he had seemed about to lose his head completely. He dismissed it from his mind, and tried to concentrate on what Karen had told him. Karen, it was still unbelievable to think she was lying asleep in his cabin, and that she had done so much, and risked everything, to warn him. He shook his head admiringly. She had been more than a match for Muir.

David Muir, he thought, must have been mad to turn his mind away from Karen, just for the chance of arresting another smuggler. What had she said? He frowned. 'Smuggling drugs.'

Suddenly, he was sitting bolt upright, his mind clear, and ice cold. If Muir had been interested in drug smuggling, it could only have been because it affected him directly, because, he paused, his eyes turning again to the portable radio, the goods were coming *in* to the country. He gasped with horror, and dropped to his hands and knees beside the shining case.

Frantically, he unclipped the back, and turned the set over on to its face, his heart thumping. For a moment he stared in confusion at the mass of coils and valves, then, with a forced calmness, he began to examine each piece individually. Slowly, he began to relax, as he found the parts in order, and revealing nothing suspicious.

Gently, he slid out the dry battery, it was a large one, and began to feel behind it. He was tapping the metal case with his finger-nail, when the boat lurched, and the battery rolled off his knee, and fell with a thud on the deck. As he picked it up, he noticed that the packing was chipped, and through a crack in the coloured cardboard he could see the glint of an aluminium container.

With a sinking feeling of helpess resignation, he began to tear away the wrapping, until eventually, he was left with a bright metal box, about a foot long, and six inches deep. It was completely sealed, and as he weighed it in his hand, he wondered how much it would be worth in cash, to say nothing of the misery it would bring in the way of human degradation.

The *Seafox* yawed in the trough of a wave, and Vivian looked up automatically towards the wheelhouse, to see what was happening. But his vision was blocked. Morrie's huge shape towered at the top of the steps, completely filling the doorway. His face was still blank and listless, but his eyes gleamed threateningly, as he stared at the box in Vivian's hands.

'What are you doing?' his voice rose to an almost crazy shout, and he started down the steps, his fingers twitching uncontrollably.

Like a cat, Vivian rose lightly to his feet, a feeling of cold, consuming rage rising within him.

'Stay where you are, Morrie!' he barked, 'I mean to get to the bottom of this.' He shook the box angrily. 'Of this filth!'

Morrie didn't apparently hear. He came on, mumbling, and reaching for the box, his eyes wild.

Vivian knew that if once he allowed himself to be taken off guard, he would stand no chance, so deliberately, he tossed the box casually on to the settee.

As Morrie lunged forward after it, Vivian stepped in close under his wildly swinging arms, and drove his fist into the heavy chin, just below his ear. He gasped with pain, as the shock of the blow travelled up his arm. It had been like hitting a wall. For a moment, Morrie staggered drunkenly, and then, as the boat rolled heavily, he pitched forward against the table, splitting it in two as he fell.

In the silence which followed, Vivian could hear someone struggling with a cabin door. All right Cooper, he thought savagely, you're next, if you want it that way!

Morrie slumped as he had fallen, a look of complete bewilderment on his features, and his mouth opening and shutting noiselessly.

'Jeeze! What the hell d'you think you two are up to?' Cooper's voice was harsh, and still heavy with sleep. He was without his jacket, and his narrow shoulders, and bright yellow braces, seemed almost indecent.

Vivian noted with relief that he was, apparently, without his pistol.

'Keep calm!' he answered coldly. 'I want a few answers out of you, and I want them now!'

Cooper's eyes suddenly fell on the dismantled radio, and they widened with shocked surprise, but quickly he recovered himself, and his normal look of cunning made his eyes dark once more.

'Well now, Cap'n, you've certainly done it this time.' He seemed to be breathing with difficulty.

In three steps, Vivian crossed the saloon, and with a jerk, seized the little man by the throat. Then, as a feeling of cold satisfaction crept over him, he began to shake him, as he had seen his cat shake a rat.

Cooper had gone deathly white, and his hands lashed the air helplessly, while his eyes bulged from their sockets.

'Now then, you little bastard!' his voice was calm, yet filled with meance, which Cooper was quick to appreciate. 'Give me the story of the drugs in that tin! Or,' he shook his doubled fist inches from the other man's nose, 'I'll give you the biggest beating you've had in your life!'

'For Chrissakes!' spluttered Cooper, his uneven teeth wet with saliva. 'It's not my fault. I've just had to obey orders.'

'Who gave the orders?'

Even as he asked, he saw Karen's frightened face behind Cooper, her hand over her mouth.

'Well?' His eyes were hard, like steel.

'Mr. Mason!' he gasped. 'He's always run this side of the business! Now please let me go!' His voice rose in a whine.

Vivian saw the quick shadow of relief cross the girl's face. She had been afraid, as he had. He felt a fresh wave of fury making his arm tremble.

'When was the last load shipped across?' He could almost feel the rise of tension in the cabin, and Cooper writhed unhappily.

'You brought it!' He swallowed heavily, as the grip on

his neck tightened. 'You remember? The two oil drums you picked up in Calais. That was a goddam big load!'

Vivian flung Cooper from him in disgust and horror, as if he had been handling something unclean.

'God! What an infernal mess!' he choked, and his eyes fell on Karen, taking in her torn stockings and bare feet, and above all, the look of anxiety on her face. He shot her a quick glance of encouragement.

'Sorry about all this,' he gestured at the two sprawled figures. 'I've just been getting a few home truths.'

The boat swerved, and rolled sickeningly, and he saw the angry wavetops rise level with the wheelhouse door.

'Can you steer, Karen?'

She nodded her head. 'Yes, Philip. Don't worry, I'll be all right now. I was afraid my uncle was behind all this.' She paused, uncertain of how to go on.

'Yes, I know,' he said quietly. 'I was, too.'

He took her to the wheel, and helped her to get the boat back on course, watching her small hands gripping the spokes with sudden firmness and confidence. Then he went back to the saloon, where Cooper was watching him anxiously, and Morrie sat broodingly in the corner.

'Now see here, you two, we don't want any more trouble. At the moment, the biggest job is to get home safely, and I'm the only one who can do that.' He let the words sink in. 'So you, Morrie, get an oilskin on, and get up on the flying bridge, and keep a good lookout.'

The big man scrambled to his feet, and shambled out on deck, dragging an oilskin behind him like a flag.

'As for you, Cooper,' he turned coldly to the other man, 'keep away from the girl, and from me!' he added meaningly.

'Gee, it's not my fault,' Cooper began.

'Maybe, maybe not. I'll find all that out, in my own good

time. Right now, you can try to make some tea, and knock up a few sandwiches.'

The little man darted a quick, anxious glance at the gleaming metal box, which lay where it had been thrown on the sofa.

'Well, what are you gonna do with that? Mr. Mason was banking on that load,' he added hastily, as if eager to be dissociated with the arrangement.

'It's going overboard! And the so-called portable radio is going with it,' he said grimly. 'Unless you have any objection?'

Cooper shrugged his narrow shoulders sulkily. 'I dunno, I dunno, I'm sure,' was all that he could say.

Vivian picked up the two articles, and walked deliberately to the wheelhouse door. As he slid back the door, the girl watched him gravely.

He smiled briefly, thinking how lovely she managed to look under these appalling conditions and circumstances, then, with a heave, he sent the tin spinning into the boiling wake, closely followed by the radio. He dusted his hands together, and breathed deeply.

'Well, that's that. I feel a bit better, now that we've got rid of that stuff.'

From the galley, he heard the sound of Cooper struggling with the kettle, and having made sure that Morrie, too, was safely occupied, he took up his position by the girl's side, and began to fill his pipe, allowing his wiry body to swing easily, as the boat creamed over each line of waves.

'Where are we making for?' she asked, after a while.

He tamped the tobacco down in the bowl carefully, his brows set in a frown.

'I think it'll have to be Ramsgate,' he answered at length. 'At least, I can't think of a better place at the moment. If Muir and his merry men are really going out of their way to catch me, there's no point in doing anything foolish.'

'What will you say to the Customs men, if they board you?'

She lifted her troubled eyes from the compass, as he answered.

'Well, as I'm supposed to be taking our two friends here on a fishing trip, I'll have to say that I've been lying off the coast until this gale has blown itself out. After all, nobody is supposed to know I've left British waters at all,' he permitted himself a brief grin, 'whatever they might really think.'

'There's the problem of you, that I've not quite settled.'

'Me, Philip? How do you mean?'

'You're not supposed to be here! And I don't want you to get mixed up with this business, now that we've got this far,' his voice was firm.

'Perhaps it will be all right. Perhaps no one will stop us.'

But as their eyes met, they knew this to be unlikely.

'That reminds me, I'd better get the fishing gear laid out, just in case. I'd forgotten all about the need for deception!'

For the first time, she laughed, her blue eyes dancing. 'You will never make a proper smuggler, Philip!'

He patted her arm, gaining strength from the brief contact. 'I'm learning fast! Will you be all right if I leave you on the wheel for a bit?'

'I'm all right, when I know you're not too far away.' She paused. 'I would not like to be alone with that man Cooper.' She shivered.

He frowned. 'I shan't be sorry to see the back of him, either.'

As he busied himself with the fishing gear, which he always kept aboard for his paying guests, he wondered how much longer he would be able to cope with the steadily mounting web of complications. Thank God it would soon be over. Perhaps then he would be able to find out what chance he stood with Karen.

He returned to the wheelhouse, as Cooper, his face pinched with the first twinge of seasickness, staggered up the steps, a tray of tea in his grasp.

'I guess I'll go and lie down for a bit,' he groaned. 'I don't feel so good.'

'All right, but be ready to put on your act when I call you.'

With a gulp, Cooper fled below, and Vivian stood the steaming mugs on the chart table.

'Here, I'll take over now. You have a drink.'

For some moments they stood in silence, watching the sea, and the scudding clouds, and enjoying the warmth of the drink.

'You will have to get me some shoes when we get in to port,' she said suddenly. 'One shoe is hardly sufficient for a girl's morale!'

He smiled at her, allowing his face to relax.

'Ah, that's better, Philip, you were looking so very grim!'

'Sorry, I'm afraid I'm not much of a companion.'

'On the contrary, I enjoy your company very much. Considering that I know so little about you,' she finished with a secret smile.

As he flushed, and stared uncomfortably ahead over the bows, she hurried on: 'It's hardly fair, you know. After all, you know all about me, but all I know of you is that you are in love with your boat, and you have what I believe is known as a chip on your shoulder!'

In a manner which was rare to him, he found himself telling her the whole story of his mixed and unusual career, and as his pent-up feelings poured out, he was amazed that he was able to speak so casually of things which, hitherto, had been his own careful secrets. He paused at one stage, to dart a quick glance at her, but found, to his astonishment, that she appeared to be genuinely interested. When he had finished, he felt suddenly exhausted and tired.

'I'm afraid there's not so much to know after all,' he said lamely.

She was looking at him in her quiet, serious way.

'Thank you for telling me,' she said simply. 'I feel better for knowing more about you.'

His heart gave an upward bound.

'But what I really wanted to say . . .' he stammered, 'what I really meant was to tell you what it means to me to have you with me like this.' He halted, confused.

'I think I know what you mean.' She laid her hand on his wrist. 'But we must not talk of it now.' Then seeing his crestfallen expression, she smiled, and shook her hair off her cheek. 'But we will talk of it later, if you still want to. Now,' she continued briskly, 'tell me about your cat. Why do you call him Coley?'

Vivian's face softened. 'Poor old Coley, he'll be wondering what's happened to me, I expect. But I'll collect him soon.' He grinned. 'Coley? Well, it means a sort of cat-fish, and as he'll eat nothing else, I thought it would suit him.'

She threw back her head and laughed, and he marvelled at her freshness, after what she had just endured.

'We are so much alike, you and I. You have no family, but a big cat. I have only Uncle Nils to worry about, and he turns out to be, not a nice, quiet, old gentleman, but a nice, quiet, old smuggler! And you,' she dropped her eyes shyly, 'are not quite what you would have people believe. In fact, you are really rather nice.'

He reached out, and held her arm, his voice husky.

'Thank you, Karen. And there is a lot I want to tell you, when we are free from all this!'

A shaft of watery sunlight began to explore the interior of the wheelhouse, and through the clouds, patches of bright blue sky began to show.

'It's going to be a fine morning, after all,' was all he said, but for each of them, it had a new meaning.

There was a sudden sliding of feet overhead, from the flying bridge, and then Morrie's heavy face appeared through the glass panel.

'Boat comin' up astern!' he shouted.

Vivian raised his glasses, and peered out of the door, the powerful lenses distorting the white wave-caps to frightening proportions. After a while, he caught a glimpse of a low, dark blue hull, shining with spray, and throwing off a creaming bow wave from the sharp, plunging stem.

'Customs boat!' he muttered. Then over his shoulder, 'Morrie, get Cooper up, and both of you get into oilskins, and start mucking about with the fishing gear. And for God's sake, try to look as if you're enjoying it!'

He turned to the girl, a worried frown in his eyes, 'You keep out of sight up forward.' He thought rapidly. 'Could you get into the chain locker?' In his mind's eye he visualized that tiny, cramped space, right against the bows, where the anchor chain was housed, and for a moment he was tempted to change his mind.

'I know it,' she answered. And before he could say any more, 'I will be like a mouse, so don't worry!' And with that, she was gone, her bare feet padding down through the forward cabin.

After a quick look at the other craft, which was rapidly gaining on them, he swept the chart off the table, and replaced it with another, identical one. Identical, but for the pencilled course, which now showed that they had kept within the three-mile limit. He took a rapid glance round. Well, here we go, he thought desperately. He gently slackened speed, and a sudden movement on deck caught his eye, as Morrie began to unwind a heavy fish-line.

Keeping out of sight in the wheelhouse, he trained the glasses on the Customs boat, now barely a cable's length away. *Pursuit*, the name was clearly visible on the bows. He wondered if he would get such a friendly visit this time. Then he stiffened, as the glasses moved to the bridge. He caught a brief glimpse of one of the white faces behind the screen. It was David Muir.

He swore under his breath. This would be interesting. No point in telling Cooper, he decided, it would make his surprise all the more genuine.

He eased the throttles lower, and *Seafox* laboured unhappily in the deep troughs. As the Customs boat bore down on him, he waved casually from the door, to show that he was waiting for them.

Morrie lumbered over to the starboard side, and lowered the rope fenders in readiness, while on the other boat, two seamen were standing by with their lines.

Both helmsmen watched carefully, judging the distance, and as Vivian felt the gentle nudge, as the two hulls bumped, he heard the thud on deck, announcing the arrival of his visitors. The lines were then released, and *Pursuit* moved away, but remained within easy reach.

The wheelhouse was suddenly crowded with figures. First through the door was the broad, red-faced boarding officer he had seen before, followed by two younger men, their brass buttons and white caps giving an air of authority to the scene. David Muir entered last, his handsome face serious and troubled.

The officer nodded curtly. 'Good morning, sir. I'm afraid I'm here on business this time!'

'Really? Well then, perhaps you'll be good enough to tell me what all this is about.' Vivian forced his voice to remain level, a habit he had learned so well in the Navy. 'And, blow me down! David Muir! What the devil are you doing here?'

'Mr. Muir is my superior officer,' said the other man quickly, as if eager to save Muir any embarrassment.

But Vivian was unwilling to let him off so lightly. 'But you are mistaken, surely!' he exclaimed.

'No, there's no mistake.' Muir's voice was flat. 'I see you're surprised.'

'Well, it is a bit confusing, you must admit.' Inwardly he thought the chap was pretty sure of himself.

'Now, if you don't mind, one of my men will take the wheel from you, sir, then we can have a nice, little chat.' The officer's gaze was shrewd and piercing.

'Yes, I bloody well do mind!' barked Vivian angrily, 'what the hell is all this?'

'Now then, sir, that'll do,' the red face was expressionless. 'First of all, I want to know why you weren't flying your "Q" flag?'

Vivian shrugged, and handed over the wheel to one of the keen-eyed young men. 'I haven't been abroad, that's why,' he lied calmly. 'I've been stuck out here in the Channel, waiting for the gale to finish. You must know that, surely?'

Muir smiled softly. 'May we go below, Vivian. My men are going to search your boat.' He paused, watching the other man's face. 'We have certain information that you have unlawful goods in your possession, namely, dangerous drugs.'

Vivian glared at him angrily. 'Rubbish. I've no drugs aboard, and I've not been smuggling!'

He allowed himself to be led below to the saloon. He saw

the officer go on deck, and speak to Cooper, while the other man began to examine the chart.

Muir sat down, calm and assured. 'You might as well speak up, you know. Now, where have you got the stuff? My men will find it, even if they have to take the boat ashore, and tear it to bits!'

'I tell you, you're mad! I've been taking Mr. Cooper out fishing. I often do.'

'But what about your trip abroad you had planned?' Muir's voice hardened. 'I'm not a fool, Vivian, and you and I both know what I have said is the truth.'

'That trip hasn't come off yet. Mr. Jensen'll tell you, why don't you ask him?'

'Perhaps we will.' He looked up sharply, as the officer came below, and raised his eyebrows questioningly.

'They deny it, of course,' he said testily.

'What d'you mean, of course?' barked Vivian. 'We're not all crooks, you know!'

'We shall see, shan't we?' said the officer pleasantly.

Then he looked over to Muir. 'All right to have a quick look now, sir?'

'Yes, go ahead.'

Vivian watched from beneath lowered lids, as the two uniformed men hurried aft to begin their search. His face felt damp with sweat, when he thought what would happen when they discovered Karen's hiding place. It made him sick with fury, to think of her name being mixed up with any suspicion of his own crime.

Muir tapped a cigarette on a silver case, his eyes mocking. 'I really am sorry about this, Vivian. It must be a bit of a shock to you.' He dusted a speck of tobacco from his immaculate grey suit. 'I made rather a good stockbroker, didn't you think?'

Vivian grinned mirthlessly. 'I'd rather not say what I

think. I've always had the greatest respect for the Customs, up until I met you!'

Muir was completely unperturbed.

Vivian heard the searchers examining the bathroom, and then the click of the deck-boards being lifted up.

'Still sure of yourself, eh? But you really haven't a very good story, now have you?' The voice was patronizing.

'I still say I didn't leave home waters,' Vivian's voice sounded flat and tired.

'Well, I don't suppose you can produce any witness?' asked Muir cheerfully.

'Unless you can call *me* a witness!' The clear voice sounded like a pistol shot in the stillness of the saloon.

Muir spun round, his jaw dropping, while Vivian could only gape with surprise at the girl's small figure, poised on the steps.

'Karen! What on earth are you doing here? And how did you get aboard?' Muir stumbled over his sentences, his calm dignity gone. 'For Pete's sake, you were with me only the evening before last!'

She allowed him to carry on for a while, his words, like his mind, thrashing about helplessly in a wilderness.

When she answered him, her eyes flashed like blue ice, and her voice was filled with contempt.

'I have been aboard here enjoying myself!' Her tone was as cold as her eyes. 'Just as Philip will tell you! But you couldn't understand that, could you, being a stockbroker, or is it Customs officer now?'

Two bright spots of colour rose in Muir's cheeks, and he bit his lip. 'This had nothing to do with the way I felt for you, Karen,' he pleaded. 'I had no idea——'

'No idea I'd find out you had been lying to me, is that what you're going to say?' In her anger, her Danish accent became more pronounced.

Behind him, Vivian could feel the two Customs officers breathing heavily, no doubt wondering what was happening.

'But, Karen, surely you realize I had my duty to do?' Muir seemed oblivious to the fascinated audience.

'All I know is,' and for the first time the girl's lip trembled slightly, and Vivian noticed her knuckles gleaming white on her clenched hands, 'you told me that you were in love with me, and that you wanted me to marry you!'

The words dropped like pebbles into a still pool, and Vivian, who had been feeling something like pity for the man, was moved to a sudden anger by this revelation.

One of the Customs officers cleared his throat noisily. 'I take it then that the boat's okay?' The question was directed at the confused Muir.

'Oh, er, yes,' he stammered. 'This is Miss Jensen. She's just stated that she's been aboard all night.' He turned back to the girl. 'Is that right?'

'Yes,' she said deliberately, 'all night.'

'But, Karen——' began Vivian hastily.

'All night!' she repeated, 'and unless you think I've been over to wherever-it-is, doing a bit of smuggling, I think you'd better go!'

Muir nodded to his men, and the boarding officer sighed deeply.

'Well, so long, Mr. Vivian, thanks for letting us look round,' was all he said, but his eyes were angry, and cheated.

Vivian watched the three officers swing aboard their own craft, and was suddenly aware of Muir by his side.

'Apparently I was wrong,' he said quietly.

'About a lot of things, I should think,' answered Vivian coldly, and as Muir turned to board his boat, he held out his hand. 'Here, you dropped this a while back!' In his palm lay the Customs identity card. 'So you see, I *did* know, and it's not likely I'd try anything stupid, knowing that, is it?'

Muir's face was white, and he took the card unbelievingly, and stared at it.

The boats moved apart, the Customs launch thrashing the water into a froth with her screws, as she manœuvred clear, but Muir didn't look back.

Vivian stood quite motionless, his heart still pounding, and his scalp tingling with sweat.

'Jeez! They've gone!' Cooper peered round the side of the hatchway.

'Oh, go to hell, and get on with your fishing!' he shouted, and stamped back to the wheelhouse.

Karen still stood by the door, but quite limp, as if her anger had drained the life out of her. At the sound of his approach, she lifted her face, and he saw that her eyes were brimming with tears. She didn't resist, as he pulled her gently against his chest, and held her tightly to him.

'It's over,' he said quietly. 'I hadn't realized it meant so much, that you were so involved.' The words sounded inadequate.

Her answer was muffled by his jersey against her mouth. 'It's all right, Philip, I didn't know what I wanted, when I met him.'

'You mean, you do now?' He spoke the words carefully, but his quick breathing betrayed his feelings, and she raised her tear-stained face to his, and he noticed the soft fragrance of her hair, the gentle curve of her lashes.

'Yes, I know now.' There was emphasis on each word. 'And I do not think that you will ever let me down!'

Then her hands were about his shoulders, and he felt her body pressing against him. Her eyes were misty, and he felt her tremble. The next instant, he pressed his mouth to hers, and a great excitement seemed to sweep down and engulf him, and send his senses racing wildly. They broke apart, and for a moment they just stood looking at each other, as if for the first time.

'My darling,' his voice sounded weak. 'Everything'll be all right now!'

Her small hands moved quickly and excitedly, to her hair, her throat, and plucked at her jacket, like two tiny, blind animals, lost and bewildered.

'Please, Philip,' she gasped. 'We must be calm!' But all at once she was laughing, and tears of happiness washed away the strain and the worry from her face. 'Oh, Philip, I'm so very happy now!'

He stepped towards her again, but she shook her head violently, her hair shimmering in the sunlight. 'No, Philip, I am going to your cabin to have a little cry.' She paused, dropping her eyes. 'And when I come up again, I will try to behave like a lady!' And blowing him a kiss, she was gone.

For a while, he didn't know what to do. He stared blankly at the chart, ran his hand over the compass, and without thinking, twisted his pipe in his grasp, until with a sharp snap, the stem broke in two pieces. He laughed aloud, his face boyish, and split into an uncontrollable grin.

Vivian steadied *Seafox* on her new course, and brought her head round until it pointed towards the grey finger of Ramsgate breakwater. A black Starboard Hand buoy bobbed and curtseyed in salute, as the sturdy, little yacht passed close by, and Vivian peered out along the deck, to make sure that Morrie was getting the mooring lines laid out. He noticed that the decks, so recently running with spray, were now dry, and steaming slightly in the bright sun, which bathed the sea, and the red-roofed houses on the shore, with warmth. The clouds had vanished with the gale, and even the surge of the tide seemed humble in its presence.

As he squinted against the glare, and pulled down the peak of his cap to shield his eyes, he noted the multi-coloured throng of people on the harbour walls. So like Torquay, he thought, and his heart warmed at the prospect of taking Karen there, to be free, and away from all complications.

His eyes softened, as he saw Karen, bright and beautiful against the blue sky, her hair rippling in the sea breeze, the skirt flapping at her brown limbs. She gripped the guard-rail, and laughed back at him, her teeth white and gleaming.

A shadow fell across the boat, as he swung her under the lee of the high wall. His watchful eye followed the tiny figure of the harbourmaster waving him to a free berth, and as the boat glided easily into the sheltered water, he stopped the engines, and allowed her to nose alongside the green, slimy piles. The fenders squeaked, and several willing hands took the warps. He cut the power, and listened to the engines shudder to silence, and at once, the sounds of the outside world, of laughter, and distant music, filtered down to him. He patted the wheel affectionately, and stepped off the grating.

'Well done, old girl,' he murmured. 'Now to get the rest of this affair straightened up.'

Karen was chatting and smiling with the harbourmaster, who was writing out the berthing ticket. He grinned a welcome.

'Hallo, Mr. Vivian, nice to see you again.'

He quickly arranged for fresh fuel and water, and watched the man climb up the long ladder to the harbour wall.

'And what were you conspiring about?' he chuckled.

'I asked him if he knew where I could get some sandals.

He said there's a place by the harbour entrance, so I can walk there in my bare feet!' Her eyes shone brightly. 'I can get you a bucket and spade at the same time!'

He waited while she went below to 'powder her nose', as she put it, and Cooper walked softly over to him, brushing furiously at his jacket.

'Looks as if I've slept in it!' he muttered bitterly. 'What are you going to do now?' His eyes were sharp and watchful.

'Well, I've got some shopping to do,' said Vivian casually. 'I suppose you'll be off to London to break the news to Mason, eh?'

Cooper rubbed his chin. 'Guess I'll 'phone him, and tell him what's happened. He's not going to like it, though.'

'He'll like it even less when Mr. Jensen closes up the beautiful partnership,' said Vivian grimly. 'He doesn't like being led up the garden. Any more than I do.'

Cooper's face darkened. 'I hope he doesn't do anything hasty, we've been kinda depending on him.'

'Well, that's all finished,' he snapped.

Cooper shrugged. 'I'm off, then.' He beckoned to Morrie, who was gazing up at the faces of the holiday-makers who were admiring the yacht. 'C'mon, bonehead! We've got work to do!'

The big man didn't even glance at Vivian, and his eyes were dull, almost unseeing.

Vivian shuddered. What a pair, he mused.

'I'm ready!' The girl was at his side, smiling at him. She had discarded her jacket, and her blouse made her look cool and carefree.

With his hand on her arm, he guided her through the jostling throng. When they reached the end of the outer harbour, they stopped, and looked back at the graceful, white hull, dwarfed by the rough stonework. Her sides glistened, and the reflected lights dappled the boat with gold. She squeezed his hand. 'Dear little *Seafox*. She has looked after us very well.'

They bought the sandals from a shop festooned with holiday-wear, postcards, and Ramsgate rock, and when she had slipped them on to her dainty feet, they made their way to a secluded 'phone box.

He squeezed in beside her, her closeness making him feel excited once more, but he forced himself to think calmly, as he sorted out the correct money for the call.

'Don't forget, Karen, tell him everything that's happened, but speak in Danish. We want to be sure that this is for his ears alone.'

They waited patiently, while the line buzzed and clicked, and then, all at once, she was speaking, and although he couldn't understand what was being said, he could tell from the exclamations from the other end of the line, that Nils Jensen was more than relieved to hear from his niece again.

She spoke quickly and carefully, the soft words rolling off her tongue like music, and occasionally, she would pause, as the old man asked her a question.

She covered the mouthpiece. 'He wants to know when we are going back to London,' she whispered. 'He is very angry about the things Mason has been doing.'

'Tell him you'll come back today. I can hire a car, it'll be quicker.'

'*Jeg rejser til London idag*,' she said, nodding her head, as if in answer to her uncle.

Vivian tapped her arm. 'Tell him to warn Felix of what's going on,' he said quickly. 'The poor chap won't know what to say to Mason otherwise!'

He'll be as relieved as I am when this is over, he thought, it can't have been any fun, sitting in an office listening to all sorts of rumours.

118

He was aware of two indignant holiday-makers queuing impatiently outside the box.

'Come on, Karen,' he grinned. 'We're holding up the works!'

'*Jeg kan ikke komme igen, Nils! Farvel!*' And with a laugh, she put down the 'phone.

They were still laughing, as they stepped out into the bright street.

'He said to thank you for looking after me,' she said at length.

'I think it was the other way about,' he answered feelingly.

They passed a shady public house, which was displaying a discreet menu, and he stopped. 'Come on, let's have a drink to celebrate.'

'What shall we celebrate, Philip?' She was mocking him, her face impish.

'To celebrate my finding you,' his voice was so sincere, and warm, that she reached up and kissed him quickly on the cheek.

He flushed. 'That does it! I'll buy you the best lunch we can get, too!'

After the meal, which they scarcely noticed, so wrapped up in each other were their thoughts and hearts, they wandered hand in hand down to the harbour, Karen clutching a paper parcel, containing a bathing suit, which she had bought on the way, and Vivian happily puffing at a new pipe. Her present to him.

Without the two other men, *Seafox* seemed friendlier, and more intimate, as they climbed aboard.

'I'll go and put on my costume,' she announced. 'You get yours, and we will have a lovely swim, before we go back to the grime of London!'

'We can go out in the dinghy!' Her happiness was

infectious, and he felt like the air itself. 'We can be alone for a bit then.'

He slipped into his swimming trunks, and padded on deck, humming to himself, as he swung the dinghy over the side, and flexing his broad shoulders in the sun, feeling the warmth seeping into his body. He lowered himself over the side, and sat back in the small boat, watching the slow movement of people along the wall, and listening to the gulls screaming for tit-bits.

A shadow crossed the dinghy, and he looked up. The next instant he was sitting bolt upright, his mouth dry, as he saw Karen walking lightly down the yacht's side deck. In the pale blue costume, with the sun caressing her young limbs, she walked with an unselfconscious grace, her skin more golden than brown, and her beauty accentuated to one of breathtaking perfection.

As he helped her down into the swaying boat, her hands rested lightly on his arms for support, and he felt the gentle curve of her breast touch him for a brief moment, which filled him with a wild yearning, and the ache of desire.

For a full second they stood motionless in the tilting dinghy, their eyes full on each other. Her lips twitched, and she smiled shyly.

'I think we had better get started, Philip, before a crowd gathers!'

Once clear of the harbour, the little boat seemed like a tiny island, intimate and private, and the crowded beaches, which jumped and shimmered in the heat haze, were part of another world.

The boat rocked, as Vivian stood up, and as if in response to a silent signal, they both dived over the gunwale, and were soon gliding and diving in the clear water.

Once, as she seized his ankle, and tried to duck him beneath the surface, he rolled over on his back, and burst up beside her, like a dolphin, and together they floundered in the trough of a wave, laughing, and so aware of each other.

It was with silent regret that Vivian rowed slowly back towards the harbour, while Karen sat quietly, dabbing at her hair with a towel, her face thoughtful and slightly sad.

'Cheer up!' he smiled, with a gaiety he did not feel, 'it'll soon be all right now.'

'I know, Philip. It's just that all this has been so wonderful today. Like . . . like . . .' she groped for the words, 'like the beginning of a new life.'

He leaned on the oars, as the boat floated gently across the harbour towards *Seafox*. Like a mermaid, he thought, as she combed the dampness from her long hair.

'Ahoy there! Mr. Vivian!'

He jumped, as the booming voice rang out from the harbour wall, shattering his thoughts. He saw the harbourmaster waving down to them.

'Telephone call for you, in my office!'

Vivian sighed, and grimaced at the girl. 'Here we go! I expect that'll be Felix ringing up now!'

They climbed up on to the yacht, feeling heavy with the sun and the swimming.

'Where's the 'phone?'

'You've got a long walk,' chuckled the harbourmaster. 'The call's come through to the main offices, by the harbour entrance!' He gestured with his head. 'You want to tell your friends to be more thoughtful!' He walked away, laughing to himself.

'Blast!' muttered Vivian. 'I'd better get up there quick, before the line gets cut off, or something.' And he dived below, pulling on his shirt, and a pair of drill trousers over his damp costume.

'I think I'll sit on deck and wait for you, Philip. I can dry my hair while you're away.'

He smiled at her, his eyes warm. 'Shan't be long.'

'Philip!' Her voice stopped him with one foot in mid-air, reaching for the ladder, and he turned, his face questioning.

'What's up?' he asked.

She crossed quickly to his side, then she halted, one hand resting on his arm.

'It's nothing,' and she shook her head. 'I just had a strange feeling, that's all,' and she shivered, as if cold.

'Well, I'll wait for you,' he smiled, but his eyes were anxious. 'We can walk up together.'

'No, really, I'm all right now. It was silly!' And she lowered her face, rubbing her cheek against his shoulder. 'But hurry back!'

He laughed. 'Before you can say "*Skal*"!' And he swung up the ladder to the wall, feeling the stones hot through the soles of his shoes.

He found the office without much difficulty, although the effort of forcing his body against a steady stream of holiday-makers had left him slightly breathless. The telephone lay waiting on the desk, and giving him a nod, the uniformed official strolled out of the office, banging the door behind him.

Vivian snatched up the instrument. 'Hallo, Vivian speaking!'

'Oh, er, good,' the dry voice crackled in his ear, 'I'm glad you found the time to come!'

Vivian frowned at the mouthpiece. 'Who is that speaking? And what d'you want?'

There was a soft laugh. 'Don't recognize me, eh? I'm surprised; after all, the last time we met, you threatened me, remember?'

'Mason!' Vivian was breathing fast. 'Well, you're wasting your time. It's finished, washed up!'

'Just a minute!' The voice became sharper, and more urgent. 'I want you to listen to me, just for a moment. So please don't hang up!'

'Well all right, but make it snappy!' answered Vivian testily.

'When you've listened to what I have to say, you'll be glad, I promise you.'

'All right, I said I was listening, but don't try making any more deals. You know what I'm talking about!'

'Well, listen carefully.' The voice hardened. 'The plates. The ones that our mutual friend wanted to get rid of. I want them!'

I'll bet you do, thought Vivian. So Jensen had told Mason off already, had he.

'Are you listening?'

'Yes, but I don't see why you're telling me all this.'

'Oh, you will, you will, I promise you! As I said, I want them. There is no point in wasting this golden chance of making money, now is there?'

'Look, will you come to the point?' Vivian snapped impatiently.

'All right, but just hang on for a second, I just have to look out of the window.'

Vivian fumed, as the receiver clicked in his ear. Blasted fool! he muttered to himself.

'Right!' The voice was sharp, and, Vivian thought, eager. 'This is what I want you to do.' He paused, his breath rasping harshly. 'I want *you* to get the plates for me! And bring them to a place which we will decide later. All right?'

'Is that what you wanted to ask me?' Vivian stared at the mouthpiece in amazement. 'You're crazy! I told you what I——'

'Wait!' It was a command. 'Get them! Or, to put it bluntly, your little girl friend will get a rather unpleasant time!'

'You try to lay a hand on her, and I'll fix you for good!' His voice shook with rage.

'Another threat?' The line buzzed with his laughter. 'We *have* laid our hands on her!' And as Vivian didn't answer: 'That's what I went to the window for. I was waiting for a signal! Do you understand, Vivian, we have her, she's all ours!'

Vivian stared blindly at the telephone, his spine chilled with a creeping horror.

'Don't do anything foolish, Vivian! Don't call the police, Vivian! Or I promise you will not recognize her again when you see her!' The voice grated on ruthlessly. 'Ever seen the results of a razor, Vivian?'

'You swine!' His throat was choked, his eyes smarted. 'You haven't, you couldn't!' He wanted to drop the telephone, and run back to the boat, but the voice held him powerless.

'We have. And could! I promise you! Don't forget. The plates. I want them, you get them. It's all so simple really, even a fool like you should understand. When you're ready to do business, hang a towel on the rail of your boat.' The laugh rang in Vivian's ears, it was a horrible sound. 'This is what comes with meddling in affairs which are too big for you!'

'But I . . .' He stopped, as the line went dead.

Dropping the telephone, he burst out of the office, his skin clammy with cold sweat, and he started to run back into the harbour. Even as he reached the deck, he knew what he had known all the time, the boat was empty. He stared into one cabin after another, calling her name, and finally, when he opened the door of his own cabin, and saw her things scattered across the bunk, he halted, his heart beating with fear and misery.

He stared about him wildly, but the boat was still, and the sound of the water against the hull seemed to mock him. In despair, his half-demented mind thrashed and reeled in a vain effort to grasp an explanation, and he fought down the sudden, overwhelming desire to kick out at the seemingly smug objects about him.

Eventually he calmed. She had gone. Karen had gone. It beat like a tattoo in his skull. He blindly picked up her jacket from the bunk, and as he lifted it, he started, as a piece of filmy underwear slithered from underneath, and fell on the deck. He went cold. Wherever she was, she was still in her bathing costume, and her assailants must have been perfectly confident of their actions. He blundered on deck, blinking in the light. Mason had been watching for a signal. He must be here, in Ramsgate! He swore horribly. He had automatically thought the call was from London. And they had been quite certain of his reactions, as they waited, and watched.

A yachtsman, leaning lazily on a mooring post, nodded pleasantly down to him. Vivian scrambled up the ladder, his mind working furiously.

'You didn't see a young lady leave, did you?' He tried to keep his voice steady.

'Sure. Went off 'bout five minutes ago, I suppose.' The man eyed Vivian curiously. 'Nothing wrong, is there?'

Vivian fought down the impulse to scream out what had happened, but remembering Mason's cold threat, 'Ever seen the results of a razor?', he shook his head, turning his eyes away. 'No, I just wondered where she'd gone, that's all.'

'Bloke came an' give her a message, and off she went!' He

grinned. 'I was watching, naturally. Couldn't help it. She looks a real gem in that swim-suit!'

'Did she know the man?'

'Oh yes, she knew him. I expect she's just gone up to the end of the wall.' He chuckled. 'Reckon you'd better keep an eye on 'er, she'd make any man weak at the knees, just to look at 'er. You're a lucky fellow, an' no mistake!'

Lucky! The word stung and jarred in his ears, as he walked hurriedly along the wall. But there was no sight or sign of her, or anything that looked suspicious.

He returned to the boat, trying to think clearly. He must see Jensen, at once, and get the plates. That would be easy. But Karen, he stopped, sweating, would Mason keep his word? The thought of her, alone and terrified, with Cooper close to her, made him sob aloud.

Must think, must think slowly! He flung on his jacket and tie, and thrust some money into his pocket. Got to hire a car, and get to Jensen, that's the first thing! Then get back here at once, and put the signal out. Hurry, hurry! He locked the boat, and set off for the shopping centre, where he eventually found a car-hire firm, who let him take an ancient Ford, at a fabulous deposit.

An hour later, as the shadows along the roadside turned to purple, he pressed his foot down hard, making the old car roar and buck along the open, deserted road. He was in a nightmare, and it seemed as if the journey would never end.

His sweeping headlights glinted on a public call-box, and with a screech, he jarred the car to a halt.

Fumbling with the coins, he screwed up his brow, trying to remember Jensen's number. It came to him, even as he jammed the money into the slot.

'Number please?'

He had to repeat the number twice, and then waited,

pounding the pile of grubby directories with his fist, while the operator's voice faded into a series of clicks and rattles.

'I am sorry. The line is dead.'

He stared around desperately. 'What, out of order?'

'I imagine so. I will make further enquiries, if you wait, caller.'

'No, no, that's all right!' And he blundered out into the darkening roadway.

No time. No time. The voices persisted in his brain. He became calmer with the strain of driving. It would be all right. Jensen would not allow things to go wrong. He would know what to do. He had been dealing with these people for years.

The road branched left, and he saw the gleam of water, as he joined a stream of traffic passing over Kingston Bridge.

'Soon now,' he muttered, and saw the high walls of the Royal Parks flashing past.

6

THE house was in darkness, as Vivian swung the protesting car into the driveway. He switched off the engine, and sat for a moment in the darkness, getting his bearings, and looking at the unlighted windows, and the high front door.

So Jensen was out, or so it appeared, so what course of action should he now contemplate? He slid from the driving seat, and closed the car door quietly behind him, then walking carefully, to avoid the dark patches of the flower beds, he turned left round the side of the house, in the direction of the lawn, which he remembered so clearly from his last visit. At the memory of holding Mason, and shaking him like a rat, Vivian trembled, wishing he had been able to foretell the future at that time. I'd have killed him, he thought savagely. He caught his foot on a piece of stone-work, and felt the crunch of the gravel path. In another second he was standing outside the glass doors of the big room, where only two days before, he and Jensen had made arrangements for that last, fateful trip.

He pressed his face against the glass, holding his hands like screens on either side of his eyes, and tried to pierce the darkness. Then he remembered the heavy curtains. If he could get in, and draw the curtains, he could have a look round. He nodded to himself, yes, that was it. He could leave a message for Jensen, if he could not find the plates.

He stopped his racing mind, angrily, but he *had* to find the plates, there was no time for doubt.

He turned slowly, examining the gardens. The housekeeper was evidently out, enjoying her night off, and he would be able to work undisturbed.

Taking a deep breath, he turned his attention back to the doors. Through the panes, he could see the catch. It should be fairly easy. Moistening his lips, he slipped off his jacket, and held it across the middle pane, then with a quick jab of his fist, he sent the glass tinkling inwards on to the carpet. It had sounded like a shop window falling out, in the stillness of the garden, but as he waited, his head craned on one side, he knew that no one would have heard.

He buttoned his jacket, and with a suddenly calm deliberation, opened the door, and stepped into the room. Once having made sure that the door was properly shut again, and the thick curtains were drawn, Vivian groped his way blindly across the room towards the door. He gasped with pain, as his shins collided with some unyielding object in his path, and then, as his hands felt the wall in front of him, he touched the light switches.

For some moments he stood blinking in the sudden, dazzling light, and rubbing his shins to ease the pain. He noted that the cause of his injury was a small coffee table. The room was much as he remembered it, with its bowls of flowers, and rich, shining furniture. As his glance fell on the heavy, oak desk by the window, he saw that most of its drawers had been left open, and various oddments of paper were scattered across the unused blotting pad. He examined them briefly, feeling a strange pang of guilt, but as there seemed to be nothing of any help to his present task, he decided to go further into the house, and find Jensen's workshop, which Lang had mentioned.

As he crossed the soft carpet, and stepped into the darkened hallway, he cursed himself for not bringing his torch, for at any moment he felt that he was about to crash into some other piece of furniture, or ornament, and accordingly, he found himself walking in the stance of a sleepwalker.

As he rounded the corner of a narrow passage, which led off the main entrance hall, his uncertain footsteps sounded loud and heavy, while the sleeve of his reefer jacket scraped eerily against the panelled wall. Then he stiffened, and stood stock still, his eyes fixed unbelievingly on a thin thread of light, which seemed to hang horizontally across his path. As he watched, his heart thumping painfully against his ribs, he realized that he was looking at a light from under a closed door.

He peered round in the darkness, listening for a sound, but there was nothing but the steady tick of the grandfather clock behind him in the hallway.

He reached out, his fingers running lightly round the edges of the door, which appeared to be heavily studded with iron bolts, and the handle, when he eventually found it, was the old ring pattern, like a huge doorknocker.

Very gently, and not daring to breathe, he started to turn the heavy handle, the metal cold to the touch, and as the mechanism clicked, he felt the door start to open in his grasp, the hinges moving with silent, well-oiled precision.

Squinting his eyes, he allowed the door to open very slowly, taking in every section of the small, cellar-like room before him. The walls were rough stone, and apart from a covering of what looked like whitewash, were completely bare. It must have been the original part of the building, he thought, as his eyes travelled across the smooth, stone-flagged floor, also uncovered, but for a few odd scraps of carpet.

A long, wooden rack had been erected at one side of the room, and from it hung several full-length travel posters, recently completed, and looking strange, and out of place. A laughing girl in a flowered dress waved to him from a steamer on the Rhine, and beside her, on a partly finished poster, loomed the grey bulk of Edinburgh Castle.

So this was the workshop. He took one last glance behind him at the dark passage, and then pushed the door wide, revealing the rest of the room. A compact mass of equipment met his startled gaze, drawing boards, piles of paper, printing frames, all scattered in orderly confusion.

The door thudded behind him, and he stood, hands on hips, wondering where to start his search.

Funny about him going off and leaving the lights on, and the door unlocked. Perhaps he would be coming back soon. His eyes fell on some old tin boxes at the back of the drawing tables, they looked as if they would be a good place to start.

He stepped lightly across to a tray of paints, their surfaces shining in the light. 'Hello,' he murmured, 'someone's upset a whole tin here.' He rounded the end of the tables, and as he glanced casually along the floor, his heart leapt, and he felt a wave of sickening horror break over him. He was looking into the frozen eyes of Nils Jensen. For a moment, he was quite unable to move, it was like opening a door, expecting to meet an old friend, and suddenly finding a frenzied maniac. The twisted body was sprawled between the legs of the tables, one arm flung out like a dancer's, and the other curled unnaturally beneath him.

Vivian forced himself to look at the face, which seemed to have shrunk to the very shape of a skull, while the thick, grey hair added to the macabre and ghastly appearance.

Gently, Vivian felt the claw-like hand, and shuddered at its cold chill, and although he had seen many dead men in his life, it was all he could do to force down the sour taste of vomit, as he turned the old man on to his side. The back of his head gaped open, like some obscene, scarlet flower.

His eye followed the dark smear along the floor, a sob rising in his throat. He had thought it was paint. And then rested on the pencil, still clutched in the thin, twisted fingers.

Vivian stood up, his brain surprisingly clear, a feeling of scalding anger making him tremble. With narrowed eyes, he tried to reset the scene. Jensen must have been sitting at the farthest table, the stool now lay where it had been thrown, and after his assailant had struck him from behind, he had crawled along the floor, to die amongst the pictures he had loved.

'Mason!' Vivian spoke the name aloud. 'I'll get you for this, if it's the last thing I ever do!'

He knelt again at the old man's side, staring unafraid at the piercing eyes, which shone in the lamplight like two pieces of cut glass, then, as if in a final salute, he reached out, and brushed the lock of hair from the wrinkled forehead. Poor, foolish, gentle, old man, he thought, his eyes moist. I hope you're with your family now.

As he stepped back gently, his elbow brushed against the end table, and for an instant his eye fell on to the loose drawing paper, with its jumbled lines, and the well-formed shadowing of several quick sketches. He must have been doing these, he thought, thinking of the pencil in the small, dead hand, he was probably quite happy. He froze, his glance fixed on one small sketch, casually drawn in one corner. For a while he was unable to grasp its significance, or the sense of familiarity it gave him. He frowned, puckering his brows. There were some planks, like a deck. A deck! That was it! He was suddenly excited, and he realized he was looking at a quickly drawn picture of *Seafox*'s engine-room. There was an engine, and by the flywheel there was a gap in the deck boards, as if to show where they had hidden the money. He bit his lip, pondering, wondering what was wrong with the picture. Then it dawned on him, it was the wrong engine. The port engine, or part of it, showed vaguely as a background. The more he looked at it, the more he was convinced that he was looking at a message. Jensen must have done it while his assailant was talking to him, and planning to kill him. A crude arrow, which before Vivian had regarded as another rough doodle on the paper, pointed away from the engines, but all that Vivian could see was a small cartoon of a cat strutting breathlessly along an invisible road, and a pile of dinner plates.

'Plates!' His hoarse voice echoed round the room. Of course, that was what Jensen was trying to tell him. He had hidden the plates under the other engine! He must have done it when I was getting the ballast, he thought wildly.

A cold sweat broke on his back, when he pictured Jensen quietly sketching, knowing that any second was to be his last, and yet still able to compile a message, which only he would understand. He groaned miserably. If only he and Karen had driven straight here, instead of going out in the dinghy, Jensen would be alive, and she would be at his side.

He found that he was suddenly shaking, his whole being quivering with an unnatural, clammy chill, and a muscle at the corner of his mouth jumped convulsively, causing him to grit his teeth, and press his hands flat on the table, until the wave of shock had passed. It was all so horrible, so unreal. He shook his head violently, it just couldn't be happening to him. He tried desperately to form a plan of action, turning his back on the terrible eyes, and using every ounce of his will-power to clear away the mist of terror which was threatening to engulf him.

Call the police, tell them there had been a murder. He

rejected the plan at once. He could almost hear the voice on the telephone, quiet, yet full of questions. A murder, sir? Where are you speaking from? Who is that speaking? And the black cars streaking through the night towards him. They would not be interested in his story of Karen. Karen, who had to be protected at all costs. Mason's words came back to him, like a blast of Arctic wind, 'Don't call the police, or I promise you will not recognize her again!'

Jensen could not be helped now. He was safe from everything. That had to be the way to look at it. If only he could call on someone to help him. Felix! He felt a pulse quicken in his throat, he might be able to assist him.

He found himself half running down the darkened corridor, his shadow dancing in fantastic shapes in the gleam of light from the workshop. Once in the study, he glanced round dazedly, until his worried eyes found the telephone. He fumbled with the instrument, his taut nerves making every task an agony.

He forced himself to sit on the edge of the desk, the telephone pressed against his ear. Nothing happened. Feverishly he rattled the telephone rest, but there was no answering click in his ear. He put it down, slowly, and with great care, as if in a final effort to stop his mind from bursting

So it was still dead. At a sudden thought, he sprang across the room, following the flex to the wall bracket. As if to mock him, the bare ends of the torn wires glinted from the carpet, where they had been torn out of the wall. He swayed slightly, and put out his hand to steady himself. The murderer had been thorough indeed.

Somewhere, far away, where life was still civilized and normal, a car back-fired noisily, and Vivian jerked his thoughts back into focus. The housekeeper, he thought, she might be coming back at any moment. He mustn't be found like this. He turned to a typewriter, which he had noticed earlier, and slipped in a piece of the headed notepaper, which lay neatly stacked on the desk. Pausing only to assemble the wild scheme which was forming in his mind, he began, clumsily, to type a letter for the housekeeper. He stated, briefly, that Jensen had been called unexpectedly to London, and would not be back for a couple of days. She was to have the telephone repaired in his absence, and she was not to worry. His lips were set in a thin line, as he typed the initials N.J. at the end, and propped the letter up on the desk, where it would be immediately visible.

Carefully he picked up the fragments from the shattered window, and slipped them into the bottom drawer of the desk, covering them with the loose papers. It was not likely that the housekeeper would be too suspicious about that, he decided. In any case, it couldn't be helped.

After several attempts, he found Jensen's bedroom, and hurriedly stuffed some clothes into a small overnight case, being careful to tidy the wardrobe when he had finished. He was about to leave the room, when a shaft of light from the bedside lamp fell on a silver mounted photograph on the dressing-table.

He almost dropped the case, and his eyes smarted. Karen's smiling face looked up at him, beautiful and happy. He picked it up, his hands unsteady. Forgive me for what I have to do, my darling, it is only for your safety, and for your happiness, that I am doing this. He returned the photograph to the table, and with a hollow sigh, snapped off the light, and forced himself back to the workshop.

The case would be all right there, and he pushed it under a pile of old art magazines. Next, he pocketed the tiny caricature, Jensen's final artistic creation, and with a quick glance at the door, to make sure that the heavy, old-fashioned key was still protruding from the outside of the keyhole, he turned off the lights, and shut and clicked the door behind him. As he pulled the front door of the house, until he heard the Yale lock snap shut, a chill breeze made him shiver, and realize just how much he had been sweating, with shock and fear.

The old car started reluctantly, and without a further glance behind him, he drove grimly down the drive, and out on to the deserted road. As he turned once more over Kingston Bridge, his tortured thoughts recalled the words of his first commanding officer, during the war. He had been trying to explain the dangers, in action, of over-confidence. 'These things don't happen to other people, Vivian, they happen to *you*!' He hadn't liked the man much, but how true his words had been then, and were now, at this very second!

Like a lonely outpost, he suddenly saw the telephone booth from where he had tried to telephone Jensen. It seemed like a century ago.

Burr-burr. 'I am trying to connect you.' It was a man's voice this time.

'Hallo? Felix Lang speaking.' The voice was thick, and heavy with sleep.

'Felix, this is Philip!' In the confined booth, his own voice was harsh and unnatural.

'Philip, for Christ's sake! What are you up to, getting a fella out of bed on a night like this?'

'Listen. I'm in a jam,' he began.

'I heard about it. Jensen told me about the spot of bother you had, but I'm jolly glad it all went off as well as it——'

'For God's sake, listen!' He was shouting. 'I've just left the old man.' Must be careful not to mention any names, a warning signal flashed in his brain. 'He's dead!' There was a gasp in the earpiece. 'They've taken the niece, they want the plates in exchange!' He stopped, struggling with his message. 'Do you understand?'

'Now, just a minute, old boy,' Lang sounded fully alert, his tone steady, and somehow giving Vivian confidence. 'I think I understand. Have you got the plates now?'

'Apparently. He left a message for me. Felix, for God's sake, what shall I do?'

There was silence for a while, and Vivian could hear Lang's deep breathing over the line.

'Look, Philip, where are you?' When Vivian had answered, his voice continued, full of strength, as if he was trying to instil a fresh confidence over the long wire between them. 'Well, drive back to your boat, and get rid of the car. Then sit tight, and wait for me. I'll come down as soon as I've squared up the business you've just left.'

'I've done that, Felix,' he said tightly.

'Phew, you have eh? Sure it's all right?'

'Yes, it'll do, I think.'

'Right, get going. I'm on my way now!'

Ramsgate was a different town when the car's headlights slashed the darkened houses and shopfronts, and even the lonely, patrolling policeman made Vivian look back with a new, fearful apprehension, until he was sure that the man was only looking at him with a professional disinterest.

He drove the car into the yard at the back of the hire firm and left a scribbled note under the windscreen wiper. Then, with his shoulders hunched, and his hands thrust deep into his jacket pockets, he started to walk to the harbour, his footsteps ringing out crisply on the still, salt-laden air.

It was low water, and he had to climb down the full length of the slimy ladder to the deck of *Seafox*.

He remembered bitterly, and with real grief, how he and Karen had climbed up the very same steps, to buy the shoes. They had laughed then, and the future had been filled with fresh hope and promise.

Seafox, too, was different, and the very noises of her loose gear, as it rattled and squeaked, seemed unfamiliar and distant.

There were no notes or messages thrust under the wheel-house door, as he had hoped, or feared, and after a rapid glance around the boat, he lowered himself into the small engine room, squatting between the silent engines. He lifted the boards by the starboard flywheel, throwing them furiously to one side, in his haste. He reached right down into the bowels of the hull, his cheek scratching against the engine's unyielding metal, and his fingers groping between the stout timbers, until he felt the rough touch of canvas, and breathing heavily, he pulled the weighty parcel into the glare of his inspection lamp. He untied the strong cord which held the canvas wrapper around the contents, and as he peeled it away, the sharp, metallic glint of the neat stack of oblong plates faced him from the deck.

He picked up the top one, turning it over in his hands, and noting the intricate lines and patterns on its surface. So these were the plates which Jensen had made so carefully, and with such patient skill. For these he had died, and for these his killers would do anything. He swallowed hard. Anything! It was fantastic, and yet so coldly logical.

He sat back on his haunches, staring at the plates. When he handed them over to Mason what guarantee could he have that Karen would be safe? Surely Mason and Cooper would not hesitate to act again.

He had to be able to bargain, even in a small way. He had to gain time. Time to get to Karen's side, to show her that he was not beaten, and that Jensen's message had not been in vain.

He looked at the plates again. One for the front of each type of bank-note, and one for the back. If he left some of them behind in the boat, and took the others to Mason, perhaps he would be able to bargain, when the time arose. It seemed a feeble hope, but it was better than doing nothing. Carefully, he selected half the plates, and then stowed the others back loosely in their hiding place, and pushed the boards back into position. Mason was no fool, but it was unlikely he would know exactly what to expect, and without a careful examination, he might accept them on their face value. Then, he would be able to see what would happen next.

He re-wrapped the package, and when he was satisfied, he climbed back into the wheelhouse, and stowed the parcel in a small locker, and turned the key.

The sight of Karen's clothes on the bunk made a fresh helplessness twist his inside in half, and he gathered the garments together, and put them carefully in a small bag in readiness.

In the saloon he found a small bottle of whisky, and poured himself a full glass, the harsh liquid burning his dry throat like fire, and helping to steady his nerves.

As he put down the glass, a paper-knife on the bookcase caught his eye. It had been given to him at a mess party in Germany, just after the Armistice, by the Guards Armoured Division. He picked it up, testing it in his hand. It was about ten inches long, with an extremely sharp point, more of a weapon than an ornament. Might come in useful, he thought, and after several experiments, he secreted it down the inside of his sock, having first wrapped the point in a scrap of paper, to protect his ankle. In that manner, he found he was able to walk quite naturally and freely.

He glanced at his watch. Felix should be here soon. It would be better to go and meet him. Anything was better than just standing still, alone with his fears.

As he mounted the ladder, and stood braced between the

guard-rails at the top, he shivered briefly in the cold air, and was thankful for the whisky's warm glow within him.

For a while he stood looking down at the yacht, and at the flapping shape of the white towel, which he had hung on the forward rail. It looked like an admission of defeat, a flag of surrender. As he watched it, his shoulders heavy with both mental and physical exhaustion, it seemed for all the world like a crude challenge, and he felt a faint stir of desperate anger rising in answer.

He noticed too that the outlines of the boat were hardening, and what before had been only indistinct, blurred shapes, began to assume their normal proportions.

So the night was all but finished, and the lightening sky, which crept slowly over the horizon in thin, grey fingers, was the visible introduction to what might prove to be his most testing day, or his last.

He shook his tired shoulders, and started to walk wearily towards the harbour entrance. A disturbed gull flapped angrily away from the masthead of a moored yacht, squawking loudly, its hard eyes watching the lone figure pass by, and in a sleeping street beyond the dance hall, a milk van rattled cheerfully on the cobbles. He paused in his stride, listening, his ears picking out the high whine of a fast-moving car.

The long Bentley swerved around the corner of the harbour road, the tyres skidding on the uneven surface, and even in the grey half-light, Vivian could see the thick coating of dust and dirt on its elegant bonnet.

A door slammed, and Lang, his thick form muffled in a belted, camel-hair overcoat, strode purposefully across to him.

'Thanks for coming,' nodded Vivian, thinking how tired and grim the other man looked. Once again, the 'old boy' mask had dropped into the background, unfitting for the new personality.

Lang smiled briefly, stretching his arms, his eyes flitting quickly around the harbour.

'Right, let's talk. I'll walk with you to the boat.' He gestured with his head towards the car. 'I've got Janice in there. She's out to the wide!' He laughed nervously. 'Poor kid's full of dope. After you 'phoned, I shot round to her place, although I still don't know what I expected to find, and she was just about going up the wall! Mason shot off in the morning. Didn't say where he was going, or how long he was going for.' He paused, fumbling for a cigarette. 'She knew something was wrong, but she still doesn't realize what he was up to!'

'You going to leave her here?'

'Well, I gave her some stuff to make her sleep, and brought her along with me. After all this is over, I'm keeping her with me, for good.'

They started to walk, Lang puffing heavily on his cigarette, not speaking, while Vivian began to relate, fully, the whole story of what, in the harsh light of dawn, could only sound like a hideous dream.

He checked himself, as Lang touched his arm.

'Have you hung out this bloody signal yet, Philip?'

Vivian pointed across the harbour wall. 'Yes, I put it up as soon as I got here.'

'We've got to be very careful about this. Mason's a proper bastard, make no mistake about that!'

He stopped suddenly, apparently having arrived at a decision.

'Look, you'll have to wait until they get in touch with you. Then, just do what they tell you. No doubt they'll want you to rendezvous somewhere.'

'But, look here——'

Lang gestured impatiently. 'Wait a minute, before you blow up! They're not a bit worried about you. They know they've got you cold! You can't go to the police, or tell anyone about it. One false move from you, and you know what'll happen!'

Vivian blanched, and Lang seized his arm.

'We've got to play it their way! Damn the plates! We've got your girl to worry about now, right?'

Vivian forced a smile. 'Sorry, Felix, I'm about all in at the moment.'

'I'm not surprised!' He flicked the cigarette in a neat arc on to the oily water below them. 'Better try to get some sleep. Until they make the first move, we're bitched!'

'I don't think Mason'll keep his word.' Vivian spoke quietly, glad to be free of the fear which had lurked in the back of his mind.

'He doesn't count on me!' Lang's voice was hard. 'If he doesn't come across, he'll have me to reckon with!' He silenced Vivian's outburst. 'I'll be right on your tail, wherever you are.' He glanced back towards the town. 'Right now, I think I'll get Janice parked up in a hotel I know. She can sleep it off there.' He turned to go. 'Soon as I've done that, I'll be right back. We sit this out together!'

'Thanks, Felix, you've made me feel a whole lot better.'

'Nuts, old boy, don't forget that I got you into all this in the first place!'

Lang sauntered away, his crêpe-soled shoes kicking up the loose sand of the stone flags. Vivian watched his broad back until it vanished around the harbourmaster's office, and then lowered himself aboard *Seafox*.

He shaved, and changed into clean clothes, and then threw himself on to his bunk, to await events. He tried to smoke his pipe, but somehow he couldn't concentrate, and he put it down wretchedly. His head was drooping, and his breathing had become slow and laboured, when the sound of Lang's heavy arrival jerked him into a state of strained alertness.

He saw that Lang had discarded his rumpled coat, and was wearing a well-cut blazer and flannels. On his feet he was wearing rubber deck-shoes, and his pink cheeks glowed smoothly, with newly shaved spruceness.

'Forgive the rig, old boy,' he grinned. 'Didn't want to cut your nice decks up with my big beetle-crushers, and I think a nautical appearance is called for!'

Around their quiet haven of seclusion, the port was now fully awake, and the air was full of the clank and rattle of a windlass, as a small timber-ship resumed the work of unloading. The walls of the harbour echoed to the stamp of feet, and the sliding grind of fish boxes, as they were trundled along the fish quay for the waiting boats.

Vivian left the saloon, and mounted the steps to the wheelhouse. He picked up the glasses from their rack, and trained them on the busy figures of the seamen and sweating dock labourers. As the faces sprang up in the powerful lenses, he studied them carefully, and then discarded them. Eventually, he turned his eyes to the hotels and seafront boarding-houses, watching the flapping beach towels hanging from the window sills, and the bathing suits drying from yesterday's swimming. God, somewhere out there, they've got her! He could picture her so clearly, still in her bathing suit, that he pounded the teak panelling with sick frustration.

He turned his head miserably, as Lang stepped softly up the steps. Something in the man's eyes made him frown.

'What's the matter?'

'Quick,' Lang snapped. 'There's someone coming!'

For a moment Vivian stared at him, not understanding, and then, his breath quickening, he crossed to his side.

'Where?'

Lang nodded to the curving wall, which bulged out astern of the boat like the side of a castle. 'That boy, see him?'

Vivian scanned the moving figures, and suddenly stiffened, as his glance alighted on the small boy who was wandering along in their direction, stopping every so often to study the names of the various moored craft. Vivian's stare became riveted on the envelope which gleamed white in the urchin's grubby hand. Scarcely daring to breathe, he waited until the boy was level with the boat, then, unable to contain himself any longer, he stepped out on to the deck, his knuckles white, as he clenched his fists at his sides, in a sweat of suspense.

The boy, his dark hair curled in an unruly mop, stopped opposite the ladder, his dark eyes wrinkled, as his lips spelled out the name on the yacht's side. Seeing Vivian watching him, he showed his teeth in a cheeky grin.

'*Seafox*, mister?'

'That's right.' His heart pounded excitedly.

'Gotta letter from a bloke up the road!' He grinned again, scratching his greasy shirt contentedly. 'Tole me ter give it yer.' Then, as an afterthought: 'Reckon it's worf a couple er bob, eh?'

As Vivian scrambled up the ladder, the boy darted forward to catch the gleaming coin which Lang had thrown from the wheelhouse door.

'Cor! Thanks, mister!' The youth's eyes were round with pleasure.

Vivian took the envelope from the grubby fist, and as the boy sauntered away, whistling, he leaned across the safety wall, feeling the stonework warm through his shirt, and tore open the flap.

The letter had been typed, and as he read the brief

contents, he found his nervousness draining away, as if his soul was satisfied at the prospect of action.

BRING PARCEL TO JUNCTION OF ROYAL PARADE AND WEST-CLIFF PROMENADE. COME ALONE AND BE THERE AT 10 A.M. IF YOU UNDERSTAND TAKE IN THE SIGNAL. DON'T FORGET, NO TRICKS.

The cool bastards, he thought, they're sure of themselves all right. He squinted at the opposite side of the harbour. They're watching me right now.

He returned to the deck, and deliberately jerked the towel from the rail.

He showed the message to Lang, who had stayed out of sight in the wheelhouse. He nodded slowly, and studied his watch.

'Two hours to go!' It sounded like a judge passing sentence. 'I'll keep below until you've gone, Philip. We don't want the swines to know all our forces!'

Vivian lifted the heavy package from the locker, and thrust it under his shirt, holding its sharp bulk against his ribs with his elbow.

'As we used to say, Felix,' he smiled meaningly, 'engage the enemy more closely!'

7

VIVIAN paused at the top of the winding flight of stone steps cut into the old cliff-side, and known locally as 'Jacob's Ladder', and as he waited for his laboured breathing to return to normal, he allowed his gaze to wander over the wide panorama of the harbour and its approaches, which were spread below him like a map. From his lofty position, the yachts and wharves, the buildings and minute, moving figures, seemed distant and obscure, and quite unattached from him, and his agony of mind.

A chill wind swept the leaves and pieces of paper along the deserted pavement in a sudden, angry movement, and while he watched the long cliff-top road, with its white-fronted boarding houses, he felt a vague sensation of hostility, as if even the holiday-makers and morning idlers had been driven away by some hidden threat.

He looked at his watch for the hundredth time. Still nearly half an hour to go, but there was no point in hanging about in the harbour, when there seemed even the remotest possibility of getting to Karen earlier.

He pulled his cap down over his eyes, to shield them from the thin powder of sand, which, even at the top of the road, swirled grittily in the wind's sharp gusts. With the small bag containing the girl's clothes under his arm, and the jagged parcel bumping heavily against his ribs, he started to stride slowly to the far end of the sloping roadway, where he knew the cross-roads to be, the place so carefully selected for the rendezvous, no doubt because of the numerous avenues of approach and escape. Even the thought that Lang was probably parked watchfully in a suitable side street, did not completely alleviate his feeling of loneliness and uncertainty. Only his quiet, controlled anger, and his eagerness for action, seemed real, and his eyes hardened at the prospect of getting his hands around Mason's throat.

A car drove slowly past, and he narrowly scanned the occupants, only to be met by the blank stares of two daytrippers, aimlessly searching for some form of distraction. He swore savagely under his breath, and unconsciously quickened his pace.

He halted by the road junction, and leaned casually against a lamp standard, letting his eyes rove around the awkward criss-cross of tarmac and white lines, of 'Keep Left' signs and pedestrian crossings. No doubt a very busy place at the height of the season, he mused, but at that moment it all seemed wasted. An occasional bus or lorry on its way to Dover, and a sprinkling of cars, but apart from a tradesman or two he appeared to be the only pedestrian in view.

A shiny, black saloon slid quietly into the main road, and halted opposite him, its engine ticking over confidently. He forced himself to look away, and tried to appear casual and indifferent.

He cursed desperately as the car's engine died, and darted a rapid glance across the road, taking in the three uniformed inmates and the bold 'Police' sign on the radiator. Faintly he could hear the steady, monotonous murmur of the car's radio, then he turned his eyes away when he realized that the sergeant in the rear seat was watching him. He steeled himself, feeling strangely guilty, without knowing the real reason, and expecting, any second, one of them to walk across to him.

Vivian's anxiety turned to a sudden, hot fury. Blast them! Why the hell don't they go away! If the others see them there, they'll drive straight on. They'll think I've called in the police.

Several more cars passed, but the police showed no signs of moving. Vivian felt his palms sweating with impatience, and he took a firmer grip on his parcels to steady himself. Already his back ached from leaning against the post, but he was afraid to move, lest he excite the curiosity of the three lawmen.

His keen ear picked out a high-pitched whine, which grew louder and more penetrating every second, and as he turned his head he saw a brightly painted motor-cycle flashing along the road, its rider helmeted and goggled and his teeth bared in a happy grin. His young pillion rider, her hair streaming in the wind, was hugging him excitedly around the waist and shouting encouragement in his ear. Must be doing about sixty, thought Vivian, as the machine roared round the corner and on to the coast road.

The effect of the snarling apparition had a startling result as far as the police car was concerned. The sergeant jabbed the driver in the back with his finger, and with a grind of gears the black car leapt from its place by the kerb and vanished in pursuit. Vivian said a silent prayer of thanks to the unknown motor-cyclist, as in the far distance he heard the tinny clamour of the police gong.

Almost immediately, another car turned the corner, and Vivian's heart throbbed painfully as he caught sight of Morrie's stony face behind the windscreen. It swung in a wide arc and ran smoothly along the kerb in front of him. The rear door swung open and he saw Cooper's beady eyes glinting at him across the wide seat.

Vivian leapt into the rear and slammed the door, keeping his body turned in the little man's direction. He was only dimly aware that the car had accelerated, and that Morrie had not even given him a glance. His feeling was one of relief, like that of a man who has sweated at the thought of a dangerous operation and then, once on the operating table, he knows that there is no longer any room for worry and fearful supposition, it is too late to turn back.

'Well, Skipper, it's been a busy coupla days!' Cooper's thin lips parted across his uneven teeth in a smugly confident smile.

'See here——' began Vivian, but the other man waved his hand in an angry gesture.

'No, *you* see here! You're through giving the orders now, we're running this show our way, so don't you forget it!' His small eyes darted quickly in Morrie's direction, as if to reassure himself. 'It's no goddam good you gettin' any ideas, cause if you try one single, goddam thing, your little sweetie has had it! Okay?'

Vivian nodded slowly, the knot in his stomach tightening, as he fought down his first impulse to smash the grinning face to pulp.

As if reading his thoughts, Cooper shook his head in mock despair. 'I'm not surprised you left the bloody Navy, it just beats me how we won the war, with guys like you messing about!'

'All right, Cooper, you've made your point,' said Vivian quietly. 'Now shut up, will you! And just remember this, if you've laid just one finger on the girl, I'll kill you!'

'Sez you!' sneered Cooper. 'D'you hear what he says, bonehead? He's tryin' to get tough.' He cackled gleefully and pulled out his cigarettes.

Vivian tingled, as briefly in the driving mirror above Morrie's cropped head he caught a glimpse of Lang's silver-grey Bentley following them down the road. A wave

149

of excitement swept over him, as he turned his attention back to Cooper's remarks.

'What's in the bag then, Skipper? You aiming to go camping, or sumpn?' He prodded the canvas bag with a nicotine-stained finger.

'Clothes,' said Vivian coolly.

'Aw gee, yes, for the little girl. Some dish, eh?' He grinned knowingly. 'Wouldn't mind a weekend with her!'

'When the time comes, Cooper, don't say that I didn't warn you!'

Cooper studied the end of his cigarette from beneath the brim of his hat, his expression shaded, but somehow giving the impression of an intense, nervous force. He looked up suddenly, his eyes bright, and Vivian felt as if a door had been opened into the little man's soul. They were the wild, excited eyes of a madman. Christ, he's really enjoying this, he thought, the more he can make me suffer, the better he'll like it. He forced his mind to be calm, and met the other man's stare coolly.

'You don't understand, do you?' He peered right into Vivian's impassive face. 'You're beat! Finished! *Kaput!*' He chuckled wildly, and twisted the cigarette viciously. 'You can't understand that people like you are nothing to the boss, nothing at all.' He waited, but as Vivian remained silent, he leaned across the seat, tapping his arm with his finger. 'You had your chance to play it straight, to fall in with us. What'd you do, eh? You just about fouled up the whole works.' He shook his head rapidly. 'The boss didn't like you chucking all that stuff into the drink, you know. That wasn't very clever, you know. But, then, you've been rather a pigeon right from the start, haven't you?'

Although half listening to the little man's yapping voice, Vivian sensed the car's increase of speed, as Morrie handled it as if it were a toy.

Pegwell Bay gleamed grey and uninviting on his left, the horizon misted by a rain squall, which within minutes was sweeping along the shining road, and hissing across the windscreen. One of Morrie's huge hands detached itself from the wheel and set the wipers squeaking across the glass and distorting the roadside houses as they flashed past.

'Well, ain't you got a thing to say?'

Vivian noticed that the pseudo-American accent tended to be replaced by a Cockney twang when Cooper became excited. Excited maybe, but dangerous too, there was no mistaking the sneer of triumph on those almost opaque eyes.

'Let's see now. You could start by explaining what's going to happen when we reach our destination, or hasn't the boss given you permission to discuss it?'

Cooper ran his tongue over his thin lips. 'Don't get wise, Mister Vivian! You'll just make it harder for yourself.' He smiled cruelly.

Vivian looked away allowing a quick glance at the mirror to ensure that Lang was still following. A signal of alarm rang in his tensed nerves. They had left the main road now and he judged that they were heading more inland to the west. To Canterbury, perhaps. The houses had already thinned out and the neat pavement had been replaced by a green ribbon of grass banking, bordered with bushes and an occasional wide gate leading into a field, or farmland. As the car twisted and turned along the almost deserted road, Lang's car fell further and further behind. Vivian gritted his teeth, forcing his eyes away from the mirror. Lang was having to pull back to avoid becoming obvious to either Morrie or Cooper, and as they swung into an even narrower road, which ran straight and empty through a rain-swept avenue of quivering poplar trees, the Bentley had all but disappeared. It only needed a sudden twist of the wheel by Morrie and they would be swallowed up in this dripping, green wilderness.

His heart sank when he realized that it was quite obvious they were making no effort to conceal their destination or route from him. They were quite confident that this was to be a one-way trip, apparently.

The muddy surface sang under the tyres, and occasionally, the nearside wheels would send a sheet of sluggish water leaping over the wings, making Morrie's eyes flicker and tighten his grip on the wheel. Suddenly Cooper leaned forward, tapping Morrie's shoulder.

'Get ready.' It was an order.

Very carefully, Cooper turned and scrutinized the road behind, smiling to himself, then, with an amused glance at Vivian, he said over his shoulder, 'Okay, bonehead, when you like.'

There was a sudden moan as Morrie changed gear, and with easy grace the big car slewed off the road, straight, or so it seemed, for a wall of bushes.

Vivian tensed himself for the impact, but as the front wheels bit into the thin branches and the leaves flapped and scraped along each side of the bodywork, the car seemed to bound through a thin layer of undergrowth, and then, as Morrie straightened the wheel, they were moving bumpily along an almost overgrown dirt road, its surface cut and runnelled by rain and what appeared to be old cart tracks. He could feel Cooper's eyes upon him, but he stared ahead, thrusting the feeling of hopelessness and defeat to the back of his mind. Of course, he should have reckoned with this situation, they were bound to make sure that they could not be followed and had obviously chosen this old, disused track with great care.

Ahead of the slowly moving car, he saw that what had first appeared to be steep banks of trees, proved to be miniature mountains of earth and gravel, overgrown with weeds and grass, and having the general air of neglect and man-made untidiness. They nosed between two of the humps, which he estimated to be about forty feet high, and through the driving lances of rain, he saw the flat, cold gleam of water. Not the blustery, uneasy swell of salt rollers, nor the clean, clear shimmering of a stream or river, but the heavy, dead, hard-top surface of unused and unwanted storage. He eyed it narrowly, and as Morrie eased the car to a dead-slow crawl and the wheels cautiously explored the uneven boards of a flimsy bridge, which linked the mainland with another forlorn section of wasteland, he realized that they must have entered one of the many disused gravel-pits, which abound in the area. From the corner of his eye, he watched Cooper's hands, as they twitched impatiently in his lap, and he tightened his grip on the bag containing the heavy plates. One false move, he decided, and he would smash them down on Morrie's skull, and then jump at Cooper before he could draw his gun, or whatever weapon he favoured at the moment.

Cooper, however, seemed more interested in the road ahead, and began to turn up the collar of his jacket, scowling at the mounting clouds.

'Be gettin' out soon,' he remarked. 'Better get your parcels ready.'

Vivian nodded, his eyes watchful. 'Quite a headquarters you've got for yourselves.'

'Only temporary. Sort of borrowed, just for this transaction, as you might say!' The furnace doors of his eyes flickered at Vivian again, as if his pent-up hatreds were getting out of control.

Vivian felt a sudden tightening in his throat. What would happen, and when? As he stepped from the car, would they be ready to shoot him down? Perhaps Karen was already dead, like her uncle? A mist crossed his eyes, as he saw Jensen's distorted features and staring, inhuman expression. No, not Karen! He ground his teeth together in anguish.

The car stopped suddenly in a small clearing, which, encircled by the banks of forgotten clay and dirt, seemed like a miniature valley.

A dilapidated, single-storey building leaned, rather than stood, alongside the twisted remains of a steel gravel scoop, its corrugated roof red with rust, and the thin, boarded walls, cracked and weather-beaten. Across the narrow door, in faded paint, was the statement 'Office and Enquiries'. His attention was taken by a sleek, red sports car which was parked nearby. It looked so entirely out-of-place that his feeling of loneliness, and the tension of being trapped, was somehow increased.

'Okay, this is the end of the line, sucker!' Cooper was grinning, his uneven teeth bared with obvious pleasure.

Morrie got out of the car and walked heavily towards the building, heedless of the rain and of them. He climbed lightly out of the car, while Cooper slammed his door and hurried, muttering, round the back, to join him.

The cool, insistent needles of rain against his tanned face cleared the mist of nervousness from his mind, and he watched Cooper with a feeling of grim resignation, mixed with a sense of unreality.

Squinting against the rain, Cooper glanced at him, his eyes, questioning, 'Come on then, ain't you in a hurry to see the girl friend?'

Swinging the two bags in his hands, Vivian followed the stooped shoulder across the rough gravel space, the wet stones murmuring under his feet. They were sure all right. They were not even watching him. Morrie shouldered his way through the door, and as Vivian stepped over the threshold, his muscles taut, expecting a sudden blow, or a shot, he again had the absurd feeling that this was not really happening to him, that there had been no murder, no Karen, no fear.

The sight of Mason sitting casually behind a rough table, eating a sandwich from a spotless napkin, only helped to heighten these impressions. Mason put down the sandwich carefully and dabbed at his lips. In the rough, deserted office, with its peeling walls and air of desolation, he looked smug and self-assured, and older than Vivian had pictured him in his mind. The harsh light filtering through the grimy windows tended to accentuate the carefully brushed grey hair and the mottled skin. Only the eyes were the same. Stony and indifferent.

'Right on time, I see.' His voice was soft and clipped. He waved a well-manicured hand around the room. 'Help yourself to a chair, we have certain business to discuss, I believe.'

Vivian stood still, his feet slightly apart, aware that Cooper had moved stealthily behind him, across the door, his hands in his jacket pockets. Morrie leaned against the wall behind Mason, his wooden face passive and without knowledge.

'Where is Karen Jensen?' The words dropped like pebbles in a still pond.

'All in good time.' Mason's voice was smooth, but his expression hardened. 'Have you the—er—goods, as we criminals would say?'

Vivian took a gradual step forward, his shoes making the only sounds in the room. Immediately, Morrie pushed himself away from the wall with one elbow, his hands hanging loosely at his sides, like an ape.

'See here, Mason, you murdering bastard, I'm through juggling with you and your rotten tribe. I want the girl now, and quickly, and then we're leaving, got it?'

155

'You're behaving rather as I expected you would, all your type are much the same, you know.' Mason smiled thinly and toyed with the napkin on the table. 'She's alive and well, in the next room as a matter of fact.' He jerked his head towards another small door at one side of the broken fireplace. 'But first, let me assure you, my foolish friend, that you'll have to keep calm and do what I tell you, or else . . .' He let his words hang in the air. 'Or else you will certainly get hurt.' As he finished speaking, he flicked the napkin on to the floor, and Vivian caught a brief glimpse of a slender automatic pistol, before Mason snatched it up and pointed the muzzle unwaveringly at his stomach.

Mason shrugged. 'You see? You haven't a hope in hell. I could read your mind, the moment you stepped in here.' He chuckled. It was not a nice sound. 'You never thought there was any danger in a frail, little chap like me, now did you?'

Vivian stared at the pistol, a sick sensation in his throat.

'No, you imagined that Morrie here was the one to watch, or Cooper, isn't that so now? We've handled tougher gentlemen than you before now, believe me.'

'Like poor old Jensen!' The cold contempt in Vivian's tone brought a flush of anger to Mason's cheeks, and the gun wavered, as if he was about to squeeze the trigger.

'Right, that's enough!' He spat the words between his tight lips, the casual and haughty veneer dropping from him like a discarded garment. 'Just drop the plates on the floor, and no foolishness, or that'll be your lot, I promise you!' His eye fell on the other bag. 'What's in there?'

'He's brought a load of clothes for his little bird.' Cooper's nasal voice was gleeful.

'Well, put those down too, just in case.'

The plates clattered noisily on the wooden floor, and as

Vivian lowered the other bag beside them, he heard Cooper chortle with satisfaction.

Mason scowled in his direction. 'All right, Cooper, just watch him, that's all. Did you make sure of everything? No police cars, or anything?'

'Nothing.' Cooper sounded hurt at being rebuked.

'Right, now back away, you two.' Mason's voice was controlled once more. 'And, Morrie, get that bag up here.'

The big man dumped the plates in front of Mason, who eagerly tore at the wrappings with a knife. As the oblong pieces of metal came to light, Vivian tensed, waiting for Mason's quick eye to notice the incomplete sets. He breathed a trifle easier, as the other man raised the first plate to the light and examined its intricate surface.

'What a job,' he breathed admiringly. 'No wonder we never have any complaints about our supplies!' He laughed shortly, and placed it back carefully on the pile.

'All right, Vivian, you can go and see your Karen now. But no tricks!'

'And then?' Vivian's eyebrows lifted slightly.

'And then,' Mason answered mockingly, 'we shall have to decide what's to be done with the pair of you.'

With a jerk he tossed the pistol to Cooper. 'Just check that bag of clothing before you hand it over. Now, take him in the next room.'

Vivian crossed to the door, caring nothing for Mason's sneer, and seizing the handle he thrust his way into the room. It was smaller than the one he had just left, and the only light was a feeble, grey glow, which filtered down from a dirt-encrusted skylight, which rattled and cracked to the monotonous beat of the heavy rain.

She lay on a low, makeshift bed of sacking and old canvas sheets, directly under the skylight, so that in the filthy and drab surroundings she seemed to shine in an unreal, statue-like pose. At first Vivian thought she was lifeless, and his heart almost froze within him, but as he watched with fearful eyes he saw the quick, unnatural breathing, the movement beneath the dust-smeared breast of the blue swimming costume which, creased and disordered, was still her only covering. The yellow tresses of hair were strewn across the sacking under her head and her face was white and strained under the tan.

'What have you done to her, you swine?' Vivian wheeled on Cooper, his face savage.

'Steady now!' The pistol rose menacingly. 'She's okay. Just a whiff of dope to keep her quiet.' He waved the gun again. 'Don't go gettin' any ideas either. As I said, she'll be all right in a bit.'

Vivian flung himself down on his knees at the girl's side and tenderly slid his hand under her shoulders, and lifting her head on to his chest, felt her rapid breathing fanning his cheek. Gently he smoothed a smudge of dirt from her cheek, and without releasing his grip slung his jacket across her legs.

Cooper tipped the contents of the bag on to the dirt floor of the room, and as the girl's underwear floated down into the dust he whistled in lecherous admiration.

'Well now,' he grinned, 'ain't they just ducky?'

From his kneeling position on the floor, Vivian stared up at him, his mind a cold knife of fury. Unconsciously he tightened his grip around the smooth, bare shoulders, a fresh determination fighting off the recurrent waves of helplessness which seemed to mock him at every turn.

How they must have laughed at him, and how simple it had all been for them to play with his stupid, naïve approach to what was rapidly developing into the most dangerous situation of his life.

Karen moaned softly against his chest, and he almost cried aloud in his misery. To have been so easily snared was folly enough, but to have brought her to the edge of disaster was enough to send a new knife turning in his bowels.

'Can't you get out?' He hardly recognized his own voice. 'You've had your little victory. You must be damned proud of yourselves!'

'I was goin' anyway. But don't think there's a way out of here, 'cause there ain't. Except through this door.' He leaned forward, his pointed shoes glinting like two misshapen claws. 'And believe me, if you try anything, nothing'd give me greater pleasure than to put a bullet into her little belly, seein' that she seems to think she's a cut above me!' As he kicked open the door, the brighter light glinted on the spittle on his thin lower lip and the savage glint in his eyes.

'Swine!' But Vivian was, nevertheless, thankful to be left alone with Karen and his thoughts.

As she lay inert in his arms, he let his mind wander back over the mad stream of events which had somehow borne him along a new course, and into a final, horror-filled climax.

It was difficult to see the situation clearly, as would an outsider. To anyone else, he must surely be a criminal, a smuggler, and probably worse. He shifted slightly, trying to ease the pain in his cramped knees as they rested heavily on the uneven floor. A criminal, he thought, it sounded strange somehow, but then he could hardly expect to notice any real change in himself. Even the people he had been working with had appeared quite ordinary; except Cooper, that was. He twisted his neck to study the inside of the room more carefully. It must be a lean-to of some sort, he mused. As he had not noticed one when he approached the building, he decided it must be tacked on to the rear, probably resting against the big bank of dirt and waste gravel. The skylight appeared to have bars across the outside, thick ones too.

A heavy, sullen rumble rolled across the building, dying away in a threatening murmur. A real, thundery storm was brewing, and already the damp air in the room was growing thick and heavy.

Carefully and gently he began to ease the girl up into a sitting position so that she sat limply on the side of the bed, her hair and arms hanging motionless, giving her the appearance of a small, neglected child.

There was a pale blue flash, and shortly afterwards, another rumble of thunder. Closer this time, and somehow giving the air a fresh edge of imminent danger.

He gritted his teeth in desperation. Come on, man. The voice inside him seemed to be imploring. Are you going to let them take you both like sitting ducks? No fight? No nerve?

Even the heavy thuds of the raindrops seemed to accentuate the growing uneasiness.

Don't panic, you fool. Think, think!

He swallowed heavily, his throat dry and raw. Then, reaching down, he took one of the girl's small, limp hands in his and began to squeeze it, gently and insistently, at the same time murmuring softly into her ear.

'Karen, Karen, my darling,' his voice was taut with anxiety, 'please try to hear me. Try to wake up again.' He kept on talking but only once did she even move and then it was only a slight shudder which ran through her.

He stood up and pulled her up against him, her hair falling across his shirt and her bare feet dragging helplessly on the dirt. Together they stood, like two weary dancers on a forgotten dance-floor waiting for the music to begin.

He darted a frantic glance at the door, but as far as he could tell the others were busy preparing some sort of meal, and he could hear the occasional clink of crockery above the roar of the rain on the iron roof.

He buried his face in her hair and crushed her slim body against him, feeling a smarting in the back of his eyes.

'My poor darling,' he spoke aloud, 'what have I done to bring this on you?'

He suddenly stiffened, aware that the weight of her body had lessened. Her feet were firmer on the ground and, even as he waited, hardly daring to breathe, her hands moved blindly, feeling at his waist, while her shoulders twisted slightly in his grasp, as if testing the strength of his hold. A long, drawn-out sigh escaped her lips and he felt another shudder run through her. He watched her cautiously as her drugged limbs seemed to come to life. When her eyes opened, their wide, almost fierce stare, all but threw him off his guard, for whereas the rest of her now seemed relaxed and calm, her eyes held, at once, the true imprint and message of the torment and agony within her. For what felt like an eternity, she stared up at him, her whole face so filled with an uncomprehending terror, entirely lacking in recognition, that his words of comfort died on his lips, he could only hold her and wait.

Slowly she opened her mouth to speak, her expression changing to one of disbelief. 'Philip?' She spoke his name as a question, as if unable to trust what she saw.

He did his best to give her a reassuring smile, and nodded dumbly.

'I've been asleep,' she faltered and swayed against his arm. 'I remember now, they drugged me!' Her eyes widened as her memory came flooding back, and her body began to tremble violently. 'Philip! Tell me it's not true about—about Nils?'

He tried to meet her penetrating gaze, but the desperate brightness of the blue eyes forced him to look away, his heart sick with fear for her, and disgust and hatred at the men who had told her.

She suddenly jerked away from his arms and seized the front of his shirt in her hands, forcing him to look at her. 'Philip, please, I have to know!'

He could feel her nails biting into his skin.

'Yes, it's true.' He tried to find the right words. 'I found him when I was trying to get to you.' He hurried on, wanting her to be rid of her fears: 'It was very sudden, I believe. He—he felt no pain.'

Still she said nothing but stood straight and still, her eyes on his face, her arms down at her sides.

'Why did it happen?' Her voice, when it came, was thin and small. 'Why did they do such a thing to him? Why?'

He took half a step towards her, but she shook her head quickly, the loose hair swinging across one shoulder.

'Tell me, can you, Philip? How did all this happen to us?' Her voice rose slightly, and it was obvious that she was only holding on to herself with a great effort. 'They killed him. Those men killed him.' It was as if she was trying to explain it to her inner self. 'And they are going to kill us too!'

Her words, though spoken so quietly, and almost drowned by the hiss and roar of the rain, burned into his mind like hot irons. She didn't seem aware of his presence, and when she spoke again her voice was almost puzzled, and only by watching her mouth could he be certain of the words.

'And we were so,' she faltered, 'so very happy.'

It was then, as she looked up, that he saw the tears beginning to pour unrestrainedly and unchecked down her face. 'They *are* going to kill us, aren't they?' He caught her

s she fell, the pent-up misery and terror making her sobs
shake and wrench her body, so that he had to hold on to
her with a fierceness, which filled him with a rising and
consuming determination, as well as new uncontrollable
hatred for those who had brought this horror to the one
person he had ever wanted to love and protect.

A sudden rumble of thunder directly overhead made
fresh feeling of urgency flood through him. If only he knew
what was happening and what Mason had said to Karen.
He rested his cheek against her hair, trying to ease the pain
of her grief.

'Listen to me, Karen,' he said softly, 'and try to remember, no matter what happens, everything will be all
right. And remember too that I love you very much.' He
stopped, and beneath his grasp he felt the sobs becoming
quieter, and more subdued.

'Right now I have to think of a way to get us out of here,
so that we can get help. If it doesn't hurt you too much,
could you tell me what you've heard? There may not be
much time,' he ended gently.

She slowly lifted her head and he was shocked by the
look of despair on her tear-stained face.

'It's no use, Philip, it's no use,' she repeated. 'That
dreadful man,' she faltered, 'Cooper, told me it was all
arranged. That we were going to be taken care of.' Her
lip trembled. 'They are going to make it look as if you
killed Nils. He was horrible, Philip, he kept boasting, but
all the time I hoped, I prayed, that he was not telling the
truth.'

The swine, he thought, the dirty, rotten, little swine.

'He's full of bluff,' he answered. 'We'll fix him, if only we
can get away from here!'

If only Lang hadn't been shaken off the trail. Vivian
wondered what Lang was doing now. Probably going back

to the boat to wait, and hope for the best. But how lon
would he wait before he called in the police? And suppose–
he shook his head angrily. This wouldn't do.'

'Look, Karen, we must get ready. The chance ma
come, it *has* to come, and then you and I will get out of th
together. Do you believe that?'

She studied him carefully. 'I believe in you, Philip.
will try not to let you down when the time comes.'

She said it so simply, so trustingly, that he wanted t
crush her in his arms, but he forced a grin.

'Come on then, my girl, get some clothes on, while
watch the door.'

He picked up her clothes from the floor, brushing th
dust from them with his hand which, he noticed, wa
trembling.

She turned her back to him. 'The swim-suit, Philip. Wil
you unzip the back for me?'

As he felt for the fastener he moved some of her hair t
one side so as not to catch it in the costume, then h
stopped, his eyes fixed to a livid, red bruise on her righ
shoulder.

'How did you get this?' His voice was strangely flat.

'That man Cooper,' she trembled, 'he tried to kiss me
but when I would not let him touch me he bit my
shoulder!'

He squeezed her arm, not daring to speak at tha
moment, and not wanting her to see his expression
Instead, he unclipped the costume and stepped away.

'All right, Karen, you get changed. We'll talk later. Bu
not about all this.' He turned his eyes to the door. In the
half light they looked like two slivers of steel.

A quick rustling of clothing behind him jolted him away
from his murderous thoughts, and from the corner of hi
vision he saw her body pale against the black walls, and h

164

knew that what he had to do had to be done carefully and with a cool head. There could be no second chance of escape.

As another peal of thunder rolled and echoed around the clouds Vivian paused in his second examination of the walls. The thick, decaying atmosphere of the room and the moist, stifling heat made him breathe heavily and he paused, with one arm resting on the rough, wooden planking, while he plucked his shirt free from his damp skin.

Behind him he heard Karen move slightly and the frown of concentration on his face deepened. Without turning, he knew that she was still sitting listlessly on the edge of the bed, as she had been for the last half an hour, while he had paced watchfully around the room and beat his brain for some fresh solution, or method of escape.

'Philip?'

The suddenness of her voice made him jump. He swung round, forcing his face to soften slightly.

'It's all right, Karen. I'm just having another prowl, to see what I can find.'

'What is the time, Philip?' Her eyes still looked frightened.

'Er, about midday.' Then as the thought struck him, 'Are you hungry?'

'I have not eaten since last night. But I am not hungry.'

He stared down at her helplessly. 'I'll tell them to get us something,' he paused uncertainly. 'You've had a bad-enough time as it is, without making yourself ill.'

She shrugged her shoulders, biting her lower lip. 'It really doesn't matter.' Her voice sounded tired, beaten.

He reached over to her and gently lifted her chin with his hand, and when she raised her gaze to his he again marvelled at the strength she seemed to give him.

'Look here,' he began quietly, 'you've been through hell.

It's my fault and I realize now that I've been a complete fool!'

She tried to shake her head, but he held her face firmly in his hand.

'Oh yes, I have. Let's not argue about that. I'd like myself to believe that I'm a blind, trusting type of chap who's been taken in by a bunch of crooks. But I knew what I was doing and I knew it was wrong. I just didn't know that I wasn't big or clever enough to pull away from their filth when I realized just how rotten they were. There's only one thing I don't regret.' He swallowed hard. 'That was getting enough mixed up with Mason and Co. to meet you.' She dropped her eyes and he hurried on, as if to purge his very soul: 'I love you, Karen—you know that already. But I swear that somehow I'll get you out of this, so that you'll be able to live your life again, free from all this misery. I'll see that Nils is avenged too.'

She took one of his hands in hers and pulled it against her cheek. 'You *are* a fool, Philip, but not in the way you mean. You are trying to tell me that if we can escape, and right now I do not see how we can, you will help me to get settled again, and then you will go away, so that I can never see you, never feel your arms about me, and all because you think that *you* have been the cause of all this!'

He flushed and started to protest, but she would not listen.

'No, Philip, it is not true. Do not deceive yourself any more. I came to you in France because I knew that I loved you then. I think I knew it when you came to the house at Hampton Court. I saw that you were different, and well'—she shrugged—'here we are.'

As he struggled for an answer, she gripped his hand with a sudden fierceness.

166

'I am all right now, Philip. When the time comes I will not let you down. This is not the first time I have been afraid, you know. When I was a little girl I remember the shooting, and the fear of others.' She stared up at him, her eyes bright and almost defiant. 'But, believe me, if I am to die here and now, I shall still be thankful for those few hours of happiness we had together before things started to go wrong.'

She reached down and picked up the beach sandals he had bought her in Ramsgate, and a brief picture flitted across his aching mind. He saw the laughing girl at his side, with her hair gleaming in the sun. Somehow he could still feel the smooth pressure of her body, as they had bathed in the warmth and happiness of their own making.

'You see?' She held them up for his inspection. 'I still have them. It *was* wonderful, wasn't it?'

He nodded, his eyes tingling.

In one lithe movement she was in his arms, pressing her full length against him.

'Now, Philip!' Her voice was a gasp. 'Kiss me hard. Just in case we do not get any more time.'

For an instant he saw the blue flame bright again in her eyes and then they were together, her mouth eagerly and desperately seeking his. He felt himself plunging into a deep, breathless wave of desire, his heart pounded wildly, and the hard pressure of her body against him seemed to sweep away the nagging feeling of despair, and he was filled with a rising flame of want which held them together, each one knowing the need of the other.

How long they clung together Vivian didn't know, but as she pulled her face breathlessly from his, a small reserve of caution sent a sharp warning to his reeling brain, and he held her gently at arm's length.

'All right, darling,' his voice was hoarse, 'I think I understand now. But do have faith because we are going to get away, and we are going to be happy, always.'

She nodded, her lips slightly parted. At her throat he could see the skin moving to the quickening of her breath, and he knew that he would never live without her.

There was a rasping click as a key grated in the door, and for a brief instant he saw her eyes widen with terror, then, as he tightened his grip on her hand, she suddenly calmed, and her whole expression became one of passive watchfulness.

The door swung open, and to his surprise he saw Mason standing casually by the entrance, his eyes widening with mock astonishment.

'Oh, so you're both up and about again, eh?' A small smile played about his thin mouth.

Vivian watched him through narrowed eyes, noting that behind the front of forced indifference, Mason somehow generated a new air of tense expectancy, or was it anxiety? As if he was eager to conclude the next part of the proceedings. This, then, was to be the show-down. He saw, too, that Mason's right hand was firmly planted in his jacket pocket. A significant gesture.

'Sorry to have kept you both waiting so long, but I've had a few more details to take care of.' He paused, darting a quick glance at Karen, who was standing quietly behind Vivian. 'Too bad about all this, but your uncle should have been a little more understanding and co-operative.'

Vivian felt her hand tremble in his, but her voice was firm and cold. 'I think he understood you too well.'

'Well, it's all over now, I'm afraid, but there's too much at stake to be spoilt by your interference.'

'I suppose this is your idea of a bargain?' Vivian spoke slowly, and with difficulty, his muscles tensing beneath his belt. 'You're even a bigger swine than you were in Germany apparently.'

Mason's cheeks flushed, and he made a quick gesture with his free hand. 'So you know about that, do you?' He shook his head pityingly. 'You see? There's no hope for you at all, is there?'

Cooper slouched into view, shaking the rain from his jacket.

'Car's ready, boss,' he said. 'Fair dropping down outside it is. Like a bloody bog!'

Mason's eyes jerked round at the interruption, and in that instant Vivian sprang forward, all the pent-up fury and suspense acting like an explosive charge behind him.

Mason emitted a half-strangled cry and pulled at his pocket, but even as the gun glinted in his hand Vivian reached him, his hands grasping him savagely by the throat. With a quick twist, he flung the twisting body against Cooper, whose expression of pop-eyed amazement changed to one of snarling rage as Mason struck him in the chest, and they both fell on to the floor in a tangled heap. Mason rolled on to his side, his voice a thin croak. 'Quick, Morrie, you fool!'

From the corner of his eye Vivian saw Morrie lumbering towards him, his face an indistinct blur. Must keep out of his reach, he thought desperately. Once in those ape-like arms, and I'm done for.

As Cooper scrabbled on the floor, dazed and cursing, Vivian lashed out viciously with his foot, and a thrill of satisfaction ran through him as he saw him fall on his back, his mouth covered in blood. Then Morrie was on him, his huge hands groping for a hold. Vivian side-stepped out of reach and swung a blow at the craggy jaw. The shock made his arm tingle, but although the other man grunted with the pain, he shook his head and came on.

One clutching hand clawed at his shirt and he felt the cloth tear from his shoulders and then, as he tried to step back, a sickening blow caught the side of his head, making his senses reel. Before he could recover, Morrie's arms had him in a vice-like hug, pressing his spine in from behind, making him gasp for breath, and lights dance before his eyes. Slowly but surely the giant increased his grip, while Vivian struggled and twisted, his arms pinned uselessly to his sides. He could vaguely see Karen's terrified face over Morrie's shoulder, until it was blotted out by the shifting bulk as he swung Vivian round, straining to increase his hold.

His breath jerked in spurts of agonized fire as he felt his resistance ebbing, and a red mist swirled before his eyes. With one final, supreme effort, Vivian drew back his leg, and then, with his last reserve of strength, he drove his knee savagely upwards into Morrie's groin.

In one jerk the crushing grip had gone and he staggered back, gasping for breath, while Morrie rolled across the floor, doubled up in agony, emitting small, short screams, his eyes shut against the pain.

A high, cracked voice pierced Vivian's thoughts as he reeled against the wall.

'Stand still! Don't make another move, or . . .' His words were unfinished, but Vivian knew at a glance that he was beaten.

Mason stood behind the girl with one of her arms twisted cruelly up her back, so that her body curved like a bow, her lips parted in pain. Her eyes were wide and staring sideways at the razor which Mason held against her cheek, the edge already threatening to slice the soft skin as it shook in Mason's unsteady hand.

Vivian dropped his hands to his sides and shook his head urgently, as if to show his defeat.

'All right, Mason, you win. Now let her go, for God's sake!'

He saw the look of relief flit across Mason's narrowed eyes. And he stood heavily, watching Cooper struggling to his feet, wiping the blood from his chin with his handkerchief and feeling in his mouth for the broken teeth.

'Take over!' snapped Mason and stepped quickly from behind Karen, the gun again in his grip, and the look of fear giving way to one of cruel composure. He closed the razor and tossed it to Cooper, who snatched it angrily.

'For once I'm glad you had that thing on you,' said Mason smoothly, 'otherwise our little friends might have got away.'

'I'm sorry, Philip,' Karen's voice was shaky. 'I couldn't——' Her voice ended in a scream as Cooper struck her twice across the face with his hand, leaving scarlet weals, and in a quick jerk he gripped her hair in the other hand and twisted it into a yellow knot, pulling her head hard back.

'Hold it!' barked Mason as Vivian moved forward. 'No more tricks or I shall shoot!' The cold eyes left little doubt.

Cooper grinned, his face distorted by the blood stains on his chin. 'What'd ya think of this, Skipper?' He ran his hand over the girl's throat and breast so that she struggled wildly, kicking out in fear and pain.

A slight scraping movement, followed by a hiss of painful breath, made Cooper shift his attention.

Morrie lumbered to his feet, his eyes red with the fires within him. He stood swaying like a tree, holding his body, and grunting loudly.

'Put your hands behind you, Vivian!' Mason's hand was steady again, the gun pointing straight and unwavering.

'Tell that swine to take his hands off her!' Vivian's voice was a sob.

'All right, Cooper, just hold her but let her be!' It was a command, and Cooper's face twisted sulkily.

'Let me handle her, boss,' he pleaded. 'I'll make the little bitch snivel!'

'Drop it, and do as you're told.'

Vivian stood silent, his limbs heavy and limp, while his eyes rested on Karen, trying to tell her that he had tried and failed. He felt his wrists jerked behind him and clumsily tied with a length of cord, which was pulled so tightly that already his fingers felt numb. Morrie spun him round, his breath hot and panting in his face. The small, stony eyes glinted murderously, although the rest of his expression was again as impassive as usual. With a quick, deliberate gesture, he tore Vivian's shirt from his body and stood back, leaving him naked to the waist, then he spat into his huge hands, never taking his eyes from Vivian's face.

'Steady, Morrie!' Mason's voice was harsh. 'Don't mark him too badly. I'm not having you hot-headed fools messing everything up now!'

Watching the other man, Vivian saw a brief shadow of childlike disappointment cross his features, then Morrie dropped his eyes, examining Vivian's body, as a dog examines a bone before taking the first bite. With a great sigh, he drew back his fist. Vivian gritted his teeth, feeling his stomach muscles bunching to take the blow. But when it came it was like a rod of hot steel, smashing down on to his unprotected skin. The lights were dancing again and there was a great roaring in his ears. Cooper was laughing, as the next blow landed beneath his heart. He heard his own voice cry out in agony, but it didn't seem to belong to him any more. He slipped to the floor and rolled on to his side.

Only dimly now, the voices, the faces, swirling round in a great vortex of pain and fire.

He saw the two gigantic feet by his face, and then he saw one of them swing back. He heard Karen scream from a long way away, and then the boot struck him behind the ear.

The all-engulfing blackness was almost a pleasure, as he plunged down into nothingness.

.   .   .   .   .

The great, black waves surged and roared in angry torment, vying with each other to drag his body deeper, pulling and sucking his sodden limbs until he could feel his lungs choking and his heart beginning to burst.

One final effort to get to the surface, one last feeble struggle to beat the savage shock of each throbbing pain in his racked body.

He became dimly conscious of a soft, continuous movement across and around his body, stroking and probing at the fire in his limbs, and bringing relief at each gentle touch. It was essential that it didn't cease, and his subconscious mind sweated with fear lest it should suddenly depart and leave him in the grip of the hot claws which tore at his inside.

He opened his eyes, the very effort making his throat constrict, and his brain spun dizzily at the vision of swirling lights and mists which danced before his eyes. It all seemed to have a pattern, a pattern centred around a pale, shining shape, which floated above him like a pure, untroubled planet.

He moved his parched lips painfully, feeling his tongue lolling against his teeth.

Immediately the pale shape floated nearer, and he felt a strange sense of elation. As he strained his eyes again, the shape became clearer, and before he plunged down once more into the sea of blackness and delirium, he saw the blue eyes and felt the soft, gentle hands moving and massaging his body, but he was still too far under the waves to feel the girl's tears against his feverish skin.

For some moments he could only gasp for breath, the sour taste of vomit in his throat, while the two small, soft hands held him firmly as each fresh tremor shook him from head to toe.

He found that his own hands were untied, and as he tried to raise himself he felt the rasp of the dirt floor against his bare skin. He threw back his head, gulping in the hot, heavy air, trying to ignore the great throbbing in his head. Gingerly he explored the skin behind his left ear and winced as his fingers contacted a ragged bruise where the boot had struck home.

'Oh, Philip! What have they done to you?' Her eyes were watching him fearfully as she pillowed his head on her knees.

He swallowed hard, and grinned crookedly. 'I'll be all right in a second or two.' A fresh dart of fire coursed through his ribs, and he grimaced. 'How long have I been out?'

She shook her head. 'It's seemed like an age.' Her voice trembled. 'They've left us alone. I have been watching you.'

He stared down at the bright red marks on his body and watched her hands resting on his chest. They fascinated him, and through the intermittent waves of pain he felt content just to stare at them, content to lie in a semi-dazed state of helplessness.

Then, like a man recovering from amnesia, his memories came flooding back, and a stream of pictures flashed across the darkness of his mind. Morrie, with his fists raised; Mason with the gun; and Cooper—he went cold—Cooper—

he saw Karen struggling in his grip, saw him pawing her lovely body, while all the time he jeered at him, his uneven teeth twisted into an expression of sadism and real enjoyment. Vivian felt the mounting sweat cool on his skin, and twisted round into a sitting position, gritting his teeth.

'Karen, you're all right? He didn't touch you any more?' His eyes explored her face desperately.

She smiled down at him, her features melting gently into a quiet mould of trust and affection. 'He has been too busy. He has been repairing the damage you did to his face!'

Vivian gripped her by the arms. 'It's been hell for you, and I let it happen,' he said thickly.

'Always we worry about each other, Philip. That is good. But now we must try to think of what to do next. Please, Philip, do not keep blaming yourself for all this. They are bad men. You are not used to dealing with such men, I think.'

He nodded. 'You're about right there.' He cocked his head at the closed door. 'I must have a word with Mason before anything else happens. I must tell him that I've still got half the plates.'

Her eyes widened. 'Half the plates? Were you going to try to make a bargain with that—that beast?'

He nodded. 'It was just an idea I had. If Lang has gone back to the boat and I send Mason running back for the rest of the plates, well, it might keep us safe for a bit and he'll run straight into trouble.'

She regarded him sadly, and then dropped her eyes. 'I'm afraid he's gone.'

'Gone? Who d'you mean?'

'Mason.'

Her voice brought another chill of angry helplessness to his feverishly working brain.

'He drove off in a car immediately after they had

dragged you back here.' She let her hand rest lightly on his shoulder. 'He is coming back, I think, to pick up the others.'

He shook his head, his face dark. 'I suppose all this really is happening? It's more like a mad dream.' He slid his arm about her shoulders and she nestled against him.

'Tell me, Karen, what made you leave the boat? Who came for you?'

'It was Morrie. He told me that unless I came at once,' she paused, 'they would kill you. I was so confused, I just followed him.' She shuddered. 'As we turned behind those big sheds something was thrown over my head and I was pulled into a car. They held me on the floor until we got here. You know the rest.'

'If only——' He stopped, listening. 'Someone's coming!' In a flash he was up on his feet, facing the door, and although his body ached in a hundred different ways his mind was clear and his eyes were steady.

Karen rose lightly and stood behind him.

Carefully the door opened and Cooper peered into the room. He stood well back from the entrance, and he held his gun straight in front of his blood-stained jacket.

'So you're all fixed up, eh?' As he bared his teeth, Vivian felt a momentary stab of pleasure at the sight of the gaps in his lower jaw. 'Well, I guess this is the end of the road for the pair of you.' There was something different in his manner, a new hardness in his whole appearance which made Vivian stiffen into fresh caution.

'Why, what's the little man got planned now?' asked Vivian coolly.

A momentary flash of fire showed in the deep-set eyes, but again Cooper controlled himself. 'Well,' his voice dropped to a soft drawl, 'I guess there's no harm in knowing what's to become of you.' He darted a quick glance from one to the other, his gun never wavering. 'We've got your car outside,' he nodded at Karen, 'and you two are goin' for a ride together.' He chuckled. It was not a nice sound. 'Only a short ride, I guess.'

A shadow fell across the door, and Morrie's face, still grey with pain, appeared over his shoulder. His features were working in dumb anxiety.

'Boss said no talk. He——'

'I don't give a damn what he said, see? He ain't here, so I'm the boss now—*got it?*' His words ended in a shout.

Morrie seemed to shrink from the fury of the little man, and he nodded his great head obediently.

Cooper turned back to the others, his face flushed with triumph. He was beginning to extract real pleasure from his little act.

'Oh boy! You sure made a big mistake when you tangled with this outfit!'

'You can cut out the Chicago manner for my part,' said Vivian wearily, 'and get down to what you're trying to say.'

Cooper grinned slowly. ' 'Kay, I'll tell you. You saw the big gravel pits around here? Well,' his face hardened, 'the car'll be found in one of 'em, with you two inside!'

Vivian felt his body grow cold, and behind him he heard the girl give a little cry.

Cooper warmed to his story, his lips growing moist.

'It'll seem as if the bridge has collapsed under the weight of the car, d'you see?'

'You're mad!' Vivian shouted. 'How do you propose to explain all this when people start asking questions?'

'Simple. I forgot to mention that the little girl here will be in the back of the car, sort of tied up. Folks'll think that you'd kidnapped her, and you were on your way somewheres, when Pfft!' He snapped his fingers. 'Bridge collapses, and you an' victim take a bath!' A horrible giggle escaped his lips. 'Neat, eh?'

'And why should I be kidnapping a girl, when everyone knows she was with me aboard my boat? It's no good, Cooper, you'll have to do better than that!'

'I reckon that a good reason'd be because she's found out you killed her uncle!'

Although Vivian had been half expecting it, the implication dropped like a bomb at his feet, and he knew he was cornered.

'Nobody'll believe it!'

Even as he said it he knew he was wrong. They'd find Jensen's body, eventually, and inquiries would start. Karen would be reported missing, and then so would he. It might be ages before they found the car, and their bodies. His mind reeled. Only Felix knew that he hadn't committed the murder, and he would be as much in the dark as anyone.

He forced himself to speak calmly. 'And I suppose you'll just carry on as if nothing has happened?'

'Well, maybe we'll take a little sea trip, till it all blows over.' Cooper grinned.

'And you're going to get me to drive into a gravel pit?'

'Let's put it another way. You'll be at the wheel, but I guess we'll put you to sleep before you start the journey.' He allowed his gaze to flicker in Karen's direction. 'I reckon I'll tame that little bitch before we start, too!'

'You bastard!'

But even as he moved, the gun-barrel dropped, until it was level with the girl's stomach.

'Shouldn't do that!' The tone was sharp. 'Pity to spoil such a swell figure.'

'Look, Cooper, there's something you don't know.'

'Yeah?' The voice was almost disinterested.

'I only brought half the plates with me. I guessed you'd try something like this, so unless you think you are going to make a fortune one dollar at a time, you'd better get hold of Mason, and quick!'

'A good try, fella. But you'll have to do better than that!'

'Well, tell me, did any one of you check to see if the plates were complete? I'll tell you. Your intelligent boss just looked at the top ones, didn't he?' He waited, watching a shadow of uncertainty cross the ferret-like face. 'Well, am I right?'

'Just supposin' I believed you, where are the others, then?'

'I gave 'em to one of the harbour officials,' lied Vivian calmly, surprised that his brain was clear, and that Cooper appeared to be swallowing his story.

'If you're playing for time, sailor, it'll be too bad for the pair of you. Especially the babe here!' He beckoned impatiently to Morrie. 'Here, bonehead, tie 'em up with that cord. I'll get on up the road and make a 'phone call. Just to see what the boss has to say.'

Vivian's heart sank and he cursed himself for not thinking that Cooper would realize the folly of leaving his prisoners untied.

Morrie stepped heavily into the room, unwinding a length of cord, his small eyes watching Vivian with hatred.

'Don't forget, one bad move, an' she gets it!' Cooper's voice was edgy. He was obviously taking no chances.

Vivian bit his lip with pain, as the cord cut into his wrists, pulling his arms behind him. With a final tug, Morrie gave a satisfied grunt and turned to the girl. As he pulled her arms back, Cooper whistled softly.

'Phew, what a dish! You're sure goin' to be nice to me when I get back.' Then harshly, 'Now keep an eye on 'em, Morrie, I'll be about half an hour.'

'Why not take her car?' Even a short sentence seemed to be an effort for Morrie.

Cooper looked at him pityingly. 'What if I'm seen driving it, bonehead? The sailor there is supposed to have pinched it when he snatched the girl, see? Fine thing if I got nicked in a hot car. I must say!' He lifted his chin, listening to the rattle of rain on the roof. 'Jeez! I'll get goddam wet though!' he added inconsequently.

Without a further glance at any of them he hurried away, and they heard the door slam in the outside office.

Morrie gestured towards the bed. 'Sit!' he commanded, and when the girl had lowered herself into a sitting position, he turned back to Vivian.

'You can kneel for a bit!' he growled and jabbed him sharply in the stomach with a half-clenched fist.

Vivian grunted and pitched awkwardly on to his knees. As he fell, a sharp stabbing thrust in his right leg made him cry out.

Morrie permitted himself a brief smile.

'That'll show you,' he muttered and stamped out, slamming the door.

'Philip, are you all right?' Her voice was filled with anxiety and fear.

He nodded, gritting his teeth. He could feel the blood beginning to run across his foot. The paper-knife that he had slipped into his sock and had completely forgotten during the last, nightmarish hours, had pierced his leg as he fell. But he hardly felt the pain any more, and as he reached backwards with his numbed fingers, groping for the hilt, a wild scheme was already forming in his mind.

8

SLOWLY and painfully he strained back, cursing the small sharp waves of cramp which took first one finger and then another, until at last he felt the smooth, rounded surface of the metal handle. In his eager excitement he almost dropped the knife, and he sobbed aloud as the thin cord bit into his skin.

It was a race. Either he cut the cord with the blunt blade, or his hands would lose all their strength and feeling. Already the circulation seemed to have stopped, and as he crouched on his knees, as if in prayer, he felt rivulets of sweat pouring down his bare chest and his jaws were clamped tight with the frantic exertion.

'Keep listening, Karen!' he gasped. 'Let me know if you hear that big brute coming back!'

She nodded quickly her body tensed as she leaned forward, as if to encourage his efforts.

Back and forth, up and down, he sawed with a fanatical desperation. The muscles across his shoulders bulged and writhed and he felt he wanted to scream out with anger and despair.

Without warning there was a sharp snap and the knife skittered across the floor. For a moment neither he nor the girl moved, and then, as he gingerly pulled at one lacerated wrist, he gave a grunt of triumph, as with a final jerk his hands were free.

A thousand hot needles pricked his arms as he rubbed urgently to bring back life and feeling to his wrists and fingers, but as he dashed the sweat from his eyes, he shot the girl a twisted grin of satisfaction and mounting excitement.

Stiffly he scrambled across to her side, and in a few seconds she too was looking in childlike amazement at the red lines on her skin, her eyes shining.

'Right, now listen Karen.' His voice was short. 'Sit just as you are, and keep your hands behind you. Our one hope is that he'll come back in here before Cooper returns. If he does, I'll try to grab him.'

He studied her face, fixing every detail in his mind, and held her hands in his, feeling their soft warmth.

'Whatever happens, no matter what I am doing, you *must* make a run for it!' He emphasized each word carefully, noticing the growing look of alarm on her face. 'When you get outside get in your car and drive like hell over that bridge!'

'But, Philip! I can't——' Her mouth quivered.

'You must! The car's a real bit of luck. God knows how they got it here, but it's too good a chance to lose.' His voice hardened. 'When I've finished in here, I'll come running!' He paused, breathing heavily, the prospect of action again filled him with a sense of savage elation. 'But you must do as I say. Do you understand?'

She bowed her head, bunching her hands until the knuckles showed white. 'I will try,' she answered in a small voice.

He bared his teeth in a grin. 'Right then. I'll take up my position.'

Stooping he gave her a quick kiss on the forehead, but as her arms reached out for him he turned away, knowing that it was his only hope. Picking up the knife he squatted

...own as before, facing the door, his hands hidden behind ...im.

He stared at the dark shape of the door until his eyes ...anced in their sockets, making him imagine that it was ...tealthily opening, or that a shadow was moving behind it.

As if at a signal the rain stopped and, but for the heavy ...rip of water from the edge of the roof, the sudden silence ...vas shattering. The violent pounding of his heart seemed to ...ill the room, and he licked his parched lips, straining every ...erve in his body.

Once a slight sound in the other room brought him to a ...oint where he almost jumped to his feet and flung himself ...t the mocking black shape of the door, but as silence fell ...gain, he sank back on his haunches, a sick taste in his ...hroat.

When Morrie entered the room it was somehow unex-...pected, and almost as if he had been waiting for Vivian ...o fall off his guard. But as he stood framed against the ...watery sunlight, his face in shadow, Vivian could sense that ...the other man was relaxed, almost to a point of being ...indifferent. He stared from one to the other, the light ...catching the gleam of his stone-like eyes. As he turned his ...gaze back to Vivian, his mouth twisted down at one ...corner, and they saw the look of hatred, mixed with one of ...animal pain.

Vivian's body, glistening with sweat, seemed to attract ...him, as if he was unable to keep his hands from smashing ...into the apparently helpless man before him.

He took a couple more steps, so that his huge frame ...blotted out the light of the door. He was so close, that ...Vivian could see the thick veins on the backs of his hands, ...which hung, half clenched, at his sides.

Vivian's heart was beating and throbbing so painfully ...against his ribs, that he thought it must be clearly audible

to the other man, and he clamped his teeth together, whil
he waited and watched for his chance. He knew that ther
could only be one such chance, one small hope for Karen t
make good her escape.

Morrie's lips moved soundlessly, while he stared dow
with a weird, fixed intensity.

'They say I'm not to touch you, but I'm the boss now
I'll make that pretty face so that nobody won't recogniz
it!' He stopped, his chest heaving rapidly.

'By God, Morrie, that was a jolly long sentence,' said
Vivian calmly. 'Cooper must have been giving you som
elocution lessons.'

It was, as he suspected, all that was needed to goad th
man into action, enough to snap the last bond of reason and
sanity. With a throaty growl, Morrie lunged forward, hi
heavy body moving with surprising agility, and Vivian fel
the hard hands wrap around his unprotected throat in a
stifling grip. The strong thumbs felt and held his wind
pipe, caressing it almost lovingly, but to hold him as he
wanted, he straddled his legs across Vivian's folded knees

'You hurt me, now I hurt you!'

And as Vivian felt the hands begin to tighten, he saw
flecks of saliva glistening on the thin lips above him.
Vivian's tensed body swayed back in the powerful grip, but
using his own neck as the pivot for his attack he whipped
both hands from behind him, and even as they flashed
upwards towards the unprotected groin, the two hands
were reshaping themselves into one moulded weapon,
which, when it landed, struck like a woodman's axe into a
tree.

The wild cry of surprise altered in pitch to a high, thin
scream of agony, and Morrie's eyes rolled upwards, showing their whites, as the vicious, chopping blow brought him
crashing down to the ground. Before he could recover,

Vivian bunched his fists and struck out again and again at the rolling, threshing figure, which flung itself around in desperation, as if to be rid of the all-consuming fires which had been started by that first, wild blow.

'Quick, Karen! Run!'

Vivian's hoarse cry was stopped, as one of Morrie's flailing fists struck him on the side of the head, exactly on top of the angry bruise already received, and before he could think, Morrie was on top of him, his kicking, clawing body forcing the wind out of him. He could smell the sour animal odour, and feel the savage, snarling breath against his shoulder. The hands, groping, feeling, fighting down Vivian's resistance, moved relentlessly upwards again for his throat. His strength seemed to grow out of his own pain, and like a mad thing, he sought to destroy his victim in one final test of muscle and fury.

Vivian kicked out frantically, and as the grip slackened slightly he called out again, 'Now, Karen!' Through a haze he saw her slim legs run past, within inches of their thrashing bodies, and he heard her crying his name.

The grip suddenly slackened and Morrie's reddened eyes widened in surprise as they lighted upon something behind Vivian's shoulder. He grabbed with his right fist, and when Vivian twisted his eyes round he saw to his horror that Morrie was holding the paper-knife, poised above his head. Seizing his wrist, he tried to keep the gleaming blade away, but in his failing grip the wrist felt like a bar of iron. Down and down. The point wavered and swayed, inches above his carotid artery.

Vivian shut his eyes tightly, feeling his last reserves of strength passing away. The foul, triumphant breath fanned his face, and the great mass of Morrie's body spread-eagled him as helplessly as a pinned butterfly.

He bit his lips, feeling the cold point of the knife scratch his skin. God, this is it. Please let Karen be safe. Let her always be safe.

He felt a muscle tremble in the other man's wrist and he knew that he was summoning the power for the final blow. Some last little piece of wild reasoning made Vivian act. He suddenly relaxed his resistance, and as the knife plunged down he twisted his neck to one side. The rough edge of the blade scored deeply into his skin, as it flashed downwards, burying itself to the hilt in the dirt.

Not giving him time to recover, Vivian kneed and punched himself clear from the sobbing, mouthing maniac, and as he staggered to his feet he crashed his hand down in a rabbit punch on the squat neck.

Blindly he blundered across the prostrate body and snatched up his jacket and ran from the room, the breath rasping from his lips in short, wheezing gasps.

For a moment he could see nothing, but when he all but fell down the short flight of steps in the front of the office he saw the car, its front wheels already against the first rough timbers of the bridge, and the girl, running towards him, her eyes wide with horror and compassion.

'Get in!' he choked. 'We've got to get out fast!'

She shook her head, the fear which marked her face forcing him to tighten his grip on his reeling senses.

'No key!' It seemed like a final blow. 'Philip, I couldn't start it!'

Behind him, he heard the crash of something falling in the hut. He was coming after them. He still had a gun. The urgent signals flashed through his brain.

'Come on, then! We must run for it!'

Together, hand-in-hand, they started to run across the bridge, Vivian realizing that she was pulling him, as he swayed in a shambling trot across the slippery timbers.

God, he hadn't realized it was such a long bridge, and

while his feet slipped and stumbled on the uneven, rain-sodden wood, he caught a glimpse of the dark, swollen water beneath. This was to have been the place for murder.

He cursed savagely, his foot tripping on a broken plank; fifty yards to go. The wet, shining trees, and the high banks of earth mocked at him.

Crack! The sound of the shot echoed and re-echoed around them. Karen faltered, but he dragged her roughly forward.

'Don't look back!' he panted. 'Must keep going!'

His words were drowned by the roar of a car engine, and even as his tortured mind grasped at the fact that Morrie must have had the ignition key, they both felt the bridge start to shake and vibrate when the spinning wheels slithered and then found their grip, sending the powerful car hurtling across the narrow bridge.

Without turning, he could imagine the bright red body tearing down on them and, as he measured up the last few yards, he knew they could not make the distance in time.

He started to pull the girl to the side, holding her panting body pressed against his own when, like a giant tree falling, the bridge gave one ear-splitting crack, and the whole centre portion reeled drunkenly on its side.

He stood transfixed, holding her face against his chest, blotting out the scene of destruction and madness. In a whirl of cracking, rotten wood, the shining shape of the car leaped into the water beneath.

As it struck the water with a tremendous splash, he saw Morrie's white face staring fixedly up at him, his jaw hanging open in a silent scream, then he was under the heaving water, and only the luggage boot was visible, hanging upright like a sinking submarine. For a few seconds it stayed motionless, until, with a gurgling shudder, it dived down into the mud.

A minute passed, and the two figures remained locked together, their feet within a yard from the jagged edge of the bridge. At the end of that time the water was again still, the surface smooth and untroubled, but for a few scattered fragments of wood.

Vivian shuddered and gently prised the girl's clutching arms from around his waist.

'It's finished,' he said slowly, 'he's gone to a better end than he deserved.'

The girl looked up quickly, her wide eyes searching his face, as if to find the reason for the new harshness in his voice. He looked down at her for a while, apparently unseeing, and she sensed the great mental and physical turmoil which was threatening to snap his last ounce of strength. She opened her mouth to speak, then, changing her mind, buried her face once more against his jacket.

Like the sun after a storm, a wintry smile crossed his lips and he patted her shoulder soothingly.

'Thank God you're safe,' he muttered. 'For a while then I thought we were done for.'

'Never!' Her voice was muffled. 'You never gave them a chance! But what you have had to go through!'

She sobbed unrestrainedly, and Vivian too felt the quickening tremble within him, the aftermath, as he knew from hard experience, of shock.

Hand-in-hand they ran shakily up the narrow lane between the brooding hills, until they came to the concealed entrance, where Morrie had driven from the main road.

And he thought it was to be *my* last ride, mused Vivian grimly.

He pulled her into the shelter of a clump of trees, while he cautiously scanned the quiet road for any trace of Cooper.

'Nothing,' he said shortly. 'That 'phone box must be further away than I thought.'

'What do we do now, Philip?'

She ran her hand through her hair, and for a moment he was caught in wonder and admiration, the mantle of weary and fearful anticipation seeming to drop away as he watched her. She stood poised and alert, yet apparently relaxed, her beauty accentuated by her stained and crumpled clothing. She saw him watching her, his eyes exploring her body, and she dropped her gaze, a slow flush spreading across her cheeks, but with a secret smile playing on her lips.

'I'm sorry,' he faltered, suddenly aware of the pounding of his heart. 'I'm afraid my mind was not where it should have been. You'll have to forgive these sudden lapses of mine.' He grinned awkwardly. 'I've not got used to being near you, if you understand what I mean. Each time I look at you I just go completely stupid and tongue-tied.'

'For one so tongue-tied, you are pretty eloquent, Philip. Perhaps I too have the same feelings as you.' She shrugged her slim shoulders, her face suddenly grave. 'But all my little dreams and hopes seem so very uncertain now. We must try to decide what we must do next. And, Philip,' her eyes clouded, 'I want to hear all about Nils, about what you found, anything you can remember'—she trembled, as if suddenly chilled—'he was so very dear to me.'

Vivian gripped her by the arm, and together they started to walk briskly along the road. Neither spoke for a while, and their shadows twisted and flitted along the dripping bushes, seeming to keep time with the slap of their feet on the wet tarmac.

'As I see it,' he said at length, 'I'd better get along to the police as soon as I can. I don't quite know how I shall start, it'll probably sound a bit of a queer story to them!'

'I wonder if Felix had gone to the police yet?'

'Hmm, maybe he has at that,' he answered thoughtfully. 'In which case, the sooner I get my story out the better. If I'm careful, I might be able to keep your uncle's name out of it. After all, they must be mainly interested in those drugs, and they were Mason's doing. And when I tell them about the rest of it, about Nils,' he breathed heavily, 'they'll be very interested!'

They found themselves at the junction of the main coast road, quite deserted but for an occasional car heading for Dover.

'The police will have to know about the money too.' Her voice was quiet, but very firm. 'They'll find out anyway, and I do not want you to be implicated any more than you are. As it is, they will understand. I will be there too.' She stifled his protests. 'It is no use arguing, Philip, you know quite well that I was not mixed up in it, so, therefore, I am the obvious one to help you. Right?' Her eyes shone in the sun.

'I don't like it,' he persisted stubbornly. 'I loathe the thought of your name being dragged through the courts, or whatever's going to happen.'

'But I *am* right, it *is* the only way. Please say you understand.' Her voice was imploring.

'If you say so,' he conceded doubtfully. 'So that means I'd better get the rest of the plates from *Seafox*. That'll at least prove that I'm trying to help.' He grinned weakly.

She squeezed his hand hard. 'You'll see, it'll all be all right.' The Danish accent became more pronounced, as it always did when she became excited. 'It was a wonderful idea of yours to hang on to half of these dreadful plates!'

'It's amazing, isn't it. A few weeks ago I don't suppose either of us had even heard of this sort of thing. Now, you and I talk quite calmly about plates, and drug smuggling, as if we'd been mixed up with 'em all our lives!'

'I don't know about *calmly*.'

'Anyway, we'll have a go.' He smiled.

He stopped in his stride and pointed upwards at a bus stop.

'See?' he grinned. 'Civilization again! Might as well wait here and try to get back to Ramsgate. By the way, do you have any money? I seem to have lost all mine back there!'

It was amazing that he could now joke about it, and keep the edge of strain out of his voice.

She found some loose change in the pocket of her jacket, and as they waited for a bus they discussed carefully the plan of action, trying not to omit any detail.

A travel-stained bus ground to a standstill, and oblivious of the curious glances of the few passengers, they climbed to the top deck, which was fortunately deserted.

As they jolted along the wind-swept road, Vivian frowned, as a sudden, disquieting thought occurred to him.

'I've been thinking, Karen,' he announced slowly, 'and I've come to the conclusion that it might be unwise for both of us to bowl into the police-station together. It'd perhaps be better if you went to the boat and got Felix and the plates, and came on a bit later.'

'But, Philip!' Her eyes filled with concern. 'I must be with you!'

He gripped her hands, his heart warm for her.

'Believe me, it is better that we go separately. After all,' he began carefully, 'they may decide to hold me in custody. I shall need all my friends then,' he finished quietly.

She turned up the collar of his jacket and handed him her own head-scarf to tie around his throat.

'No one will see that you do not have a shirt on now. We do not want people to think you are a pirate!' But her sad expression belied her brave words.

'We're nearly there. Now promise you'll be careful. I'll carry on into the town and get this business off my chest.'

'I will be all right.' She nodded gravely. 'It is you who needs to be careful.'

The bus slowed down as it swung in towards the cliff top. Beneath them the harbour lay like a white horseshoe.

'I will hurry, Philip,' she said softly. Her lips brushed across his mouth, then she was gone.

The bus lumbered on its way and began to fill up with chattering holiday-makers, but Vivian stared at them unseeingly, his mind elsewhere and conscious of the sinking feeling in the pit of his stomach.

He found his way easily enough to the dark, red-brick building, with its large blue lamp outside. He walked past it twice, glancing up at the solid, helmeted policeman who stood indifferently in the doorway.

He swallowed hard, clenching his fists that he had thrust deep into his reefer pockets. His knuckle touched a small, hard shape, and he pulled out a sixpence, which had some-how got itself lost in the lining. He glanced round, his eyes falling on a small café opposite the police-station. A quick cup of tea, he thought. That'd do the trick. It might be just emptiness which was making his inside boil and quiver so sickeningly.

He sat in a corner of the café, at one of the marble-topped tables, watching the policeman across the road. Soon be over, he thought, soon be cleared up, one way or the other.

A fat, jolly man, his face and neck burned by the sun to a fiery, lobster-like glow, heaved himself up from a neigh-bouring table, where he'd been feeding his two noisy

ildren with cakes and ice cream. As he pushed a small
ece of silver under a plate he caught sight of Vivian,
tting taut and grim-faced and toying with his cup and
ucer. His broad, Yorkshire features split into a grin.

''Ere you are, lad! 'Ave a dekko at the paper, it'll cheer
ou oop!' He thrust the afternoon paper across to him and
uckled. 'It's right good, I can tell you; another bloody
ar goin' to start any second, and my horse 'as coom in
urth at Hurst Park! I dunno, I'm sure!'

Vivian nodded to him, and watched the man shepherd-
g his children out of the café.

Ah well, time to see the gentlemen across the road, he
ought, no good putting it off. He finished his tea and
ood up. As he did so, his eye fell casually on a side column
f the front page. The café spun about his ears and he
ached out to stop himself from falling across the table.
here was a great roaring in his head and he had the
reatest difficulty in preventing himself from crying out in
stonishment and horror.

With a frightened glance round, to see if he had attracted
ny attention, he sat down again and forced his eyes and
rain to work slowly and carefully across the bold type.

MAN MURDERED AT HAMPTON COURT

arly this morning, in response to information received, police
ent to the 16th century riverside home of Mr. Nils Jensen, well-
nown Danish head of the Europa Travel Agency, where they
ound his body lying savagely battered to death and hidden in an
ld cellar, used as a studio by the deceased man. There were signs
f a violent struggle and of a forced entry having been made.
Miss Karen Jensen, the dead man's niece, is missing, and it is
elieved that she may have been kidnapped by the murderer,
whom she is believed to know. A senior police official told our
eporter that he is confident of an early arrest, although he was not

prepared to state his own views of the reason for the murder at th
stage. It was later announced that Chief Inspector Laidlaw, we
known for his recent success in the Brighton Cellars murder cas
is in charge of investigations. Police are anxious to trace th
whereabouts of Philip Vivian, who they feel may be able
help in their inquiries.

Vivian's head swam and his throat felt as dry as dust. I
a semi-dazed state, he read the rest of the announcement
which included his own full description, as well as a smilin
photograph of Karen. He tried to think back, rememberin
the broken glass from the window, that he had thrust int
the desk drawer. His fingerprints were probably every
where, he realized. He swore silently, remembering too
what Mason had said, and how he had boasted of th
success of their plan for laying Jensen's murder at his door
There had been only one hitch so far, for by rights he an
Karen should now be lying in the slime and mud at th
bottom of the gravel pit. His thoughts crowded in on hin
and he stared blindly down at the newspaper, tremblin
with the fury of a trapped animal.

Almost without realizing it he jumped to his feet, anc
with the paper clenched in his hand, he blundered out o
the café. For a moment he stood unsurely on the edge of the
pavement and then, bracing his shoulders, he marchec
grimly across the road, and with his heart pounding, pas
the policeman, into the front office of the station.

If anything, his reception was one of anti-climax. The
office was high and cool, its pale green, distempered wall:
covered with notices and bills, and the many bookshelve:
crammed with tall, dusty ledgers. There was a long, well-
polished counter across the entrance, and in the centre o
the room, a plump, elderly station-sergeant sat writing
carefully in a heavily bound book, a thick briar pipe
hanging from his mouth.

At the counter, a young constable, looking somehow strange without his helmet, was pouring tea into a succession of cups on a battered tin tray. He looked up briefly, and smiled cheerfully.

'Shan't keep you a minute, sir. Just dealing with an essential duty.'

God! If I don't get this thing sorted out, I shall go raving mad! Vivian swayed on his feet and placed his hands flat on the counter to control himself. He cleared his throat, his firm chin jutting forward in a certain pathetic defiance.

'I'm Philip Vivian,' he announced flatly. 'I understand you think I've done a murder!'

There was a hard chink as the spout of the teapot clattered against the cups, and a sharp intake of breath from the constable, who stared at Vivian, his eyes wild, and seemingly unable to release the metal pot from his grasp.

The sergeant put down his pen and with slow deliberation removed the pipe from his mouth. Vivian noted with surprise that the man's eyes were china blue and unwavering.

'Er, what's that you were saying?' he asked, his tone conversational. 'Something about a murder, wasn't it?'

'I'm Vivian,' he repeated it wearily. 'It's in the paper here.' He planked it down on the counter.

The sergeant was on his feet, methodically buttoning his jacket. His eyes never left Vivian's face, but his expression remained calm and unruffled.

'I see,' he said at length. 'Well, perhaps you'd better come inside the counter here, so that I can have a look at you.'

Nobody moved as Vivian lifted the wooden flap and walked into the room, and stood quietly by the desk.

He was a good few inches taller than the old man, but the

sergeant seemed to fill the room. He sensed the goggling stare of the constable who had at last succeeded in ridding himself of the teapot, and he observed that the other one who had been standing by the door, was now inside blocking the entrance.

'Take a chair!' The sergeant's voice held a ring of authority. 'And, Collins, finish pouring the tea. I've a feeling we'll all be needing a cup.' He turned to Vivian and after a slow scrutiny, he perched himself on the edge of his desk. 'You're the man all right,' he said slowly. 'I think you'd better just sit here quietly while I get things organized.'

He pressed a button on the desk, and Vivian heard a door open behind him.

'Tell Peters to get on to Information Room about, er,' he glanced quickly at a pad of messages, 'message number seven. Tell them we have man answering description in the station. All the usual to Chief Constable, and our own people. And make it snappy!'

'Very good, Sergeant.'

The door closed, and seconds later Vivian heard the rattle of a teleprinter. He found that he was breathing heavily. It was all too calm and too normal.

The door opened from the street and his heart leapt: perhaps it was Karen already. But it was only a small man inquiring about a lost umbrella.

As he watched the slow, patient proceedings, the sergeant giving no hint that he was already dealing with a suspected murderer, Vivian heard the door open behind him again. This time, two men in civilian clothes walked into his vision.

One, a dark, thin-faced man, jerked his head. 'Okay, upstairs, you!'

Vivian felt himself flushing. 'Look, who the hell d'you

hink you're talking to?' he snapped. 'I've come here of my
own free will to explain what's happened!'

'Okay, okay, don't get excited!' The man was taken off
his guard by this outburst. 'Just come up to the C.I.D.
office so that we can get the preliminaries over. The chief
inspector from the Yard'll be here to see you as soon as
he gets the wire, and he'll want all the loose ends cleared
up.'

The other detective, a gaunt, ungainly figure, with a
permanent blink in his left eye, grunted surlily. 'And no
tricks!' he added unnecessarily.

Wearily, Vivian followed them to the C.I.D. office. A
room crowded with desks, filing cabinets, and ash-trays. A
room which spoke of constant and unceasing use.

'Look,' he said suddenly, 'I'd rather not say anything
until I can see this Chief Inspector Laidlaw. What I've got
to say is big stuff, and I've just about had enough trouble
lately to last me a lifetime!'

The two men exchanged glances.

'Right,' snapped the first detective. 'Sit down there and
we'll get on with the job in hand.'

The door opened slightly and the station sergeant thrust
his head into the room.

'All right, gents?' he grinned broadly, as if it was all one
huge joke. 'The chief's on his way and so's the tea! I see
you were in the Navy?' he asked, quite inconsequently.

'Yes,' replied Vivian, surprised.

'My son was too. Went down on the old *Prince of Wales*.'

'I'm sorry.'

'Yes. Er, d'you take sugar?'

When he had gone, Vivian sat back and began to worry.
Karen should be here by now. Something must have gone
wrong. Perhaps Lang had found out about the allegation
of murder and was getting legal aid, or perhaps he'd not

been aboard *Seafox* when Karen got there. He cursed silently for not going with her.

The time passed, the tea was brought and consumed without any further attempt at conversation, and all the while he writhed inwardly at the delay, and with the all-consuming desire to set the wheels in motion to place Mason in the position he now occupied himself.

Eventually, one of the detectives looked up from his desk, his head cocked. Below, some car doors slammed and the rumble of voices drifted up the stairs.

'He's here,' he announced.

Vivian sighed deeply, not with tiredness, but with that odd, empty feeling that he had felt before going into a fight, or whilst awaiting the dentist's chair.

Chief Inspector Bruce Laidlaw, followed by two other men, entered with a suddenness, and with such an air of brisk decisiveness, that the very room seemed to come alive with his presence.

Although above average height, his square, compact shoulders and short neck gave the impression of stockiness, a growing paunch beneath his neat, grey suit adding to the general appearance of heavy middle age. He swept a trim, green trilby from his head, and for a moment ran his stubby fingers through his cropped, greying hair. Then, for the first time, he let his eyes rest on Vivian. They were dark brown, and unlike the rest of his body, they held all the secrets of his immense vitality and energy, as in a few, quick glances, he took in the other man's appearance, as if tabulating each small fact as it came to life.

Vivian began to stand up, but one pink hand waved him down again.

'No, no, Mr. Vivian, you can remain seated. We have certain details to discuss.'

It was a quiet, even voice, with a small hint of harshness,

nd like many policemen's it bore no trace of any particular ccent.

He nodded to the two local detectives. 'I'll be taking an fficial statement shortly. In the meantime, you can wait in he other office.'

It was neither an order nor a request. It was a statement f fact. It revealed to Vivian the whole machinery of this nan's remarkable method of dealing with his job. He ealized he was face to face with a professional policeman, . detective at the top of his already brilliant career. He sat low, facing Vivian, one leg crossed over the other, and his lands resting in his lap like two pink crabs. He had taken ver. He asked for no help or guidance from anyone else. As if realizing this, the two local men left the room.

Laidlaw looked briefly at the other men. 'This is Sergeant Arnold, my assistant, and this is Dr. Mortimer, who has also been assisting me.'

He waited while Vivian looked at each of the others in urn. The detective-sergeant, had he seen him in other urroundings, would have made him think of a professional athlete. Wide shoulders and slim hips, and with his dark air lopped into a crew-cut. His cold eyes and thin mouth howed little mercy and no compassion.

The doctor, on the other hand, was a friendly looking, ittle man, in an ill-fitting, tweed suit, and he nodded at practically everything that Laidlaw said.

Altogether, he decided, they were a very ill-assorted trio.

Arnold walked quickly to a desk behind Vivian, drawing a notebook and pencil from his dark-blue suit.

'Now we're all settled, perhaps you'll tell me, in your own words, why you killed Nils Jensen,' said Laidlaw calmly.

It was like a sharp slap in the face, and Vivian had to hold on to himself to stop a wild flood of denials pouring from his lips. This was obviously to be the method of interrogation, he decided, so it must be taken carefully and warily.

'I didn't kill him. He was dead when I got there.' It sounded weak and incomplete.

Laidlaw examined the toe of one well-polished shoe, his lips puckered into a small frown of concentration.

'Start from the beginning. From the time you forced the window,' he added.

Vivian began again. 'I found him lying on the floor of the studio. He was already dead. I couldn't have killed him. I was too fond of him!'

'You knew him well, then?'

'Yes. Both as my employer and as a friend. I——'

'Yet you broke into his house? Hid the evidence of entry in the desk, and when you left you moved the body, packed some of the old man's clothes and left before anyone should discover you. Right?' The deep, liquid eyes rested on him steadily.

'Of course I didn't want anyone to know. His niece had been kidnapped, they threatened that if I went to the police about anything, she would be killed!'

The chief inspector's eyebrows lifted very slightly. 'So she was already kidnapped, then?' He prompted. 'And where is she now?'

'She's on my boat in Ramsgate harbour, and she'll vouch for my innocence!' he exploded angrily.

'So she was there when you say you found the old man dead?'

'No, she was—I mean, I don't know where she was,' Vivian stumbled.

'Then there was the business of the typed note on Jensen's desk. I suppose you did that to put off the discovery of the body long enough for you to make good your somewhat hasty departure, eh?' He asked the question mildly, but there was scorn in his eyes.

'I keep telling you,' Vivian's voice rose to a shout, 'she's safe on my boat, or she's on her way here now, with some definite evidence!'

'More evidence, is there?' The voice hardened. 'Now see here, Vivian, we're wasting time, so I'll tell you how I see it, then you can fill in the gaps afterwards. If there are any,' he added meaningly.

He pulled a sheaf of papers from the inside of his jacket, and leaned back comfortably.

'You worked for the deceased as a charter yachtsman, who apparently gave you the job because of your war record, and because you own a new boat. You were broke at the time, due to a bad season, and due to the high premiums you were paying off on the boat. I gather, however, that you got rather deeply involved in other directions.' He paused, his eyes flickering up. 'I am talking about smuggling!' His face was hard, and Vivian felt himself sweating. 'You must understand that I am fully aware of the actions of my colleagues in the Customs!' He let the words sink in. 'It appears, however, that Jensen got wind of your little game and got particularly upset, apparently because you had been getting rather close with his niece, for some reason or another!'

'You hired a car, here in Ramsgate, from the Everest Garage, and you drove to Jensen's house. I think that when you broke into the house you thought you'd made it look like a robbery. You knew that if Jensen talked to the police about you, and he intended to, if only to prevent you from marrying his niece, you were all washed up. So you surprised him in his studio and killed him with a heavy instrument, which we have not yet found! But we will, Mr. Vivian!'

His voice jumped from a calm softness to sudden snap. 'I think you killed him to save your own, rotten skin!'

Vivian gripped the arms of his chair, his eyes gleaming fiercely. 'It's a damned lie!' The words choked in his dry throat. 'I tell you, he was dead when I got there!'

Dear God. Why doesn't Karen come? His whole body felt soaked with sweat as he tried to marshal his thoughts.

The door clicked back and a head poked round the edge. Laidlaw lifted a questioning eyebrow, but the other man merely shook his head without speaking and shut the door. He turned his attention back to Vivian, his manner once more smooth and urbane.

'Not a bad case, eh? Now perhaps you'd like to make a statement. We'll take it down, naturally, but this is just an unofficial one. We can get it sorted out later.' He nodded over Vivian's shoulder and Sergeant Arnold lifted his notebook.

Vivian found that he was trembling. This was the moment for extreme caution. Laidlaw had deliberately excited and unnerved him before asking for a statement. He knew full well that if Vivian lied in one story, it would be extremely unlikely that he could conceal it in another, at a later time.

'Mason killed him.' His voice was quiet but firm. 'He was doing a two-way trade. Drugs into the country and forged money out, so that he was paying his way, and getting rid of the money at the same time. He used the travel bureau as a complete cover.'

'Where did he get the forged money?'

'Jensen had some plates.' He faltered. 'He was a famous engraver in Denmark. He had been doing it for the Germans. They forced him,' he added defensively.

'Hmm, no one was forcing him this time, I imagine.' The detective's face was expressionless.

Vivian shrugged wearily. 'He didn't know about the drug part of it though. When he did find out he decided to wind up the whole business, he'd intended to for some time. He'd been afraid Karen, his niece, would find out.'

'She knew nothing at all about it?'

'Nothing.' He leaned forward, his eyes desperate. 'Mason killed him to get the plates. He couldn't find them, so he kidnapped the girl to force me to get them for him. I took half of them to an agreed place, and Mason told us he was going to get rid of both of us and make it look as if it was an accident. As if it happened while I was running off with the niece,' he ended hoarsely.

'How did you know where these plates were? And how did you happen to find them, if Mason, who I understand is a co-director of the firm, could not?'

'Jensen managed to leave a message for me before he died.'

A flicker of interest darted across the detective's eyes. 'Where is it? What did it say?'

'It was a picture of where he'd hidden the plates. A drawing,' he added.

'You've lost it?'

'Yes.' It sounded flat and final. 'You don't believe a word of it, do you? But when Karen gets hold of Lang they'll tell you the same story.'

'Have you got all that?' Laidlaw glanced at the watchful Arnold.

'Good. Now let's get on a bit. You mentioned Lang, he's the manager of the firm. What's he got to do with it?'

'I told him about the murder and the kidnapping.'

'When?' The word was sharp, like a thin knife.

'This morning, when he came down to my boat.'

The two pink crabs rose violently from their resting

place and slapped down hard on Laidlaw's knees. He leaned forward, his eyes blazing.

'You're lying!' His lip curled in contempt. 'How d'you suppose I got on to the Murder Squad? By sitting on my arse listening to fairy stories?' He dropped his voice to a low, menacing purr. 'Firstly, you killed him because of what I just explained. Next, the girl followed you in her car. You didn't expect that, so you had to kidnap her, to keep her mouth shut!'

'What are you saying?' Vivian's face drained of colour.

'Her car was seen shortly before the time given by Dr. Mortimer as the time Jensen was killed! Mason was in Ramsgate at that time. I have already seen him, and I've checked his alibi. He was, in fact, having a Turkish bath!' He smiled thinly. 'As for Mr. Lang, I understand he's on holiday, on a boat of some sort. I don't know quite where at the moment, but I do know he was not aboard your boat today, and'—he paused, his face grim—'he's not there now! My men have checked!'

It was like a savage blow at the heart, knocking him speechless and numbing his senses into a whirl of incredulity. Vivian felt a cold numbness creeping up his spine as he struggled with his spinning mind, and he shook his head as if to clear himself from the mist which brought a smarting to his eyes.

Not there. Karen was not there. The words hammered at his brain. He was alone, helpless and shattered by the detective's ruthless attack.

Then, like a blinding light, it came to him, and he found he was shaking with shock, and the torture of his realization. He had sent Karen to Lang! Lang! Lang! The name echoed around the trapped confines of his mind. The inspector had said Lang was on holiday, on a boat. He remembered the yaching clothes Lang had been wearing.

Who else had known about Jensen's death, about the broken glass in the desk drawer? Who, in fact, was the only other person who had the opportunity, the motive, and God, what a motive! His head swam. The others in the room sat silent, watching him like fascinated cats by an injured mouse.

'Lang!' The name exploded from his lips, and he stared at them wildly. 'It was Lang!'

'So it's someone else now?' Laidlaw's small teeth bared in a mock grin. 'You just can't take it, can you?'

'For God's sake! Can't you understand? I've sent her to certain death!' He was shouting wildly. 'Unless we can get to her now!'

He jumped to his feet, but as he moved two arms, like bands of steel, pinioned his arms from behind.

'It's my unofficial opinion,' Laidlaw's eyes were like two pools of brown fire, 'that you've killed the girl too already! But we'll find out!' He turned to the doctor. 'Have a look at that cut on his head. It's probably where Jensen hit him before he died.'

His whole expression was filled with cold contempt. 'I'm glad I do this job sometimes. Even if it's just to catch up with swine like you!'

9

LONG after they had locked him in the small, white-tiled cell, Vivian stood stock-still, his muscles stiff and his brain frozen into immobility. At first his ears had strained after the heavy, retreating footsteps, but as the silence closed in on him, so too the gleaming walls seemed to move inwards, mocking him, so that he involuntarily stepped back, pressing his back against the studded door.

He was conscious of his own heavy breathing, and he found himself listening to its irregular, panting beat, unable as yet to take in and appreciate his surroundings.

The cell measured about eight feet by ten, and was brightly lit, more by the harsh glare of the electric light than by the feeble rays of fading daylight, which were reluctantly allowed to filter through a massive window made entirely of glass bricks and which was placed high up, next to the ceiling.

The cold, unyielding touch of the door seemed to bring him to his senses, and as he pressed the palms of his hands against it he felt a wave of helpless revulsion run through him, bringing his body out in a fresh, icy sweat.

For the very first time in his life he felt completely broken. In the past he had shied from a steady, routine life, in house or office, and always returned to his first love, the sea, with its constant movement and many kinds of freedom. Now, as he felt the great pressure of the walls, as they strained inwards, he felt a surge of sudden terror, mingled with the frantic desire to scream, and kick out at the impassive door, which was keeping him from his most precious possession.

When the convulsion had passed he lowered his head weakly against the well-worn metal, smoothed by countless prisoners, who had stood, and hoped, and cursed, in this self-same spot. He found comfort from its touch, and he stared blindly down at the concrete floor, trying desperately to project his mind and soul out and beyond the confines of the police-station, back in time, to the moment he had gone into the café. When he had made some sort of plan, when he had felt that a new future was at last possible.

Even as he tried to think, the voices came flooding back, blotting out all other thoughts in a mental sandstorm, choking his brain with their cruel insistence. And all the time, the loudest voice of all shouted Lang! Lang! Lang! until his eyes smarted with tears of frustration and mad fury.

After the chief inspector had finished his cross-examination, he had handed Vivian over to the other detectives, and had watched him contemptuously while they searched and finger-printed him. At the memory, Vivian glanced at his fingers, which still showed the signs of the finger-print ink.

'You'll be taken to court tomorrow,' Laidlaw had announced coldly. 'You'll be formally charged then. You can rest assured that you'll be remanded for a couple of weeks after that, so that I can complete my inquiries.'

'For the last time, aren't you going to look for the girl?' Vivian felt he wanted to fling himself at the other man. 'D'you think I'd have walked into this place and given myself up if I'd really done a murder, and if I'd known Karen's in danger?'

Laidlaw watched him through narrowed eyes. 'As I said, all inquiries will be made. But not into a trumped-up yarn like that!'

Something had snapped inside him, and in the red haze which swam about him, he couldn't see Laidlaw, only Felix Lang's smiling face, and he thought he heard his smooth voice. 'Well, old boy, it's nice to be working with someone I can trust!'

He couldn't remember much about the short journey to the cells. He had vague impressions of a policeman searching through a large bunch of keys, and of the old station sergeant dropping his eyes as they had marched past, gripping his arms. A thin, cracked voice, raised in some obscure song, had stopped as if to listen, as they had arrived breathless outside the cell. This cell. It must have been some drunk, already locked up for the night.

What did it matter now what happened to him? He had failed her again. Karen. Karen looking up at him in the bus, her eyes grave. 'It is you who needs to be careful.' Her words rang and echoed around his skull.

He couldn't even remember how long he'd been in the cell, or even in the police-station. Several times he had glanced automatically at his wrist, only to be confronted with a band of pale skin where his watch had once been. They had even removed that when they had searched him.

The scarf around his throat tickled his chin and he pulled it off, running it through his hands, remembering how she had looked that first time on *Seafox*, when she had found him holding this very one. He suddenly flung himself face down on the bed, trying to shut out the light, and trying to hold on to the picture of her face. It was useless. All the time he saw Lang, and heard only his mocking laugh.

Occasionally, a fresh realization stabbed his aching mind.

No wonder Morrie and Cooper hadn't worried about being followed. They *knew* they were being followed. By the faithful Lang, who was making sure that no one else was following to see his 'friend' being led docilely to his own funeral.

Escape. He stared round his little prison. Escape. The very word, let alone the idea, seemed ridiculous. The men who designed and built such places left nothing to chance.

He tried to think of what Laidlaw had said.

Going to court in the morning, wherever that was. Going further and further away from Karen. Being cheated of one last chance of saving her.

He faced the blank, tiled bricks of the wall. Stop fooling yourself! Stop thinking that you're in control of the situation! Can't you see that there *is* no last chance? He shook to his torrent of silent rebukes.

The more he thought, the more simple it became. It seemed impossible he had not suspected it from the beginning.

Lang had used him ruthlessly from the very start. It hurt him so much to believe it, that his racing mind tried to find a small loophole, but all the time he knew there was none.

Lang had wanted those plates, and all that went with them. When Mason had told him about the drugs being thrown overboard, and of Vivian's impending visit to Jensen, Lang must have raced straight round to the old man's house, to make some sort of bargain, but when Jensen had told him that he had already spoken to Vivian and his niece on the telephone, and that they were on their way up to see him, Lang must have realized that unless he could get the plates there and then, his dreams would be shattered.

Vivian twisted his hands in agony. He could well imagine

Lang losing his temper, as he had seen him do often enough during the war. He probably started to threaten Jensen, only to be told that the plates were in Vivian's possession anyway. Having given himself away, and to no purpose, Lang must have acted instantly. Vivian saw in his mind's eye, the desperate Lang, telephoning Mason, and giving his terse instructions. Like giving orders at sea. Get the girl. Jensen knows too much now. He has to be taken care of. Taken care of. Like Patterson had been. And how well I played my part for them thought Vivian wretchedly.

No doubt Lang had waited until he knew Vivian was well on the way to the house, and then he too had gone back, probably on the excuse to renew his pleas, or threats. Jensen must have seen the real danger too late, as he doodled calmly on his drawing-board, while his once trusted friend and saviour had circled behind him. Only the staring travel posters had been silent witnesses to the savage drama of man's greed.

The more he thought, the clearer it became, like a bad film slowly developing in the tray. Only Lang could have thought calmly of what was to be done next. Karen's car to be driven near the house, where it was well known. Vivian's behaviour, blinded to everything but Karen's safety. The bait, the catch, and the execution.

Once he had believed that the pair of them had been disposed of, he must have started the ball rolling with the police.

For a brief moment there was a small flicker of hope, and he tensed his body forward on the edge of the bed. Lang must have got a terrible shock when Cooper reported their escape. He fell back, weak and deflated. What did it matter? The story still fitted. The fact that he was in the cell, was living proof. Lang, wherever he was, knew that he only key to the real story was Karen. And he, Vivian, had sent her straight to his grasp.

It seemed obvious that the police would only be interested in the murder. They probably considered the case closed already. And later, at the trial, how would his word stand against the evidence of Lang and Mason? He sweated when he thought of how the police case would stand.

He could almost see the brief smiles on the lips of the jury, the contempt in Mason's eyes. And Lang! He doubled his fists helplessly. He'd just shrug his shoulders and say, 'Well, old boy, you've got to look after Number One!'

The strain of thinking had left him weak, and even the entry of a policeman carrying a tray of food failed to rouse him from the depths of despair.

The policeman returned later and stared at the untouched tray. 'Tch! Tch! This won't do, old man,' he said, not unkindly. 'You must keep your strength up, y'know.'

Vivian turned his head heavily. The constable was a sturdy young man, and his eye fell on the faded row of medal ribbons on his serge jacket. He smiled grimly.

'What's the joke, then?'

'Nothing, nothing.' He shook his head. But all the time, he was thinking. Lang, this constable, and myself. All heroes together. Can the years have changed us so much, or were we as we are now? The P.C. picked up the tray casually, but Vivian noticed how he stayed facing him, and he sensed the presence of another man outside the door.

A new feeling ran through him, and as he watched the heavy door begin to close he felt a tide of resentment and bitter fury engulfing his whole body and sweeping away the heavy weight of self-condemnation and surrender.

He knew at that moment that he would take the first opportunity, no matter how slight or small, to make a bid for his freedom. He could not, would not, wait for any obscure miracle. He had in the past shunned society, and now that very society was taking the word of a liar, and a murderer, against his. He must escape, if only to get his hands on the one man he had always trusted and admired, and the one man who had taken from him his one chance of happiness and life itself.

He lay on his back, seeing and hearing nothing, and when the cell light was switched off from the outside he continued to stare up at the invisible ceiling, his whole being throbbing with this new, consuming fire of destruction.

Vivian awoke from his sleep, dull and listless, until his puzzled eyes fastened upon the unfamiliar surroundings of the police cell. The door was open. It must have been the grating of the key in the lock which had summoned him back from his exhausted state of collapse. As he watched, with dulled eyes, a constable banged a tray of food on the floor and nodded to him.

''Mornin',' he grunted. 'Breakfast. When you've 'ad it, you can come along 'er me and get a shave. Reckon you'll need it!' And so saying, he slammed the door.

Vivian rubbed the bristles on his chin. Must be damned early, he pondered, there was hardly any gleam through the thick glass of the window, only a suggestion of greyness.

He picked up the tray of food and realized suddenly that he was extremely hungry. As he munched steadily through the sausages and baked beans, and washed them down with an enamel mug of sweet tea, he began to think more clearly, his brain sharp, and his heart filled more than ever with an almost insane desire to break out, to find, and to kill Felix Lang.

Unlike the previous night, however, when he had been torn apart mentally and physically, he was able to look at the situation in a coldly calculating way, which would have surprised him, had he considered it. He had nothing to lose but his life, which already seemed to have been disposed of by everyone else, and to gain, he had the satisfaction of revenge, brought about by this new and savage hatred.

Two constables escorted him along to the end of the passage, and while he shaved in lukewarm water, he caught a glimpse of their stolid but watchful faces in the glass.

The whisper of caution which seemed to come from the vigilant faces of the two policemen was not lost on him. He realized only too well that they would be watching his every move. As far as they were concerned, he was a murderer of the very worst kind, and one small, careless move on his part would lessen his chances of escape one hundred per cent.

He wiped his tingling skin carefully with the towel. 'Bit of an early start this morning?' he observed casually. 'I suppose that's the usual thing in these places, is it?'

The two men glanced at each other, their faces blank. Then one of them smiled briefly, understanding crossing his face.

'Of course,' he nodded, 'he means it's dark.' Then to Vivian: 'You wouldn't know about it, being in a cell. I mean, we've got the worst fog in the Channel we've had for bloody ages!'

'Really?' Vivian prayed that his voice concealed the mounting excitement he felt.

'Yes, it may be dark, but it's nigh on eight o'clock.'

'Er, what time'll I have to be leaving, d'you think?' Vivian lowered his eyes as he folded the towel.

'Pretty soon, I should say. They won't be using the van this weather. You'll have to go by car.'

'Yup, the chief inspector'll take you in 'is,' added the other one.

As they headed back to the cell Vivian's heart pounded noisily and he shuffled his feet heavily, in case they might notice any sudden change in his manner, or any expression of hope in his appearance. They passed another policeman shepherding a small, watery-eyed man in a rumpled, blue suit, who pressed himself against the wall as Vivian went by. There was a mixture of fear and curiosity in his dirty face, and Vivian concluded that he must be the singing drunk from the night before. Also on his way to court, no doubt.

That was just one of the many curious glances he was to get when, shortly afterwards, he was accompanied to the main building. He was led into a high, bleak room, labelled 'Charge Room', behind the front office, and even in there he could sense the air of excitement and expectancy as the groups of policemen studied him with interest.

He was able to ignore them. His whole attention was taken by the overpowering and almost threatening gloom which hung over, and even invaded, the police-station. As a sailor, he knew that this fog was one of real menace and strength. But at that moment he knew that it was his only possible ally.

His thoughts were interrupted by the bustling entrance of Chief Inspector Laidlaw, his eyes darting everywhere, and his lower lip thrust out belligerently.

The uniformed policemen fell back respectfully, and the hum of conversation died away.

Sergeant Arnold followed his superior, his arms clutching a file of papers, and his face dark and impassive.

Laidlaw was wearing a light raincoat, and Vivian's keen eyes noted the heavy drops of moisture on the collar. It was a real fog all right.

'We're off soon,' snapped Laidlaw. 'We shall come back here after the hearing, and then you'll be collected by prison officers and taken to a safer place while you're on remand.'

Vivian inclined his head, the detective's eyes were too dangerous to meet.

'I suppose you don't feel like altering your statement?'

'I have told you the truth,' Vivian answered quietly.

Laidlaw looked at him thoughtfully. 'We shall see,' he said slowly. He turned to speak to his sergeant, and then as a thought came to him, he swivelled his eyes back to Vivian. 'By the way, if you're thinking of anything, don't! I thought I'd mention it.' His face hardened. 'My boys are pretty used to this sort of thing!'

Vivian shrugged angrily, and pretended to read one of the notices on the Charge Room wall.

Perhaps the detective always gave warnings like that. Maybe he had been unlucky once with a prisoner. It made Vivian realize that if and when his chance came, it would be his only opportunity of escape, and unless pressed with a ruthless determination it would easily be cut short by a man like Laidlaw.

His attention was taken by a new voice and he saw a constable, his peaked cap glistening with moisture, speaking to the detective.

'Car's out back, sir,' he reported. 'We'll have to take it slow, but it shouldn't take more than 'alf an hour.'

A small procession clattered past. The drunk was being escorted out of the rear of the station.

'He's goin' in the other car,' explained the driver. 'We shall be followin' him all the way.'

A fine contrast, thought Vivian grimly. A drunk and a murderer. All in a day's work for the police, it seemed.

When, a few moments later, Sergeant Arnold touched his sleeve, he felt an icy thrill run through him, and as he was led to the massive door, which opened out on to the enclosed yard, he had to fight hard to keep the tenseness out of his arms.

The fog swirled in on them, its thick, moist breath caressing them, and its dark tentacles filtering between and around them, causing Arnold to change his grip on Vivian's arm, his cold fingers twisting the bottom of his cuff into a tight and effective handcuff.

Laidlaw led the way and they stumbled down the steps to the waiting car, its vague shape broken only by the dull eyes of its headlamps. Laidlaw flung himself into a corner seat, and Vivian found that he was squeezed between him and the sergeant, who sat back cursing, and rearranging the papers which had threatened to slide under the car. The upholstery felt cold and clammy to the touch, and the windows were already black with dirt from the fog's embrace, the windscreen wipers squeaking ineffectually on the filthy glass.

The driver hunched over the wheel, and another uniformed man sat beside him, the back of his head and casual stance, typical of one who is neither concerned nor responsible for possible events.

A faint, pink glow lit up the fog as the other car's rear lights backed towards them, then with a snap of gears, both vehicles started to move forward, passing between the dark, indistinct shapes of the main gates, and both drivers watching and responding to the white gauntlets of a traffic policeman, who, seconds later, was swallowed up by the seemingly impenetrable grey clouds.

Vivian's heart quickened. They were out and on their way. With narrowed eyes he peered ahead, watching the black shape of the car in front. Several times they lost it and then the driver would brake violently, as the twin red lights loomed up under his bumper. Like ships in convoy, he thought, remembering the chaos as one ship would tear down upon another, terrified of the fog, yet even more afraid of being left alone.

He was aware of Laidlaw watching him from the corner, and out of the corner of his eye he could see the big man leaning back on the cushions, as if to keep as much of him under observation as possible.

The driver swore savagely, and the car lurched again.

'Blast!' Arnold stirred uncomfortably, easing his long legs under the bucket seat. 'Pity we weren't in front.'

'Pity we're here at all!' commented Vivian, amazed at his own calmness.

He seemed to feel the tension slacken within the car's sweating atmosphere. It was almost as if his simple remark had caught them all off guard.

Laidlaw blew his nose noisily, and snorted with disgust, as he stuffed the handkerchief away. 'The blessed stuff gets right inside you,' he grumbled.

The rear lights loomed up again, and once more the driver slammed on his brakes, swearing under his breath and rubbing the windscreen with his sleeve.

They waited while the engine raced impatiently. A door slammed, the sound muffled and distorted, and dimly they could see some dark shapes moving away from the other car.

'What the hell's going on now?' Laidlaw studied his watch. 'We'll be damn late at this rate!'

'Seems as if they're goin' off the road for something.' The other constable had spoken for the first time. His lazy voice confirmed Vivian's previous opinion of his indifference. 'They've left the car doors open though, so I don't s'pose they'll be long.'

'Well, get out and see, you fool!' barked Laidlaw, his patience completely gone.

And with a hurt glance over his shoulder, the man began to put on his helmet while the driver, now humming tunelessly, snicked back the hand-brake and killed the engine.

As if to show his feelings the constable threw back the door, and as he lumbered away into the murk he left the door hanging open, allowing the fog to sweep into the small, private world of the car, making their breath steam in small clouds to mingle with the encroaching vapours.

'For Christ's sake, shut the door!' barked Laidlaw, coughing angrily.

And without thinking, Vivian leaned forward across the curved back of the bucket seat, his fingers groping for the edge of the door. He felt the seat give slightly under his weight and he gripped the driver's seat with his right hand to steady himself.

As he grasped the door his eyes fell on the damp tarmac of the roadway. So near—and yet so far. In a flash it dawned on him. This was the moment. This was it!

With a wild sob of excitement he heaved with his right hand, pulling his taut body forward with all his might, and at the same time grabbing the edge of the open door with the other. The bucket seat collapsed under his weight, folding submissively forward, and in a flash he was clawing and kicking over the top, diving head first for the roadway.

A hand gripped his ankle in a vice of steel, but he kicked back savagely, his heel connecting with something hard; there was a grunt of pain, and once more he was free.

Everything was happening at once. He heard Laidlaw's

voice, seemingly right above him, calling on the others to hold him, and the next instant he felt his hands scrape on the road. He rolled over, and like a cat, landed on his feet. A door burst open, and as he ran round the car he met the driver, his face distorted by the fog and the pale gleam of the headlamps. He raised his arm, and Vivian saw the truncheon swinging towards him. He side-stepped quickly, his thigh bumping against the car wing, and drove his fist into the pale, frightened face. More shouts and the stamp of feet in the roadway. He almost fell over the crouching body of his fellow prisoner, who was busy being sick in the roadway. So that was the cause of the delay. The drink last night, the worry of going to court, and the taste of the fog had had their effect. Vivian blessed him briefly, and then, as a blue figure loomed in front of him, he swerved wildly, knocking down another groping shape before the man could recover his wits.

He ran desperately down the white line in the middle of the road, his rubber deck shoes making no sound, and with his eyes wide and staring, searching for a way of escape. Behind him, he heard the blast of a whistle, doors slamming, and the sounds of car engines starting, but already they were muffled, and part of another world. He tried to ignore them and concentrated instead on the steady pad of feet, close on his heels, and as his breath laboured in his lungs he forced his body forward with wild desperation, the wet, clinging air soaking his face and chilling his heaving chest, bared by his torn jacket.

The car engines were getting louder and he cursed himself for staying on the road. He almost stumbled as he swung in to the pavement, dodging a looming lamp-post and losing valuable ground. And all the time, the other footsteps sounded nearer, slowly but relentlessly overtaking him.

Only one of them, he thought wildly, but it only needed one to hold him long enough for the others to close in.

If only he could throw him off. Neither of the cars had been wireless cars; it would be some time before a general alert could be called, he might be able to make it, if only—he cursed aloud, as the kerbstone dipped into a small gravel incline. He turned left, his breath coming in great, sobbing gasps, and he found he was blundering down some sort of small pathway between what appeared to be wooden walls, lock-up garages probably, anyway, off the main road.

He almost cried out as a high wall brought him skidding to a halt, his throat dry and his body pounding with exertion. Blindly he ran from side to side, but there was no other way, it was a cul-de-sac.

He peered up at the top of the wall. About eight feet high. As he gathered himself for a spring, the fog wall behind him darkened, and a figure padded towards him, half crouched in readiness.

Sergeant Arnold halted, his chest heaving, his tie hanging loosely from his jacket.

In silence they peered at each other, like wild animals looking for an opening to make a kill. Both tensed, as a freak cloud of mist swept between them, distorting their bodies and making their shapes twist and writhe in distorted shadows.

The car engines revved louder, and another whistle shrilled its urgent message.

'Well, you bastard! Are you going the easy way, or the hard way?' Arnold was speaking through his teeth.

Vivian backed against the wall, feeling its rough surface scratching his jacket.

He couldn't speak, he just stood gasping in the clammy air. Behind him, one jump could take him to some sort of safety, but he knew that as soon as he turned, Arnold would have him down. Somehow he knew that the other man would enjoy doing it.

A voice boomed unnaturally and without warning down the little road. 'Are you there, Sergeant? Do you hear me?'

Arnold grinned, his teeth gleaming in the darkness, and he twisted his head half round to answer.

With a sob of desperation Vivian sprang forward, propelling himself from the wall in one quick movement. His wildly grasping hands felt the detective's tie, and before the man could cry out, he jerked him off his balance, pulling him forward with all the strength he could muster.

Together they rolled over on the roadway, hitting out at each other in short, vicious jabs, each grunting with pain as the blows went home. Arnold kicked out his long legs, gaining a purchase on the ground, and slowly but surely forcing himself on top of the other man. Their arms locked and their faces were inches apart, Vivian feeling the warm breath on his neck. He felt Arnold drawing back a knee, preparing for the crippling blow, and with a final, anguished heave he twisted one hand free, making the vicious movement impossible, and causing Arnold to temporarily lose his balance. With his palm open, Vivian struck downwards, the edge of his hand striking below the hairline, and as he rolled from under the suddenly limp body, he knew that it was over.

Somehow he pulled himself up and over the wall, only once glancing back at the still form on the road, then, as he dropped silently to the ground he peered round, getting his bearings, and finding that he was apparently in another side road, he started to run again, but more slowly and with more confidence, as all sounds of pursuit were swallowed up and lost behind him.

He ran his hand shakily through his hair, pushing it

back from his contorted face. He could run no more, and when a pillar-box suddenly appeared in his path he stopped altogether, and leaned weakly against it, letting his body fight its gasping battle. His face and neck were soaking wet. When he felt a little easier he took stock of his surroundings and cocked his head on one side, listening. Hearing nothing, he started to walk on, trying to recognize a landmark, or see something which would give him a clue to his whereabouts. Sometimes he thought he was walking in a circle, and sometimes he would turn down a road, only to stop dead, as if his instinct was guiding him and warning him of a wrong direction.

He was walking downhill most of the time, and whether it was that, or whether it was the sea calling him back to his own, proper element, he found that he was progressing with an unaccountable sureness, although most of the time he could see nothing.

He saw several hurrying figures with heads bowed and squinting faces, and each time he was able to keep his distance, but for the most part Ramsgate seemed dead and deserted. No doubt the hotels and boarding-houses were finding difficulty in turning their reluctant guests out into the streets under such conditions.

Once he stiffened as the figure of a policeman moved slowly along the deserted pavement, but the man's attention was elsewhere, or perhaps he just did not know what was happening.

He was just beginning to feel an edge of despair when all at once, mingling with the acrid stink of the fog, he detected something else. He halted, wrinkling his nose, and then hurried on, following the scent of the salt air, the sharp, clearly defined tang, that told him he was getting near his first destination, and automatically, the need for greater caution transmitted itself to his brain.

A dim tobacco kiosk, a little island of colour, which he had visited many times in the past, pinpointed his position. Without further hesitation, but walking more slowly, he made his way from the kiosk towards where he knew lay the main harbour entrance. There were a few more people here. In ones and twos, they wandered disconsolately up and down, while some of the more daring groped their way along the shining stonework of the harbour.

He stopped once more, forcing himself to think before taking another step. He was so keyed up, that thinking had become an effort of will-power. His actions now seemed to be automatic, or governed by instinct.

It was likely that there would be a guard on his boat, he thought. They would not assume that he'd make for the boat, but it was possible that they might want to keep sightseers away. Anyway, he could take no chances.

As he stood pondering, he heard a car slowly drive to the harbour wall and stop. He could not see it, and he marvelled at the determination of the driver. As he listened, a voice, very close, said quite conversationally, 'Look, Jane, a police car.'

Vivian shrank back, straining his ears.

A heavy crunch of boots halted, apparently by the car, and he could even hear the man clearing his throat.

'All correct, Sergeant!' a voice said.

'Very good. Keep your eyes skinned at this entrance, will you. No need to go along the outer harbour, just watch this bit.'

'All right, Sergeant,' the other man answered obediently. 'D'you think he'll come this way?'

'Not likely. What'd be the point?'

The constable laughed. 'Poor devil! He must be about all in.'

'So'll you be if he gets hold of you!' The voice was grim. 'He's just laid out a sergeant from the Yard!'

'Serve him right,' muttered the other man surlily. 'Why can't they let us get on with it?'

The sergeant laughed, and a second later the car moved stealthily away, its lights glinting feebly.

Vivian breathed out slowly, waiting for the policeman to move back to his position of observation.

After a while he started off in the opposite direction, until he found himself overlooking the inner harbour, which was mainly used as a yacht basin.

He could not see the water, but a seemingly disconnected forest of small masts swayed and bobbed at him along the edge of the wall. Feeling carefully with his feet, he crept down the first stone steps leading to the water, a scheme forming in his mind. He was so busy with his thoughts that he almost stumbled over the sitting figure on the last step. A lonely fisherman, the sea lapping practically over the tops of his rubber boots.

'Lousy morning!' he commented without looking round, his face turned towards the invisible end of his rod. 'Still, it keeps the bloody kids away!' He chuckled hoarsely.

'Pretty thick,' agreed Vivian casually, stepping back slowly to hide his wild and ragged appearance. 'Been here long?'

The fisherman spat. 'Since an hour before high water. 'Bout two hours, I suppose. Haven't caught a blessed thing!' he added bitterly.

Vivian took another step back, feeling the stones with his heel.

'Tell you something, though. I wish I'd been here a bit sooner.'

'Really?' Vivian tried to sound interested.

'Yes.' The man laughed shortly. 'My mate, Jim Gibbs,

'ou may know him? Well, he was here all night. Eels, he was after,' he added scornfully. 'As if you'd get eels here!'

Vivian was half-way up the steps now and the other man's shape was fading.

'Well, Jim was tellin' me that some silly ass of a yachtsman put out to sea just before the fog came down.' He shook with silent humour. 'Reckon he must be stuck out ere right in the middle of it now, eh?'

Vivian stiffened, suddenly wide awake and alert.

'What yacht, d'you know?'

But as he asked, he knew that it had to be the one. It had to be Lang. If the police had been watching his own boat, and Lang had not been aboard he must have been very close at hand, to catch Karen as she entered the harbour. Where else but right here? He stared at the blank wall of fog, his head spinning.

'Don't know the name of the boat. Jim said there was a pansy-looking chap in a bow-tie up in the bows, shining a torch on the harbour wall as he went out, afraid he'd hit it, I expect.'

Vivian caught his breath. Cooper! No wonder they were in a hurry. They had what they wanted. The girl, the plates, and the method of completing their alibis!

He muttered something to the fisherman and hurried up the steps. There was still a chance. There had to be. As if in answer, a doleful clang sounded from the fog bell at the harbour entrance.

Somehow he found the end of the inner wharf, and without pausing for further thought, he stripped off his jacket and trousers and stood naked on the edge of the slippery stonework. With the clammy mist exploring his body, he lowered himself down one of the mooring chains, gritting his teeth as the cold, oily water moved up and around his body. When the water lapped across his back

225

he pushed away from the green slime of the wall with hi
feet, hardly making a sound as he drifted clear of the old
chains and weather-worn piles along its edge.

As is often the case, the visibility was better near to the
surface and he started to swim, strongly and easily, across
the invisible harbour. It was a queer, unnatural experience.
Occasionally he would hear a snatch of conversation, or a
laugh, apparently quite close, and odd, unexplained noises
and bumps echoed and muttered through the water
around him. He was swimming almost exactly from north
to south, from the end of the inner harbour to the eastern
arm of the horseshoe-shaped outer wall.

The bottom half of a dark blue hull—the top was
invisible in the swirling mist—seemed to drift past him, but
it was the reserve lifeboat resting peacefully at her moorings, just as he had anticipated. He rested for a moment,
supporting himself by one of the boat's slip-wires. So far so
good, he breathed. The next stretch was more difficult
because there would be no more obvious guides, or, in fact,
any visible guides at all. He would be depending entirely on
his sense of direction.

His flesh tingled as he pushed himself forward again, and
his body felt refreshed rather than tired. He knew that
could be deceptive, and was careful not to use up all his
strength. Instead, he maintained his steady crawl, his eyes
keeping a constant watch on the fog-banks ahead, which
rolled across the dead water like great creatures in a dream.

He was in the widest part of the harbour now, and he
could feel the strong surge of the current's undertow
pulling at his legs. He swam on, losing all idea of time and
praying that he was still heading in the right direction. The
steady boom of the fog bell was no help at all, as its source
seemed to change its bearing with devilish cunning.

His arms and legs were beginning to ache, and his body

It heavy and unresponsive to his efforts. He knew, only too well, that if he had made a mistake in direction, he might easily have been carried through the harbour entrance already, and be swimming out towards the open sea. He spat out salt water as his head ducked wearily under the slight swell, and he concentrated grimly on his stroke. It would be very simple to be unnerved by wild fears and go blindly off on another, even more fruitless, search.

Clang, clang! The bell was nearer. Or was it behind him? He swore breathlessly and stopped, treading water. There was a longer patch of grey on his left and he stared at it without comprehending, and wondering what fresh twist of distortion had caused it. Unlike the rest of the fog, it didn't seem to move, or alter, and he was tempted to turn towards it.

His heart bounded as a shrill whistle cut through the heavy air, followed by the harsh bark of a command over a loudspeaker. Of course! That explained it! The grey shape was a ship, the naval fishery protection vessel in which he had often enjoyed a drink with the officers when he had called at Ramsgate in the past. The sound was that of a bosun's pipe announcing part of the daily routine. Thank God! He knew now that his own boat was about fifty yards further on.

At eye level, he saw the sleek, shiny curve of *Seafox's* hull, her shape strengthening at every stroke of his arms, and he almost floundered under with his excitement.

The white hull felt good under his wet palms, and he eased his way along the side, to the bobbing dinghy moored under her stern. For a moment longer he waited, listening. There were a few hurrying footsteps along the wall but they soon passed, leaving only the gurgle of water under the boat.

He heaved himself over the gunwale of the little boat, h
limbs suddenly heavy, and his teeth chattering.

The tide had swung the dinghy round at right angles, s
he was able to climb aboard the yacht, keeping the coac
roof, and part of the wheelhouse, between him and the wal
His sodden deck shoes squelched noisily along the deck, an
he wondered why he had not discarded those along wit
his other clothes. He shivered slightly as the fog move
eerily round his wet, naked body.

The next instant he had the wheelhouse door open an
he was standing on the smooth deck, in a widening pool c
water. His heart was pounding wildly, with relief or excite
ment, he couldn't say, but as he stood listening intently, th
sight of the gleaming wheel and binnacle, and the othe
familiar objects about him, made a lump form in his throat

His boat, where all the trouble had started. He found i
difficult to believe that outside the comfort and feeling o
security it gave him the rest of his world had smashed, an
he was, even now, being hunted.

He moved swiftly about the darkened interior, his action
ordered and compelled by the need for haste and care. A
he passed a scuttle, or wheelhouse window, he ducke
down, after taking a quick glance at the top of the wall, t
make sure no one was taking an interest which might prov
dangerous.

He pulled on a clean pair of drill trousers and a shirt
feeling the material rub and cling to his damp limbs. He
had neglected to dry himself, and had paused only long
enough to run a comb through his matted hair, wincing as
it touched his bruised head.

All the while he was filled with the wild driving force of
urgency. The desperate need to get out of the harbour
before the fog lifted was more than a wild scheme. It was an
overpowering obsession.

If only he could just press the starter buttons to his two powerful diesels he would take his chances on the fog. He knew that at their first roar some curious onlooker, or prowling policeman, would give the alarm. He cursed himself repeatedly for not remembering to question the fisherman more about the yacht Lang was using. It might be fast or slow, old or new. One thing: he was firmly convinced that it was not much bigger than *Seafox*. The moorings indicated by the vague sweep of the fisherman's arms were not deep enough for large craft. A really big yacht would entail additional crew too, and it was unlikely that Lang would want to involve others at this stage, nor would he use a fool like Cooper unless it was absolutely necessary.

He padded on deck again, unwinding a coil of thin, nylon tow-line, which, although very light to handle, was as tough as an ordinary rope many times its size. This was to be the tow to end all tows, he thought grimly.

With a quick jerk, he made one end fast to the yacht's capstan and carried the rest back to the stern, paying it out over the boat's side as he went. With a careful heave he dropped the remainder into the dinghy, and climbed down after it. Working fast he secured it to the stern of the dinghy, and cast off the painter holding the little boat to its parent ship.

With his heart in his mouth he scrambled back aboard the yacht, crouching low until he was sure that he was still unobserved, then with a few rapid tugs he slipped both the mooring ropes holding the yacht to the harbour wall. He paused, appalled at the apparent noise he was making. In the distance a dog barked, and quite near a man's loud laugh bellowed unnaturally through the fog. Nothing else happened. With his legs braced, Vivian pushed away from the mooring posts with all the strength of his arms and shoulders, and obediently *Seafox* drifted out on to the black water.

Vivian ran aft and jumped into the dinghy, which had floated free on its long line. With powerful strokes on the stubby little oars, Vivian pulled round ahead of the yacht, watching the nylon rise, dripping and slack, until it slowly took the strain of the tow. The line tautened and Vivian lay back on the oars, his eye measuring the distance between the two craft. The sharp, raked stem of the yacht seemed to tower over him, and but for the tiny ripple at the water-line, it was as if they were both motionless and suspended in space. He gritted his teeth and pulled harder, feeling the jerk of the line protesting against its load. *Seafox* yawed from side to side, but he was making her move, and now that he had started there was no turning back, even if he had wanted to.

Several times his aching arms made him slacken his stroke, and the white, ghost-like shape of the yacht bore down on him, and it seemed an age before he had it under control again.

The fog bell was louder now and he pulled slightly away from it. One false move here and the yacht would scrape along the wall, or come to a full stop on the stone piles at the last curve of the harbour's embrace.

His head and neck ached from constantly looking over his shoulder and back at the tow, without allowing the pace to slacken.

A faint, yellow glow appeared over his right shoulder, and for one frightful moment he thought it was the light of a ship, but in a flash he realized that it must be the harbour-master's office and signal station, right on the tip of the harbour. He watched it float by and vanish behind him. He was out. The heavier swell, which lifted the dinghy easily on its back, was enough to tell him that he was on the open sea.

He pulled on, not caring about the direction, his arms

tearing free from their sockets, and hot knives stabbing at his spine. Eventually he realized he could go on no further. He would have to chance someone hearing him start the engines.

As the yacht glided to a halt, and lay wallowing uncomfortably, he made the dinghy fast to the stern again and climbed aboard. He could only faintly hear the fog bell, so he estimated he was quite some distance from the harbour. His brain worked surprisingly clearly, and he was able to concentrate on the business of moving the boat with a coolness that had often come to his assistance in the past.

With the tide ebbing, he was drifting further away from Ramsgate every minute, roughly north-east, he decided, towards the North Goodwin Lightship. With a bit of luck, he would be able to leave it a little longer before he got under way.

The boat rolled widely on the long Channel swell, making various loose articles rattle and bang, and he had to steady himself against the chart table. He stared around, feeling rather at a loss, and trying to push the nagging murmurs of futility out of his thoughts. Now that he had made good his escape, the aftermath of shock was making his next moves difficult to formulate, and even the effort of concentration seemed additionally hard.

He scrambled down into the engine-room, switching on the pilot light as he did so. Lifting the boards by the silent flywheel he groped downwards with his hand, his knuckles grazing against the ice-cool planks of the rounded hull. The remainder of the plates had gone. He cursed slowly and coldly. Lang must have had a good search of the boat after he had left, or, most probably, he had slipped across the harbour by dinghy, after Karen had unwittingly blurted out the secret.

Wearily he climbed back to the wheelhouse, slamming the hatch bitterly behind him. Peering out of the misted windows he felt additional qualms about the soundness of his plan to leave the harbour at all. Suppose the fog lifted suddenly. Any fast launch, or helicopter, would find him within minutes. The alarm might have already been started. He shrugged his shoulders at the hopelessness of his fears. Perhaps Lang wasn't even on that particular yacht which had hurried out to sea. After all, many yachtsmen were stupid enough to disregard a fog warning, any life-boatman would tell you that. His eyes glinted suddenly, thinking of the 'pansy-looking chap in a bow-tie'. It was more than a coincidence. It had to be the one. The question was, where had he gone?

Switching on the light of the chart table he spread the local chart over the lighted glass and studied it carefully, trying to estimate and mark his exact position.

He shivered, the fog had got into his lungs. There was still some whisky in the saloon and he poured a large glass, downing it in one gulp. He refilled the tumbler, and absently held it up to the cabin lamp, watching the warm, amber fluid, and feeling the neat spirit burning his throat. *Seafox* gave an even heavier roll than before, and a book thudded on to the carpet.

He bent to pick it up, raising his eyebrows when he found it to be his copy of the A.B.C. time-table. Straddling his legs against the boat's slow wallows, he stood looking at it dazedly, remembering how he had looked up the fatal train which had taken him from Torquay to London. It was a century ago, and in a sudden, blind rage, he held the book up, looking for somewhere to throw it, as if by destroying it he could blot out the memories for ever.

As he did so, he noticed the edge of a match-stick wedged in between the pages. His natural curiosity acted upon his temper, like water on a fire, and putting down the glass, he flicked open the book, scanning the two pages with dulled interest.

A tremor of excitement sent a cold chill up his back. Against the town name of Margate was a line of pencilled figures, and as he held the book up to the light, his hands shaking, he noted that they appeared to be a collection of train times. Trains from Margate to London. He banged the book down, sending the glass shattering across the cabin. Of course! What could be simpler? Lang must have sat here, idly checking the train times, whilst waiting for Vivian to get on his way with the plates. He slapped his forehead with an open fist. He had sailed for Margate in his boat, just to make it far enough from Ramsgate not to attract attention. Then up to town, a quick switch to the anxious employer, doing his best to help the police!

He ran back to the chart, his mind racing hard. He'd be there by now, but he'd have had to anchor a good way out in this weather. It was unlikely that he'd risk rowing ashore either, he thought, remembering his own nightmare in Ramsgate.

He stopped dead, his thumb poised over the starter buttons, the breath stilled in his throat. Karen! How easy it would be to get rid of her on the trip round the North Foreland.

Deliberately he pressed the buttons, and one by one the engines roared to life, the shattering rumble settling down to a steady, confident beat. He hardly noticed them as he eased the gear levers ahead, his mind was coldly steady again, his heart filled with consuming hatred.

He spun the varnished spokes in his hands, feeling the yacht cant over and settle on her new course, the bows climbing over each roller, and cutting a white wake through the oily water. He checked the course, and watched the swaying compass card, as it danced in its small pool of light.

'Come on, old girl!' he breathed, between his set lips. 'Don't let me down now!'

With a steady pressure, he eased the twin throttles wide open, a thing he would never think of doing under normal circumstances, until the whole boat shook and trembled as she leapt through the invisible sea. The needles on the revolution counters crept higher and higher, as the screws bit deeper and deeper, thrusting the sharp stem forward with almost savage force.

10

IT WAS a weird experience. A blank wall of fog surrounding the boat, and the bows only just visible from the wheel, as she hurtled into what appeared to be a solid mass, which clawed and clutched at the hull as if to slow her passage.

He switched on the Automatic Pilot, and having satisfied himself that it was behaving correctly, he started his other preparations. If another ship was coming straight for him, he'd never see it, and above the scream of the engines no fog-horn could warn him in time.

He tipped the First Aid box impatiently on to the side seat, giving a grunt of satisfaction as the long automatic pistol fell glinting evilly on to the cushions. With an ease which he had forgotten he possessed, he pulled back the slide, his eyes expressionless, as the little bullet slid forward into the breech.

You'll be sorry you gave me this, Felix!

He stuck the weapon in the top of his waistband, only pausing to consider the depths to which he had been brought. Next, he found another sort of pistol, his Very Light gun, which was always near to hand in case of real emergencies. He slit open the packet of flares, and inserted one of the fat, red cartridges into the pistol's wide breech, and clipped it shut.

If I'm in a position to call for help, I'll need it fast! he mused.

He took a look around the boat, realizing that it might well be his last. Then, again by the wheel, he settled down to watch the boat's progress.

The fog showed no signs of thinning, and he ducked involuntarily as a large, grey cloud reared over the stem. He glanced at the luminous clock on the dashboard. About another ten minutes before he altered course towards the west, a course which should take him well clear of the treacherous Foreland and in towards Margate. Provided his calculations were correct, as he told himself repeatedly, while he studied the thin, pencilled lines on the chart.

Treading carefully on the spray-washed planks, he climbed up on to the forward deck, tasting the salt on his lips, and feeling the clammy moisture clinging to his face and hair. Rising and falling to the powerful thrust of the boat, he steadied himself against the guard rail, listening intently. The thunder of the engines was deadened up on the sloping deck, and he noted with satisfaction the throaty blare of a distant fog-horn. He counted the intervals. North Foreland lighthouse, he observed.

It was easy to lose all sense of time and direction. He stood right up in the bows of the yacht, his legs taking each plunge with ease, while the bow wave hissed and sparkled beneath him. It was as if he was flying through the air, skimming over the surface, like an avenging sea-bird. He wiped his streaming face, his eyes and ears playing him tricks, which he knew well enough to ignore, but his mind wandered in vague fantasies that could not be so easily cast aside.

Suppose he just took one step forward? If Karen had gone, life was no more use to him anyway, so why prolong an agony which was certain to destroy him?

He imagined the boat driving on, smashing him down with her keel, guiding him into the racing screws. With her course held by the Automatic Pilot, she would drive on alone, a ghost ship, until she dashed herself on the shore, or was found abandoned by some wondering persons elsewhere.

He swayed slightly and tightened his grip on the rail. Fool! he cursed, there is one thing you have to do yet.

Another blast of a horn sounded out of the fog, nearer this time it seemed, but he knew that it must really be well over to port.

He returned to the wheel, and, as he noticed the clock, he cursed and spun the wheel on to her new course. The minutes ticked by, minutes charged with mounting tension and a fierce, growing determination.

The engines slowed, and the yacht ran on more quietly, while Vivian, with every window open, peered ahead, waiting calmly for the sight of any small vessel which might be anchored here to ride out the fog. He knew that somewhere over the salt-caked bows lay Margate, and here, in the Road, he would find Lang. He wasn't quite sure how he could be so definite, he just knew.

The area for yacht anchorage only measured about two miles in length, so it would be a job for the dinghy again. He lifted his head higher, hearing the plaintive squawk of the fog-horn guarding the end of Margate's tiny harbour. Getting pretty close, he decided, and slammed both engines into neutral, allowing the boat to glide forward silently, the water slapping against the sides in protest. The tide was running out fast, and he knew that in a while the area beyond the small, stone breakwater would be just a mass of treacherous mud.

Taking his time, he went once more on to the forward deck, and when the bow wave had died to a sullen ripple, he started to lower the anchor, swearing softly at the grating clink of the cable, as it ran jerkily through the fairlead. He felt the chain slacken, as the swinging flukes dragged along the sandy bottom, and as the boat moved away crabwise with the current, he carefully paid out more and more cable, until the boat swung gently to her moorings.

Thoughtfully, he strapped a small compass on his wrist. Rowing a dinghy in the fog, in a definite direction, would be difficult enough as it was, without adding to his troubles.

With a sigh, he lowered himself into the little boat, which bobbed obediently astern. He checked his two weapons, and shoved off from the yacht's side, experiencing a strange curdling feeling in the pit of his stomach.

He chased all other thoughts out of his head, and pulled off strongly, the dinghy feeling light and free without the yacht dragging behind it, and within seconds he had lost sight of *Seafox*, although he could still hear the chafing clink of her taut cable.

Occasionally he rested on his oars, checking his compass, and listening so carefully that it hurt. He reckoned that he was pulling about half a mile from the beach, or probably less, and even allowing for the current, he should still be parallel to it.

Twice he swerved to avoid what he thought was a moored and unmarked vessel, but each time it was a thicker bank of fog, which seemed to jeer and mock at his desperate efforts, which, as the time wore on, appeared fated and hopeless.

He rested again, the silence closing in on him like a blanket. Nothing. He lowered his head, watching the water swilling about under the boat's bottom boards.

'No boat here,' he said, as if addressing the silence. 'Not one bloody thing!' His shoulders slumped, and he felt himself drifting sideways across the busy current.

What a damned fool I am, he pondered. I don't even deserve to live!

Ding! Ding! Ding! Ding! The tinny note of a bell, being struck with inexperienced vigour, brought all his senses alert, and he found himself craning round, trying to trap the sound, to hold it and plan its direction.

He waited, the glistening oar blades poised inches over the water. How well he understood that sound, a ship's bell being rung to denote she was lying at anchor in a fog. He knew that he had another minute to wait before the next few strokes, provided the person doing it was abiding strictly by the rules.

There it was again. His heart pounded with excitement, as he pulled slowly and silently towards it, the blades biting deep into the water.

Like a stalking hunter he moved, waiting for each new group of sounds before he pulled onwards. His head was strained round over one shoulder, his eyes staring into the fog, regardless of the salt smarting under his lids and the ache in his neck.

Ding! Ding! Ding! The ringer must be getting tired. Much nearer now, he decided, it would be any second and he would find this invisible vessel.

As he lay on his oars, waiting for the bell, two things happened at once. The bell clanged, apparently overhead, and at that very instant, before the notes had time to fade away, he saw the swaying shape of a yacht's stern, only feet away. He watched her in silence, hardly daring to breathe, and licking his dry lips in cold anticipation of what he had to do next.

She was quite a large yacht, from what he could see, about five to ten feet longer than *Seafox*, and with tapering, twin masts to carry her auxiliary sails. Her dark blue hull gleamed dully even in the fog, showing her metal sides, and the name *Grouville* in bold letters across her stern.

As he waited, a figure detached itself from the dark hump of the yacht's wheelhouse and stamped noisily to the rail. Then, with an impatient glance at his wrist-watch, he moved back again, his shape merging with that of the boat. Another loud ringing clanged and rolled around the fog, and Vivian realized that the man, whoever he was, would be remaining on deck to maintain the constant signal. He bit his lip angrily. There was nothing for it but to swim for the yacht's side. At the first scrape of the dinghy alongside, the alarm would be given in a second. He'd just have to let the boat drift away on its own, there was nothing else that he could do, he concluded.

He hardly made a splash as he slid into the water, and floating on his back, he watched anxiously, as the dinghy curtsied and bobbed out of sight.

In a few strokes he was feeling his way under the bulging curve of the stern, his knees scratching along the rough, encrusted waterline and one foot touching a protruding propeller. Being a steel boat, there was little to hold on to, and a pang of anxiety caused him to move more quickly along the high side, which rose above his face like a sheer wall. Three square, window-like ports, blazing with light, glared out from the middle of the boat, and he reached up cautiously, the tips of his wet fingers exploring the edge of the first one. There was a small flange at the bottom, so with both hands he pulled himself bodily out of the water, until his eyes rose above the level of the brass overhang.

At first he could see nothing, the glass was caked and smeared with salt and fog stains, then as he hung with his ribs rubbing against the cold, steel plates, he saw a figure move rapidly across his vision. He swallowed hard. It was Mason, his face twisted into a frown of anger or fear, as he paced to and fro, tossing remarks to someone sitting against Vivian's side of the boat, and who was out of his range of view. Faintly, through the thick, toughened glass, he heard only snatches of Mason's high, agitated voice.

'How did he escape? That's what I'd like to know.' And, 'If it's all so damned foolproof, why are we squatting out here like this?'

Vivian grimaced with the pain in his arms and fingers. He could feel his grip slowly slipping from the tiny, brass ledge, but he hung on, determined to hear as much as possible. They must have heard about my escape on the radio, he thought. Once Mason glared straight at him and Vivian froze, but he continued his pacing and storming without interruption, so he stayed where he was, feeling the swell of the water pulling at his dangling thighs.

While he watched, Mason took a decanter from a well-stocked sideboard, and filled two glasses with a shaking hand.

Of course, the yacht's name came back to Vivian's racing brain, it was one of the travel agency's hire yachts. Lang had mentioned it to him when they had been discussing the subject in the first place.

The very thought of Lang made a great surge of anger tear right through him, nearly making him lose his last precarious hold. He was about to slide back into the water, to look for a fresh method of boarding, when an arm reached forward to take the other glass from the table.

For the short time it took, he saw again the plump, fresh-complexioned face, and smooth, well-groomed hair. Even after Lang had leaned back again, out of sight, Vivian still stared, his eyes cold with hatred.

It was almost a relief to feel the embrace of the sea, as he slid back down the smooth side, and paddled further along the yacht's length.

'Soon, soon,' he breathed, 'I'll make it even with you, Felix!'

There was nothing within reach, so he swam to the anchor cable, and, hand over hand, pulled himself up to the high stem, straining and sliding his streaming body over the wide flare of the bow, to roll, panting, on the deck. Breathless though he was, he was up, and crouching behind the capstan before he had time to realize he was aboard, and before the man by the bell had finished his last stroke.

He crouched, counting the seconds until the bell started to jangle again, and at the first stroke he scrambled noiselessly along the wide deck, and as the bell stopped ringing he flung himself down flat on the wet planking, taking his weight on his hands. He listened, his heart thudding in his breast, so that he thought it must be heard. He caught the scraping sound of a match, and lifting his head only slightly, he saw Cooper's face bent over a cigarette, his eyes squinting against the flame. He was standing on the other side of the wheelhouse, as Vivian had anticipated, and the sight of him made him clench his fists, as the memories came flooding back.

He turned his face away, concentrating on the lighted glass of a deck skylight, which should, he thought, be right over the saloon. He eased his body forward, until his nose was practically touching the coaming, and when the bell jangled its message once more, he peered over the edge. Lang was talking now, his voice sharp, but completely at ease.

'. . . and so that's it,' he was saying. 'We've taken years to build this thing up, and to break away from the other people in the game; why,' he shrugged expressively, a gesture that sent a shaft of pain through Vivian as he watched, 'it's madness to let anything or anyone spoil it now!'

A girl's voice made Vivian start, and twist his head further round. At the other end of the saloon, slumped on the wide settee, was Janice Mason. Her eyes were red, as if she had been crying for a long time, and she looked completely miserable. From the slur in her speech, he observed that she was also very drunk.

'Whyja do it?' she said, looking desperately at Lang. 'You didn't tell me you were going to kill him.' She sniffed loudly, and lowered her eyes to her empty glass. 'He was such a nice old man,' she added, almost to herself.

'Well, we're all in it!' Lang sounded quite cheerful. 'You too, Janice!'

'But I——'

'Don't forget, you drove the girl's car up to the house, with the horn blaring, a very convincing double I thought! Oh yes my girl, we're all in it!'

'You swine.' She said it without emotion. 'I've been a fool!'

'Nonsense! We're all right, I keep telling you. What does it matter if he has escaped, eh? Only makes it look more convincing if he runs away for a bit. He doesn't know where we are, so what the hell!'

Mason refilled all the glasses. He seemed a bit calmer now.

'So you say, Felix. I must confess that when you explain it, it does seem a bit easier.'

'Mind you, old boy, I must say that even I had a few nasty moments! When that girl came running up to me in Ramsgate, well! I had just been giving this boat the once over, and she damn near fell on me! Phew, I'd never have believed that old Morrie would fall down on the job. I'm glad we've got rid of him!' he added callously.

'Anything else? What other thing did the great man miss?' The girl's voice was getting thicker every moment.

243

Lang ignored the interruption. 'Then there was this, old boy.' He fumbled in the pocket of his blazer. 'This little scrap of paper.' He smoothed it down on the table, directly beneath Vivian, and he saw Jensen's last desperate message, the drawing of the engine-room. 'Found it on Vivian's boat when I was nosing around. That's how I found the rest of the plates.' He chuckled. 'Bit of luck I found them, old boy, I might have thought you were trying to double-cross me, what?' He laughed as if it was all a huge joke.

Mason stared at the paper. 'What's the idea of this little drawing of a cat?'

'Don't you get it, old boy? Old Jensen was no fool you know. You've got to hand it to him, really you have!' He gulped down his drink. 'Remember the cartoons we used to go and see before the war, when we were kids? You know, when cartoon films were a real novelty.'

Understanding dawned on Mason's thin features. 'By God! I've got it, Felix the cat!' he shouted. 'Felix! He was trying to tip off the name of his murderer!'

Vivian's heart was ice cold, when he realized how he had overlooked the most important part of poor Jensen's warning. Without taking his eyes from the little group below, he reached down to his belt, and pulled the automatic pistol up to his face. Resting the muzzle on the coaming, he lined up the fore-sight with Lang's stomach, which even now was shaking with silent laughter. There was no mercy in Vivian's eyes, and none in his heart, as he curled his finger round the trigger.

Had anyone else been in a position to make a plea for Lang's life, the words would have fallen on deaf ears, but it was Lang himself who caused Vivian to falter, to allow the pistol to waver dangerously on the edge of the skylight.

'I suppose I'd better go and have a look at our little Karen, just to make sure she's all right. By the look of things,

I'll have to take care of her myself. My partners don't seem to be very reliable on that score.'

Vivian's eyes misted over, and he lowered his head weakly against the wood coaming. She was alive! Karen was still safe! The words hammered at his brain, until his throat trembled with pent-up emotion. He stared round the murky deck, a feeling of wild elation almost throwing him off his guard, as Cooper moved uneasily by the bell. She was aboard, somewhere quite close to him.

'Cooper!' Lang's voice boomed up through the half-opened skylight.

He heard Cooper clatter down the steps of the companion-way, which led from the wheelhouse, and next he heard his voice from the saloon.

'Carn I leave off banging that flippin' bell, boss?' he whined. 'My head's bursting!'

'I'll burst it, in a minute,' laughed Lang ominously. 'Here, catch this key! Go and see if the little Danish miss is safe and sound.'

'Gee, thanks!' Cooper sucked his teeth noisily. 'I'm sure gonna enjoy this!'

Vivian's grip tightened on the butt of the pistol. You're not, you know! He slipped into the wheelhouse, and waited, bent double, at the top of the varnished stairway.

Cooper stepped out of the saloon, and before he shut the door, a beam of light revealed the wolfish grin on his face. He scurried down the narrow passage-way between the cabins, and paused outside the last door, excitedly jamming the key into the lock. As the lock clicked back, Cooper paused, and adjusted his bow tie with a well-practised flick, and without looking back, to where Vivian moved like a shadow at the foot of the companion-way, he thrust open the door. He was excited, that Vivian could see, his face muscles trembling with uncontrollable emotions that he could only imagine, although the wild light of lust in the dark eyes left little to the imagination.

'Well, hiya!' Cooper leaned against the door-post, grinning at the girl who sat hunched on one of the lockers, in what appeared to be a store cabin. Vivian's mind noted all these details, as he crept forward, his breath held in tightly, until his temples throbbed painfully. It was all he could manage to tear his eyes away from her face, as she stared at Cooper, her face a picture of horror and disgust.

'You'n me are goin' to have a nice little chat,' continued Cooper.

'And so are we.' Vivian spoke softly, yet it was as if the other man had had a gun exploded in his ear.

He swung round, his beady eyes popping out of his head. He couldn't speak, but his Adam's apple bobbed up and down, almost comically, over his bow tie.

'Nothing to say, eh?' Vivian's voice was like ice. 'But, then, you've said enough, haven't you?'

He pushed the man back into the passage, screwing his strong fingers into the pale blue suit to get a better grip. Behind him he heard an incredulous sob, and a blaze of anger flooded through him.

Cooper was still emitting gurgling sounds, when the butt of the pistol struck him between the eyes. Vivian lowered him to the deck and stepped back into the cabin, reaching out blindly for the girl, as she flung herself into his arms.

For a long moment they clung together, each unable to believe that the other really existed.

'Philip! They're all here! It was Felix . . .' she stumbled over the words.

'I know,' he murmured soothingly, 'I know it all now!'

The tiny warning flashed through his mind, which had become dulled by the feeling of warmth and love which flooded his heart, and he knew that there was no time to be lost.

'Come on, Karen, we must get away now, while they're busy up there.'

He fumbled with the wrist compass, strapping it on to the girl's tiny wrist, while she still stared at him wonderingly.

'We may have to swim for it! If you keep an eye on this, and swim due south, you'll be on the beach in a few minutes!'

He studied her face anxiously. 'Can you make it all right?'

She flung off her red jacket, her soft mouth pressed into a tight, determined line.

'Do not worry, I will do it!'

'Right. Let's go!'

He gripped her elbow and guided her round Cooper's prostrate figure, to the end of the passage-way.

From the saloon came the murmur of voices, and the sound of a chair squeaking back against the bulkhead.

'What the hell's Cooper up to?'

Lang's voice was so close, that the girl paused with one foot on the first step.

'Quick,' Vivian hissed. 'Make a dash for it!'

As she reached the top of the darkened stairway, she flung back the small double doors, and a blinding shaft of sunlight burst in on them like a comet. He staggered after her, gasping incredulously at the bright sunlight, which sparkled and flashed on the short, grey waves. Like a white gull resting on the water, *Seafox* lay less than a mile away, her glass scuttles and brasswork shining, reflecting the sunlight from every angle, as she swung at her anchor. Of the fog, not even a wisp remained.

A door banged beneath them, followed by a stifled oath and the sound of someone running along the passage-way.

'She's gone! Quick, on deck, you silly fool!' Lang's voice cracked like a whip.

Vivian glanced round desperately for a new means of escape. The pale golden sands of the distant beach sparkled in the sunlight. It appeared to be deserted of holiday-makers, who had probably not had time to take advantage of the change of weather. He raised the pistol, pointing it down the companion-way.

'Quick, Karen, now!'

'But, Philip! What about you?' Her wide eyes stared at him imploringly.

'Soon as you're clear. Must keep you covered, otherwise he'd get us before we were half-way to the shore!' He spoke shortly, each sentence clipped by the realization of their danger.

'Please, darling. Now!' The words were torn from his lips.

She ran lightly to the rail, unclipping her skirt as she went. He saw it flutter to the deck, and from the corner of his eye, he caught the gleam of her brown legs and the flash of yellow as her hair blew out behind her. For a moment longer she waited, poised on the rail like a statue. Then she was gone, her body hardly making a splash, as she struck out for the shore. He looked across at her for a second, watching her hair floating on the surface and her hands spearing forward into the spray.

'She's jumped for it!'

Mason's face appeared over the deck, his pale eyes blinking against the light. As his glance fell on Vivian, his jaw sagged open, and losing his footing, he slithered down the stairway, calling to Lang in an almost hysterical voice.

'Just stay where you are!' barked Vivian. 'I've got a gun and I'll use it if necessary. We'll just sit here and wait for the police to arrive!'

There was a quick murmur of voices below, and then

silence. Vivian waited, wanting to look across at Karen, but not daring to take his eyes off the gaping void of the hatchway.

'Now listen, old boy,' Lang's voice floated up to him and he stiffened. 'Let's not go off at half-cock over this!'

'Forget it, Felix. Don't waste your breath!' His voice sounded cool, but the blood was churning like water in his veins.

'I'm coming up, old boy. I shouldn't behave too foolishly, if I were you. Perhaps we can make a little bargain.'

The step creaked, and Vivian laid the fore-sight in line with the top edge of the coaming.

'I'm warning you, Felix!'

At that instant he heard the scrape of metal against glass. He whirled round, cursing himself for forgetting the skylight. Mason's pale face gleamed distortedly through the angle of the small panes, his eyes wide with desperation and fear.

The crack of the shot was deafening, as the top of the sky-light shivered to fragments of wood and glass. Mason's face disappeared with a wild yell.

Vivian swung the pistol back to the hatchway, but too late. The world exploded in his eyes, with a bright yellow flash, and he felt a terrific numbing blow in his right shoulder. Dazedly he watched the pistol spin uselessly across the deck, a deck suddenly speckled with bright red drops, which gleamed and multiplied even while he stared with helpless fascination.

Then, the pain came swooping down on him, crushing his resistance and making the boat rock wildly under his feet. His will to fight, his very manhood, collapsed under the cruel onslaught and he dropped heavily to his knees, feeling the warm blood coursing down his arm.

Lang watched him narrowly, the gun still smoking in his

fist. 'That's that!' he said slowly, then, with a jerk, he turned to the wheelhouse. 'Come on, Mason! Shake yourself, we're getting out of this!'

Dimly Vivian saw Mason lope past, his face ashen, his mouth wet with saliva.

'What are we going to do?' he babbled. 'It's all up now!'

'Shut up, you fool! We've got the plates and enough dope abroad to see us pretty for life. Are you going to chuck it all away now?' Lang seemed to fill the deck with his presence, his thick neck thrust out commandingly, as he stared fiercely at the whimpering man who faced him.

'I can't go through with it.' There were real tears in Mason's eyes and, as if in prayer, he twisted his hands together. 'Please, Felix! Let's just get out, do anything, but please don't ask me to go through with it now!'

Through the roaring in his ears, Vivian heard the light step of the girl on the deck, and her exclamation of horror. Then he felt her unsteady hands trying to pull his shirt from around the wound. He saw her face very clearly against the clear, blue sky, her eyes filled with terror.

Over her shoulder, Lang's voice drawled calmly. 'I suppose that goes for you too?'

She nodded dumbly, her face made old by fear.

'Right!' Lang's voice sounded settled. 'Get the plates up here on deck, and quick!'

'What are you doing?' Mason paused in the hatchway.

'I'm getting out,' answered Lang quietly, 'and I'm taking the whole lot ashore with me.' He jerked his gun at Janice. 'Get that dinghy in the water. I'll give you a hand.'

Vivian groaned softly, as the others moved out of his immediate vision. He tried to think clearly, but his strength seemed to be failing fast. He smiled to himself. Karen's safe. Whatever else happens, she's safe now. Nothing more to harm her.

The deck shook under his pain-racked body as Mason breathlessly dumped two large suitcases, and that familiar, waterproof bag, which he knew held the plates, down beside the break in the rails, where a line secured the yacht's dinghy alongside.

Lang appeared to be breathing heavily, with the suppressed excitement of one about to carry out a fantastic scheme. He controlled his voice with an effort, his words clipped and strained.

'This is good-bye, then?' He laughed shakily. 'I'm going over to the *Seafox*, and I'll run her ashore somewhere. They won't catch me!' His eyes danced wildly. 'Now get below, the pair of you!'

He stifled their protests with a wave of the gun, and Vivian heard the slam of a door below, as Lang locked them in a cabin.

A shadow fell across his body, and he raised his head with an effort, studying Lang's glistening face through heat-waves of pain.

'So long, old son! Pity it had to be like this!' Lang shook to a tremor of silent laughter.

He's mad, raving mad, thought Vivian dully. But it didn't seem to matter. He watched as Lang burst open the package, and thrust the gleaming plates into his jacket and trouser pockets. He was humming to himself, and entirely immersed in the job he was doing. He didn't seem to hear the shouts from below, the pounding fists on the locked door. He stood looking blankly at two small plates.

'Blast! Can't get 'em in! Still, they're only cheap ones!' And he placed them carefully on the deck.

Quickly he flung the suitcases down into the dinghy, and with a last glance round, he strode over to Vivian.

'Come on, old boy, better get you into the saloon.'

Vivian struggled feebly, biting back the scream of agony,

as Lang dragged him down the companion-way, and pitched him on to the saloon deck.

As Lang slipped the key into the outside of the door, Vivian rolled over on to his side, the sweat breaking out on his face with the effort.

Lang's teeth gleamed white in his pink face. 'Forgot to mention that I'd opened the sea-cocks!'

The door slammed, and seconds later footsteps thudded overhead, followed closely by the squeak of the dinghy's fend-offs. The yacht was suddenly quiet, even the others down aft seemed to be listening.

Already it felt heavier in the water, and as each swell lifted under the keel, she responded only sluggishly. She was going down fast.

He swore aloud in his agony. If once Lang could get to the *Seafox*, he might well get clear. The excitement of a sinking yacht would draw all eyes and hands from the shore.

Inch by inch, he pulled himself across the thick carpet, his left hand doing the work of two. He fell once on his side and something sharp jabbed into him. He gasped excitedly, clawing inside his shirt. The Very Pistol! There might be still time.

He pulled it out, and dragged himself snakewise over the settee berth under the square ports. He was sweating profusely now, and each small move was an agony of fire.

Blindly he lashed out at the thick glass, feeling the pieces shiver around him. Suddenly, the warm sunlight was on his upturned face, and the quiet water lapped only two feet below him. He thrust out his arm, regardless of the jagged teeth of glass gashing his skin, and only vaguely aware of Lang's expression of surprise and bewilderment, as he pulled on the dinghy paddles.

Gritting his teeth with determination, Vivian pointed the bell-mouthed gun straight up at the untroubled sky, and pulled the thick trigger. There was a loud click. Nothing more.

Lang rested on his oars, fumbling in his coat. The light caught the gleam of steel in his hand.

As if it weighed too much for his arm, Vivian lowered the useless weapon, its barrel swung down like a signal of defeat. It was curious how everything had turned against him. He had even been finally beaten by a damp flare. He felt like laughing crazily.

Lang swayed on his seat, as he levelled his pistol, his eyes narrowed to points of hard light.

At that moment, the gun in Vivian's hand came to life. There was a soft hiss, followed by a dull thud, and he felt the handle wrench itself from his grasp.

He squinted his eyes to shield them from the small island of fire which blossomed out of the middle of the placid water. It was bright enough to dull the sun's rays, and the heat scorched his cheek, as the faulty flare changed Lang's dinghy into a raging inferno. Dimly Vivian heard Lang's screams, and saw the heavy shape, with tongues of flame licking from his legs, jump wildly into the water. The plump hands thrashed the water into a white froth, the up-turned face was empurpled with fear, as the gaping mouth choked and gurgled at the sky.

Vivian watched Lang's crazed efforts in a sort of detached wonder, as with one last, piercing cry, the face sank below the water, the shape becoming an indistinct, pink blob, and finally disappearing completely.

Vivian knew the answer to many things; he knew, for instance, that Lang had died of greed. Dragged to the bottom by the plates he had cherished above all other loyalties, even love.

Vivian's arm slipped from the scuttle, and he fell head-long on to the settee.

He had won his battle. He didn't try to fight the tide of darkness which closed him in its cloak, nor did he hear the screech of metal, as the powerful launch ground alongside decanting its cargo of blue-uniformed figures on to the sinking yacht's deck.

Philip Vivian was at peace with his conscience.

EPILOGUE

Only a few people braved the cold, Atlantic wind which whirled the pieces of paper from the streets and sent the lonely seagulls squawking angrily from their perches. The windows of the hotels stared blankly at the tossing white-horses across the bay, adding to their general air of empti-ness and desolation.

The boats in Torquay harbour huddled together at their moorings, as if for comfort, while the uneasy stir of the waves made their masts spiral and bob in miserable har-mony. Everywhere, the covers were on, the unnecessary gear stowed away, to await another season, which now seemed a long way away.

Only one boat in the harbour looked fresh, and com-pletely at home in the grey surroundings. She lay alongside the lower jetty, rolling easily, contemptuous of the wind and the weather. Old Arthur Harrap took a last look round and nodded, apparently satisfied with his work, and thought-fully shook the deck mop over the side. He smiled quietly, as a big black-and-white cat rubbed itself round his legs, purring noisily.

'Glad to 'ave yer 'ome back, are yer?' he wheezed. 'Won't be long now, I reckon.'

He squinted his watery eyes along the jetty, as a taxi pulled up with a jerk. He watched them narrowly, as they walked slowly down the stone steps.

He was looking paler, and carried his arm in a sling. And she, well, he shook his head in admiration. He gave the ca another pat, and slipped quietly over the rail of the yacht hunching his shoulders to meet the wind.

As his steps rang out on the stonework, he was whistling softly. He'd go back later, when they'd settled down.

After all, he reflected, they were in love.